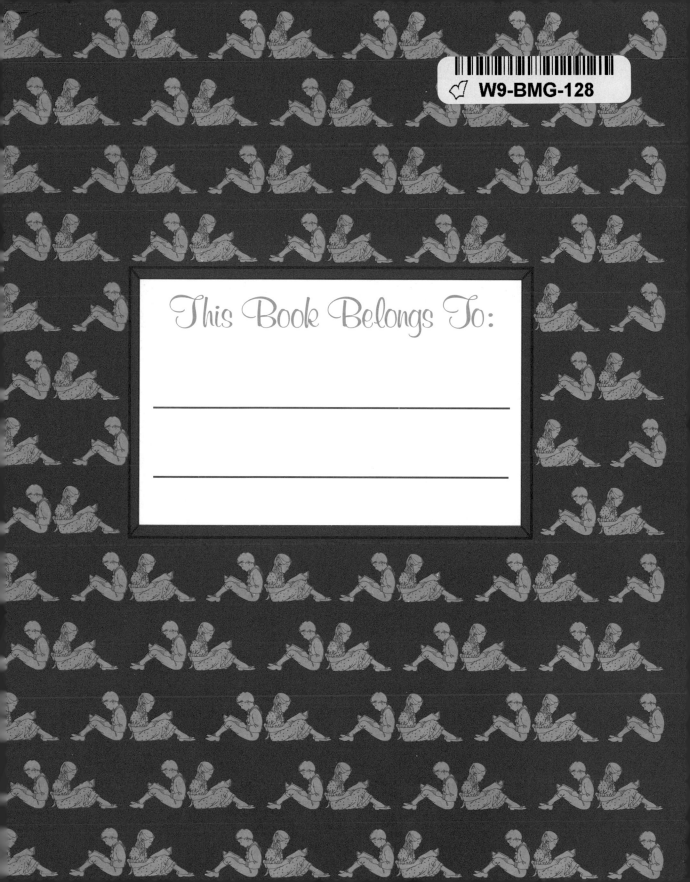

This Book Belongs To:

_____

_____

GRIMM'S
FAIRY TALES

GRIMM'S FAIRY TALES

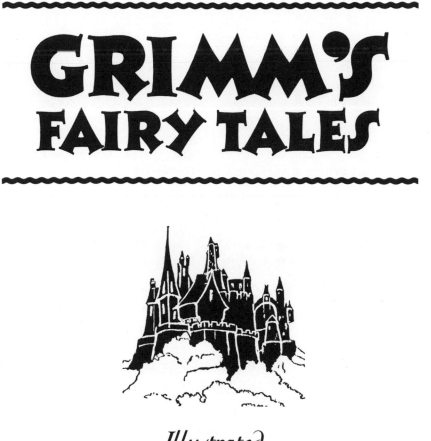

Illustrated
by
Noel Pocock

LONGMEADOW PRESS

This book is printed on acid-free paper. It surpasses the standards set for Performance of Paper for Printed Library Materials.

∞™

Copyright © 1987 by dilithium Press, Ltd., Children's Classics Division.

This 1987 edition is published exclusively by Longmeadow Press, 201 High Ridge Road, P.O. Box 10218, Stamford, CT 06904, by arrangement with Outlet Book Company, Inc., 225 Park Avenue South, New York, New York 10003.

Printed and bound in the United States of America

ISBN 0-681-40312-8

10 9 8 7 6 5 4 3 2

Cover design by Madge Schultz
Cover illustrations by Noel Pocock.
Front cover: illustration for "Hansel and Gretel" (page 70).
Back cover: illustration for "Snow-Drop" (page 100).

CONTENTS

LIST OF COLOR ILLUSTRATIONS

FOREWORD

Reading *Grimm's Fairy Tales* is like walking in a forest and making an unexpected turn to see a flower luxuriantly blossoming in the darkness. These stories are as alluring and as mysterious as that flower, appearing with their own exuberant beauty out of the tangle of everyday concerns of generations past. This volume, a representative collection, contains the most popular of Grimm's fairy tales. Reading this treasury, we are in a boundless world where magic is very real, where the youngest son always triumphs, and virtue is always rewarded. Though some of these stories are ingeniously comical, most of them concern a young person—male or female—who struggles against great odds. Thus, fairy tales have been recognized by psychologists as being an important part of childhood. Dr. Bruno Bettelheim, in *The Uses of Enchantment: The Meaning and Importance of Fairy Tales* (Vintage Books, New York, 1977), points out that these stories, in beautiful images, encourage us to meet the challenges that each successive stage of life brings us.

We are fortunate indeed that the illustrator of this book, Noel Pocock, had an intense vision that captures so well the spirit of these tales. The dwarfs he painted seemed to spring out of the ancient, rocky landscape, having in their faces knowledge half human and half magical. His people are more real than real, often portrayed with rounded forms that seem to bear the weight of the ages. But what is so remarkable are his depictions of the fateful encounters upon which the stories turn—when knowledge is gained or deception is practiced, which we can read in the characters' eyes or the movement of their bodies. Rarely has an illustrator so perfectly balanced the fantasy and reality to be found in *Grimm's Fairy Tales*. The magic is so real we can touch it.

What is not generally recognized nowadays are the many moments of beauty and tenderness described in these stories. A young queen's hopes for her child are unforgettably described in the beginning of "Snow-Drop" ("Snow White"):

> It was in the middle of winter, when the broad flakes of snow were falling around, that a certain queen sat working at a window, the frame of which was made of fine black ebony; and as she was looking out upon the snow, she pricked her finger, and three drops of blood fell upon it. Then she gazed thoughtfully upon the red drops which sprinkled the white snow, and said, "Would that my little daughter may be as white as that snow, as red as the blood, and as black as the ebony window-frame!"

"Ashputtel" is a more haunting version of "Cinderella", and begins with a reminder of the mother's enduring love. And "Ashputtel" is perhaps a more humane story—the young heroine's eventual triumph comes as result of her loyalty to her dead mother. We are shown that the mother's care continues after her actual presence is gone.

Many of these fairy tales are as luminous as the stones, shining in the moonlight, strewn by Hansel in the forest to show him the way home in "Hansel and Grettel." Who can forget the alarm of the youngest princess in "The Twelve Dancing Princesses," as she alone, of all her eleven sisters, hears the snap of branches caused by the invisible soldier who is secretly following them in their hidden, underground world? This moving moment shows the princess's shock of awareness in the midst of her dream-like state. And the feeling of loss, as the young girl stands on the threshold of a new stage of life, is poetically created.

The nature of love is beautifully illuminated in a very concrete manner in "The Water of Life." A princess has a gold road built and tells her people that her true suitor will ride straight up its center, but her false ones will ride by its side. The two eldest sons of a distant king see the shining road and ride to the side, so that it may not be marred. But the youngest son

> journeyed on, thinking of (the princess) all the way, and rode so quickly that he did not even see the golden road, but went with his horse straight over it.

His is true, all-consuming love. He is welcomed by the princess.

We can imagine the sense of revelation and delight these fairy tales must have offered to the generations of folk who originally heard them told aloud at firesides. But these stories fell into disrepute with the educated classes, ashamed of reminders of what they imagined to be a barbaric past. It was Jacob and Wilhelm Grimm who brought these stories into print, revealing their beauty and strength.

Jacob and Wilhelm were born in 1785 and 1786 in the small German principality of Hesse-Cassel, and spent their later childhood in Steinau, a small town dotted with medieval monuments. Theirs was tightly knit family, and the two brothers, who were unusually close, developed a deep love of tradition. As adults, they collected the fairy tales mostly from friends and neighbors. The first volume of these stories was published by Christmas, 1812, and the second appeared in 1814. Murray B. Peppard in *Paths Through the Forest, A Biography of the Brothers Grimm* (Holt, Rinehart and Winston, New York, 1971), quotes Jacob, who wrote that the fairy tale "is a poetry which belongs to the childhood of the race—and therefore children take to it so readily."

Some of the characters in these fairy tales indeed combine the adult and the child. Rumpelstiltskin is spinner beyond compare, turning straw into gold, but, in the end, he dissolves into infantile rage. Dr. Bettelheim points out that the dwarfs in "Snow-Drop" toil daily but do not understand romantic love. Perhaps it is the father in "The Three Children of Fortune" who gives his sons what may be the most essential advice from the old to the young: "Only seek out for a land where what you have is as yet unknown, and your fortune is made."

Though some of these fairy tales contain violence, it is never gratuitous, but a fitting punishment for an evil-doer. Dr. Bruno Bettelheim, the noted child psychologist, writes,

> ...such retribution reassures the child that the punishment fits the crime...he wants those who cheat and degrade him...most severely punished. If they are not, the child thinks that nobody is serious about protecting him; but the more severely the bad ones are dealt with, the more secure the child feels.

These stories are little masterpieces of condensation. Within one paragraph, a character may travel far and face tests of wit. Or, as in "The Twelve Dancing Princesses," a puzzle may be laid out:

> There was a king who had twelve beautiful daughters. They slept in twelve beds all in one room; and when they went to bed, the doors were shut and locked up; but every morning their shoes were found to be quite worn through, as if they had been dancing in the night...

We feel we have in our hands an exquisitely tied knot which we may turn all around, but whose secret we cannot fathom.

There are also wonderful dialogues in these stories. Children love to reenact Red Riding Hood's questioning of the wolf and his replies, for the scene has a tantalizing but ritual-like quality. Equally as satisfying is the maiden's guessing of Rumpelstiltskin's name, a give-and-take that also underscores young children's feeling that naming something gives them power over it.

And humor abounds. It often deals with misapplied knowledge. Hans, in the second part of "Hansel and His Wife Grettel," takes home various gifts, applying the advice given him for taking care of each possession only to the next thing he carries, always with ludicrous results. In addition to making us laugh, this story makes us marvel at what promises to be a series of errors stretching into infinity. We also enjoy the images of the ridiculous that poke fun at people's pretensions—thus, the long string of villagers forced to keep up with Dummling, carrying the golden goose to which they have become stuck out of greed, ambition, or idle curiosity.

Several of the tales in this volume are also better known by other titles. "The Travelling Musicians" is widely called "The Bremen Town Musicians," "Rose-Bud" is "Sleeping Beauty," and "Snow-Drop" is "Snow White." "The Lady and the Lion" is similar to "Beauty and the Beast." Some stories in this edition are variants of others, in that they combine several tales—thus, "Roland and May-Bird" is formed of large sections of "Hansel and Grettel" (also included here separately) and the lesser-known "Sweetheart Roland" (not in this volume); "The Young Giant and the Tailor" contains the entire story "The Young Giant" as well as elements of "The Valiant Little Tailor" and "The Cunning Little Tailor" (neither included here). The three parts of "Hans and His Wife Grettel" often stand alone as stories, and do not refer to the renowned classic "Hansel and Grettel," which is included here separately.

"Small as this fairyland looked from without, it seemed within to have no end," we are told in "The Elfin Grove." And so it is: reading these fairy tales, we feel again our youthful sense of anticipation, the delicious expectation that at any moment, we may come upon something extraordinary. We find ourselves confronted with surprising but necessary recognitions in enchanted settings. These stories are imbued with a super-reality—be it with romance, action, or humor, they touch us deeply. *Grimm's Fairy Tales* thus becomes a vital part of the heritage of childhood.

ELLEN S. SHAPIRO

Brooklyn, New York
1988

GRIMM'S
FAIRY TALES

Hans in Luck

HANS had served his master seven years, and at last said to him, "Master, my time is up, I should like to go home and see my mother; so give me my wages." And the master said, "You have been a faithful and good servant, so your pay shall be handsome." Then he gave him a piece of silver that was as big as his head.

Hans took out his pocket-handkerchief, put the piece of silver into it, threw it over his shoulder, and jogged off homewards. As he went lazily on, dragging one foot after another, a man came in sight, trotting along gaily on a capital horse. "Ah!" said Hans aloud, "what a fine thing it is to ride on horseback! there he sits as if he was at home in his chair; he trips against no stones, spares his shoes, and yet gets on he hardly knows how." The horseman heard this, and said, "Well, Hans, why do you go on foot then?" "Ah!" said he, "I have this load to carry; to be sure it is silver, but it is so heavy that I can't hold up my head, and it hurts my shoulder sadly." "What do you say to changing?" said the horseman; "I will give you my horse, and you shall give me the silver." "With all my heart," said Hans: "but I tell you one thing,—you'll have a weary task to drag it along." The horseman got off, took the silver, helped Hans up, gave him the bridle into his

7

hand, and said, "When you want to go very fast, you must smack your lips loud, and cry 'Jip.'"

Hans was delighted as he sat on the horse, and rode merrily on. After a time he thought he should like to go a little faster, so he smacked his lips, and cried "Jip." Away went the horse full gallop; and before Hans knew what he was about, he was thrown off, and lay in a ditch by the road side; and his horse would have run off, if a shepherd who was coming by, driving a cow, had not stopt it. Hans soon came to himself, and got upon his legs again. He was sadly vexed, and said to the shepherd, "This riding is no joke when a man gets on a beast like this, that stumbles and flings him off as if he would break his neck. However, I'm off now once for all: I like your cow a great deal better; one can walk along at one's leisure behind her, and have milk, butter, and cheese, every day into the bargain. What would I give to have such a cow!" "Well," said the shepherd, "if you are so fond of her, I will change my cow for your horse." "Done!" said Hans merrily. The shepherd jumped upon the horse, and away he rode.

Hans drove off his cow quietly, and thought his bargain a very lucky one. "If I have only a piece of bread (and I certainly shall be able to get that), I can, whenever I like, eat my butter and cheese with it; and when I am thirsty I can milk my cow and drink the milk: what can I wish for more?" When he came to an inn, he halted, ate up all his bread, and gave away his last penny for a glass of beer: then he drove his cow towards his mother's village; and the heat grew greater as noon came on, till at last he found himself on a wide heath that would take him more than an hour to cross, and he began to be so hot and parched that his tongue clave to the roof of his mouth. "I can find a cure for this," thought he, "now will I milk my cow and quench my thirst;" so he tied her to the stump of a tree, and held his leathern cap to milk into; but not a drop was to be had.

While he was trying his luck and managing the matter very clumsily, the uneasy beast gave him a kick on the head that knocked him down and there he lay a long while senseless. Luckily a butcher soon came by driving a pig in a wheel-barrow. "What is the matter with you?" said the butcher as he helped him up. Hans told him what had happened, and the butcher gave him a flask, saying "There, drink and refresh yourself; your cow will give you no milk, she is an old beast good for nothing but the slaughter-house." "Alas, alas!" said Hans, "who would have thought it? If I kill her, what will she be good for? I hate cow-beef, it is not tender enough for me. If it were a pig now, one could do something with it, it would at any rate make some sausages." "Well," said the butcher, "to please you, I'll change, and give you the pig for the cow." "Heaven reward you for your kindness!" said Hans as he gave the butcher the cow, and took the pig off the wheel-barrow, and drove it off, holding it by the string that was tied to its leg.

So on he jogged, and all seemed now to go right with him; he had met with some misfortunes, to be sure; but he was now well repaid for all. The next person he met was a countryman carrying a fine white goose under his arm. The countryman stopped to ask what o'clock it was; and Hans told him all his luck, and how he had made so many good bargains. The countryman said he was going to take the goose to a christening;

"Feel," said he, "how heavy it is, and yet it is only eight weeks old. Whoever roasts and eats it may cut plenty of fat off it, it has lived so well!" "You're right," said Hans as he weighed it in his hand; "but my pig is no trifle." Meantime the countryman began to look grave, and shook his head. "Hark ye," said he, "my good friend; your pig may get you into a scrape; in the village I just come from, the squire has had a pig stolen out of his stye. I was dreadfully afraid, when I saw you, that you had got the squire's pig; it will be a bad job if they catch you; the least they'll do, will be to throw you into the horsepond."

Poor Hans was sadly frightened. "Good man," cried he, "pray get me out of this scrape; you know this country better than I, take my pig and give me the goose." "I ought to have something into the bargain," said the countryman; "however, I will not bear hard upon you, as you are in trouble." Then he took the string in his hand, and drove off the pig by a side path; while Hans went on the way homewards free from care. "After all," thought he, "I have the best of the bargain: first there will be a capital roast; then the fat will find me in goose grease for six months; and then there are all the beautiful white feathers; I will put them into my pillow, and then I am sure I shall sleep soundly without rocking. How happy my mother will be!"

As he came to the last village, he saw a scissor-grinder, with his wheel, working away, and singing

> O'er hill and o'er dale so happy I roam,
> Work light and live well, all the world is my home;
> Who so blythe, so merry as I?

Hans stood looking for a while, and at last said "You must be well off, master grinder, you seem so happy at your work." "Yes," said the other, "mine is a golden trade; a good grinder never puts his hand in his pocket without finding money in it:—but where did you get that beautiful goose?" "I did not buy it, but changed a pig for it." "And where did you get the pig?" "I gave a cow for it." "And the cow?" "I gave a horse for it." "And the horse?" "I gave a piece of silver as big as my head for that." "And the silver?" "Oh! I worked hard for that seven long years." "You have thriven well in the world hitherto," said the grinder; "now if you could find money in your pocket whenever you put your hand into it, your fortune would be made." "Very true: but how is that to be managed?" "You must turn grinder like me," said the other; "you only want a grindstone; the rest will come of itself. Here is one that is a little the worse for wear: I would not ask more than the value of your goose for it;—will you buy?" "How can you ask such a question?" replied Hans; "I should be the happiest man in the world, if I could have money whenever I put my hand in my pocket; what could I want more? there's the goose!" "Now," said the grinder, as he gave him a common rough stone that lay by his side, "this is a most capital stone; do but manage it cleverly, and you can make an old nail cut with it."

Hans took the stone and went off with a light heart: his eyes sparkled for joy, and he said to himself, "I must have been born in a lucky hour; everything that I want or wish for comes to me of itself."

Meantime he began to be tired, for he had been travelling ever since day-break; he was hungry too, for he had given away his last penny in his joy at getting the cow. At last he could go no further, and the stone tired him terribly; he dragged himself to the side of a pond, that he might drink some water, and rest a while;

so he laid the stone carefully by his side on the bank: but as he stooped down to drink, he forgot it, pushed it a little, and down it went plump into the pond. For a while he watched it sinking in the deep clear water, then sprang up for joy, and again fell upon his knees, and thanked heaven with tears in his eyes for its kindness in taking away his only plague, the ugly heavy stone. "How happy am I!" cried he: "no mortal was ever so lucky as I am." Then up he got with a light and merry heart, and walked on free from all his troubles, till he reached his mother's house.

The Travelling Musicians

or The Bremen Town Musicians

AN honest farmer had once an ass, that had been a faithful servant to him a great many years, but was now growing old and every day more and more unfit for work. His master therefore was tired of keeping him and began to think of putting an end to him; but the ass, who saw that some mischief was in the wind, took himself slyly off, and began his journey towards the great city, "for there," thought he, "I may turn musician."

After he had travelled a little way, he spied a dog lying by the road-side and panting as if he were very tired. "What makes you pant so, my friend?" said the ass. "Alas!" said the dog, "my master was going to knock me on the head, because I am old and weak, and can no longer make myself useful to him in hunting; so I ran away: but what can I do to earn my livelihood?" "Hark ye!" said the ass, "I am going to the great city to turn musician: suppose you go with me, and try what you can do in the same way?" The dog said he was willing, and they jogged on together.

They had not gone far before they saw a cat sitting in the middle of the road and making a most rueful face. "Pray, my good lady," said the ass, "what's the matter with you? you look quite out of spirits!" "Ah me!" said the cat, "how can one be in good spirits when one's life is in danger? Because I am beginning to grow old, and had rather lie at my ease by the fire than run about the house after the mice, my mistress laid hold of me, and was going to drown me; and though I have been lucky enough to get away from her, I do not know what I am to live upon." "O!" said the ass, "by all means go with us to the great city; you are a good night singer, and may make your forture as a musician." The cat was pleased with the thought, and joined the party.

Soon afterwards, as they were passing by a farm-yard, they saw a cock perched upon a gate, and scream-ing out with all his might and main. "Bravo!" said the ass; "upon my word you make a famous noise; pray what is all this about?" "Why," said the cock, "I was just now saying that we should have fine weather for our washing-day, and yet my mistress and the cook don't thank me for my pains, but threaten to cut off my head to-morrow, and make broth of me for the guests that are coming on Sunday!" "Heaven forbid!" said the ass; "come with us, Master Chanticleer; it will be better, at any rate, than staying here to have your head cut off! Besides, who knows? If we take care to sing in tune, we may get up some kind of a concert: so come along with us." With all my heart," said the cock: so they all four went on jollily together.

They could not, however, reach the great city the first day; so when night came on, they went into a wood to sleep. The ass and the dog laid themselves down under a great tree, and the cat climbed up into the branches; while the cock, thinking that the higher he sat the safer he should be, flew up to the very top of the tree, and then, according to his custom, before he went to sleep, looked out on all sides of him to see that everything was well. In doing this, he saw afar off something bright and shining; and calling to his companions said, "There must be a house no great way off, for I see a light." "If that be the case," said the ass, "we had better change our quarters, for our lodging is not the best in the world!" "Besides," added the dog, "I should not be the worse for a bone or two, or a bit of meat." So they walked off together towards the spot where Chanticleer had seen the light; and as they drew near, it became larger and brighter, till they at last came close to a house in which a gang of robbers lived.

The ass, being the tallest of the company, marched up to the window and peeped in. "Well, Donkey," said Chanticleer, "what do you see?" "What do I see?" replied the ass, "why I see a table spread with all kinds of good things, and robbers sitting round it making merry." "That would be a noble lodging for us," said the cock. "Yes," said the ass, "if we could only get in:" so they consulted together how they should contrive to get the robbers out; and at last they hit upon a plan. The ass placed himself upright on his hind-legs, with his fore-feet resting against the window; the dog got upon his back; the cat scrambled up to the dog's shoulders, and the cock flew up and sat upon the cat's head. When all was ready, a signal was given, and they began their music. The ass brayed, the dog barked, the cat mewed, and the cock screamed; and then they all broke through the window at once, and came tumbling into the room, amongst the broken glass, with a most hideous clatter! The robbers, who had been not a little frightened by the opening concert, had now no doubt that some frightful hobgoblin had broken in upon them, and scampered away as fast as they could.

The coast once clear, our travellers soon sat down, and dispatched what the robbers had left, with as much eagerness as if they had not expected to eat again for a month. As soon as they had satisfied themselves, they put out the lights, and each once more sought out a resting-place to his own liking. The donkey laid himself down upon a heap of straw in the yard; the dog stretched himself upon a mat behind the door; the cat rolled herself up on the hearth before the warm ashes; and the cock perched upon a beam on the top of the house; and, as they were all rather tired with their journey, they soon fell asleep.

But about midnight, when the robbers saw from afar that the lights were out and that all seemed quiet, they began to think that they had been in too great a hurry to run away; and one of them, who was bolder than the rest, went to see what was going on. Finding everything still, he marched into the kitchen, and groped about till he found a match in order to light a candle; and then, espying the glittering fiery eyes of the cat, he mistook them for live coals, and held the match to them to light it. But the cat, not understanding this joke, sprung at his face, and spit, and scratched at him. This frightened him dreadfully, and away he ran to the back door; but there the dog jumped up and bit him in the leg; and as he was crossing over the yard the ass kicked him; and the cock, who had been awakened by the noise, crowed with all his might. At this the robber ran back as fast as he could to his comrades, and told the captain "how a horrid witch had got into the house, and had spit at him and scratched his face with her long bony fingers; how a man with a knife in his hand had hidden himself behind the door, and stabbed him in the leg; how a black monster stood in the yard and struck him with a club, and how the devil sat upon the top of the house and cried out, 'Throw the rascal up here!'" After this the robbers never dared to go back to the house: but the musicians were so pleased with their quarters, that they took up their abode there; and there they are, I dare say, at this very day.

The Golden Bird

A CERTAIN king had a beautiful garden, and in the garden stood a tree which bore golden apples. These apples were always counted, and about the time when they began to grow ripe it was found that every night one of them was gone. The king became very angry at this, and ordered the gardener to keep watch all night under the tree. The gardener set his eldest son to watch; but about twelve o'clock he fell asleep, and in the morning another of the apples was missing. Then the second son was ordered to watch; and at midnight he too fell asleep, and in the morning another apple was gone. Then the third son offered to keep watch; but the gardener at first would not let him, for fear some harm should come to him: however, at last he consented, and the young man laid himself under the tree to watch. As the clock struck twelve he heard a rustling noise in the air, and a bird came flying that was of pure gold; and as it was snapping at one of the apples with its beak, the gardener's son jumped up and shot an arrow at it. But the arrow did the bird no harm; only it dropped a golden feather from its tail, and then flew away. The golden feather was brought to the king in the morning, and all the council was called together. Every one agreed that it was worth more than all the wealth of the kingdom: but the king said, "One feather is of no use to me, I must have the whole bird."

Then the gardener's eldest son set out and thought

to find the golden bird very easily; and when he had gone but a little way, he came to a wood, and by the side of the wood he saw a fox sitting; so he took his bow and made ready to shoot at it. Then the fox said, "Do not shoot me, for I will give you good counsel; I know what your business is, and that you want to find the golden bird. You will reach a village in the evening; and when you get there, you will see two inns opposite to each other, one of which is very pleasant and beautiful to look at: go not in there, but rest for the night in the other, though it may appear to you to be very poor and mean." But the son thought to himself, "What can such a beast as this know about the matter?" So he shot his arrow at the fox; but he missed it, and it set up its tail above its back and ran into the wood. Then he went his way, and in the evening came to the village where the two inns were; and in one of these were people singing, and dancing, and feasting; but the other looked very dirty, and poor. "I should be very silly," said he, "if I went to that shabby house, and left this charming place;" so he went into the smart house, and ate and drank at his ease, and forgot the bird, and his country too.

Time passed on; and as the eldest son did not come back, and no tidings were heard of him, the second son set out, and the same thing happened to him. He met the fox, who gave him the same good advice: but when he came to the two inns, his eldest brother was standing at the window where the merrymaking was, and called to him to come in; and he could not withstand the temptation, but went in, and forgot the golden bird and his country in the same manner.

Time passed on again, and the youngest son too wished to set out into the wide world to seek for the golden bird; but his father would not listen to it for a long while, for he was very fond of his son, and was afraid that some ill luck might happen to him also, and prevent his coming back. However, at last it was agreed he should go, for he would not rest at home; and as he came to the wood, he met the fox, and heard the same good counsel. But he was thankful to the fox, and did not attempt his life as his brothers had done; so the fox said, "Sit upon my tail, and you will travel faster." So he sat down, and the fox began to run, and away they went over stock and stone so quick that their hair whistled in the wind.

When they came to the village, the son followed the fox's counsel, and without looking about him went to the shabby inn and rested there all night at his ease. In the morning came the fox again and met him as he was beginning his journey, and said, "Go straight forward, till you come to a castle, before which lie a whole troop of soldiers fast asleep and snoring: take no notice of them, but go into the castle and pass on and on till you come to a room, where the golden bird sits in a wooden cage; close by it stands a beautiful golden cage; but do not try to take the bird out of the shabby cage and put it into the handsome one, otherwise you will repent it." Then the fox stretched out his tail again, and the young man sat himself down, and away they went over stock and stone till their hair whistled in the wind.

Before the castle gate all was as the fox had said: so the son went in and found the chamber where the golden bird hung in a wooden cage, and below stood the golden cage, and the three golden apples that had been lost were lying close by it. Then thought he to himself, "It will be a very droll thing to bring away such a fine bird in this shabby cage;" so he opened the door and took hold of it and put it into the golden cage. But the bird set up such a loud scream that all the soldiers awoke, and they took him prisoner and carried him before the king. The next morning the court sat to judge him; and when all was heard, it sentenced him to die, unless he should bring the king the golden horse which could run as swiftly as the wind; and if he did this, he was to have the golden bird given him for his own.

So he set out once more on his journey, sighing, and in great despair, when on a sudden his good friend the fox met him, and said, "You see now what has happened on account of your not listening to my counsel. I will still, however, tell you how to find the golden horse, if you will do as I bid you. You must go straight on till you come to the castle where the horse stands in his stall: by his side will lie the groom fast asleep and snoring: take away the horse quietly, but be sure to put the old leathern saddle upon him, and not the golden one that is close by it." Then the son sat down on the fox's tail, and away they went over stock and stone till their hair whistled in the wind.

All went right, and the groom lay snoring with his hand upon the golden saddle. But when the son looked at the horse, he thought it a great pity to put the leathern saddle upon it. "I will give him the good one," said he; "I am sure he deserves it." As he took up the golden saddle the groom awoke and cried out so loud, that all the guards ran in and took him prisoner, and in the morning he was again brought before the court to be judged, and was sentenced to die. But it was agreed, that, if he could bring thither the beautiful princess, he should live, and have the bird and the horse given him for his own.

Then he went his way again very sorrowful; but the old fox came and said, "Why did not you listen to me?

If you had, you would have carried away both the bird and the horse; yet will I once more give you counsel. Go straight on, and in the evening you will arrive at a castle. At twelve o'clock at night the princess goes to the bathing-house: go up to her and give her a kiss, and she will let you lead her away; but take care you do not suffer her to go and take leave of her father and mother." Then the fox stretched out his tail, and so away they went over stock and stone till their hair whistled again.

As they came to the castle, all was as the fox had said, and at twelve o'clock the young man met the princess going to the bath and gave her the kiss, and she agreed to run away with him, but begged with many tears that he would let her take leave of her father. At first he refused, but she wept still more and more, and fell at his feet, till at last he consented; but the moment she came to her father's house, the guards awoke and he was taken prisoner again.

Then he was brought before the king, and the king said, "You shall never have my daughter unless in eight days you dig away the hill that stops the view from my window." Now this hill was so big that the whole world could not take it away: and when he had worked for seven days, and had done very little, the fox came and said, "Lie down and go to sleep; I will work for you." And in the morning he awoke and the hill was gone; so he went merrily to the king, and told him that now that it was removed he must give him the princess.

Then the king was obliged to keep his word, and away went the young man and the princess; and the fox came and said to him, "We will have all three, the princess, the horse, and the bird." "Ah!" said the young man, "that would be a great thing, but how can you contrive it?"

"If you will only listen," said the fox, "it can soon

be done. When you come to the king, and he asks for the beautiful princess, you must say, 'Here she is!' Then he will be very joyful; and you will mount the golden horse that they are to give you, and put out your hand to take leave of them; but shake hands with the princess last. Then lift her quickly on to the horse behind you; clap your spurs to his side, and gallop away as fast as you can."

All went right: then the fox said, "When you come to the castle where the bird is, I will stay with the princess at the door, and you will ride in and speak to the king; and when he sees that it is the right horse, he will bring out the bird; but you must sit still, and say that you want to look at it, to see whether it is the true golden bird; and when you get it into your hand, ride away."

This, too, happened as the fox said; they carried off the bird, the princess mounted again, and they rode on to a great wood. Then the fox came, and said, "Pray kill me, and cut off my head and my feet." But the young man refused to do it: so the fox said, "I will at any rate give you good counsel: beware of two things; ransom no one from the gallows, and sit down by the side of no river." Then away he went. "Well," thought the young man, "it is no hard matter to keep that advice."

He rode on with the princess, till at last he came to the village where he had left his two brothers. And there he heard a great noise and uproar; and when he asked what was the matter, the people said, "Two men are going to be hanged." As he came nearer, he saw that the two men were his brothers, who had turned robbers; so he said, "Cannot they in any way be saved?" But the people said "No," unless he would bestow all his money upon the rascals and buy their liberty. Then he did not stay to think about the matter, but paid what was asked, and his brothers were given up, and went on with him towards their home.

And as they came to the wood where the fox first met them, it was so cool and pleasant that the two brothers said, "Let us sit down by the side of the river, and rest a while, to eat and drink." So he said, "Yes," and forgot the fox's counsel, and sat down on the side of the river; and while he suspected nothing, they came behind, and threw him down the bank, and took the princess, the horse, and the bird, and went home to the king their master, and said, "All this have we won by our labour." Then there was great rejoicing made; but the horse would not eat, the bird would not sing, and the princess wept.

The youngest son fell to the bottom of the river's bed: luckily it was nearly dry, but his bones were almost broken, and the bank was so steep that he could find no way to get out. Then the old fox came once more, and scolded him for not following his advice; otherwise no evil would have befallen him: "Yet," said he, "I cannot leave you here, so lay hold of my tail and hold fast." Then he pulled him out of the river, and said to him, as he got upon the bank, "Your brothers have set watch to kill you, if they find you in the kingdom." So he dressed himself as a poor man, and came secretly to the king's court, and was scarcely within the doors when the horse began to eat, and the bird to sing, and the princess left off weeping. Then he went to the king, and told him all his brothers' roguery; and they were seized and punished, and he had the princess given to him again; and after the king's death he was heir to his kingdom.

A long while after, he went to walk one day in the wood, and the old fox met him, and besought him with tears in his eyes to kill him, and cut off his head and feet. And at last he did so, and in a moment the fox was changed into a man, and turned out to be the brother of the princess, who had been lost a great many many years.

The Fisherman and His Wife

THERE was once a fisherman who lived with his wife in a ditch, close by the sea-side. The fisherman used to go out all day long a-fishing; and one day, as he sat on the shore with his rod, looking at the shining water and watching his line, all on a sudden his float was dragged away deep under the sea: and in drawing it up he pulled a great fish out of the water. The fish said to him, "Pray let me live: I am not a real fish; I am an enchanted prince, put me in the water again, and let me go." "Oh!" said the man, "you need not make so many words about the matter; I wish to have nothing to do with a fish that can talk; so swim away as soon as you please." Then he put him back into the water, and the fish darted straight down to the bottom, and left a long streak of blood behind him.

When the fisherman went home to his wife in the ditch, he told her how he had caught a great fish, and how it had told him it was an enchanted prince, and that on hearing it speak he had let it go again. "Did you not ask it for anything?" said the wife. "No," said the man, "what should I ask for?" "Ah!" said the wife, "we live very wretchedly here in this nasty stinking ditch; do go back, and tell the fish we want a little cottage."

The fisherman did not much like the business: however, he went to the sea, and when he came there the water looked all yellow and green. And he stood at the water's edge, and said,

> "O man of the sea!
> Come listen to me,
> For Alice my wife,
> The plague of my life,
> Hath sent me to beg a boon of thee!"

Then the fish came swimming to him, and said, "Well, what does she want?" "Ah!" answered the fisherman, "my wife says that when I had caught you, I ought to have asked you for something before I let you go again; she does not like living any longer in the ditch, and wants a little cottage." "Go home, then," said the fish, "she is in the cottage already." So the man went home, and saw his wife standing at the door of a cottage. "Come in, come in," said she; "is not this much better than the ditch?" And there was a parlour, and a bed-chamber, and a kitchen; and behind the cottage there was a little garden with all sorts of flowers and fruits, and a court-yard full of ducks and chickens. "Ah!" said the fisherman, "how happily we shall live!" "We will try to do so at least," said his wife.

Everything went right for a week or two, and then Dame Alice said, "Husband, there is not room enough in this cottage, the court-yard and garden are a great deal too small; I should like to have a large stone castle to live in; so go to the fish again, and tell him to give us a castle." "Wife," said the fisherman, "I don't like to go to him again, for perhaps he will be angry; we ought to be content with the cottage." "Nonsense!" said the wife; "he will do it very willingly; go along, and try."

The fisherman went; but his heart was very heavy: and when he came to the sea, it looked blue and gloomy,

though it was quite calm, and he went close to it, and
said,

"O man of the sea!
Come listen to me,
For Alice my wife,
The plague of my life,
Hath sent me to beg a boon of thee!"

"Well, what does she want now?" said the fish. "Ah!"
said the man very sorrowfully, "my wife wants to live in
a stone castle." "Go home then," said the fish, "she is
standing at the door of it already." So away went the
fisherman, and found his wife standing before a great
castle. "See," said she, "is not this grand?" With that
they went into the castle together, and found a great
many servants there, and the rooms all richly furnished
and full of golden chairs and tables; and behind the castle
was a garden, and a wood half a mile long, full of sheep,
and goats, and hares, and deer; and in the court-yard were
stables and cow-houses. "Well," said the man, "now will
we live contented and happy in this beautiful castle for
the rest of our lives." "Perhaps we may," said the wife;
"but let us consider and sleep upon it before we make
up our minds:" so they went to bed.

The next morning, when Dame Alice awoke, it was
broad day-light, and she jogged the fisherman with her
elbow, and said, "Get up, husband, and bestir yourself,
for we must be king of all the land." "Wife, wife," said
the man, "why should we wish to be king? I will not be
king." "Then I will," said Alice. "But, wife," answered
the fisherman, "how can you be king? the fish cannot make
you a king." "Husband," said she, "say no more about
it, but go and try; I will be king!" So the man went
away, quite sorrowful to think that his wife should want

to be king. The sea looked a dark grey colour, and was covered with foam as he cried out,

"O man of the sea!
Come listen to me,
For Alice my wife,
The plague of my life,
Hath sent me to beg a boon of thee!"

"Well, what would she have now?" said the fish. "Alas!" said the man, "my wife wants to be king." "Go home," said the fish; "she is king already."

Then the fisherman went home; and as he came close to the palace, he saw a troop of soldiers, and heard the sound of drums and trumpets; and when he entered in, he saw his wife sitting on a high throne of gold and diamonds, with a golden crown upon her head; and on each side of her stood six beautiful maidens, each a head taller than the other. "Well, wife," said the fisherman, "are you king?" "Yes," said she, "I am king." And when he had looked at her for a long time, he said, "Ah, wife! what a fine thing it is to be king! now we shall never have anything more to wish for." "I don't know how that may be," said she; "never is a long time. I am king, 'tis true, but I begin to be tired of it, and I think I should like to be emperor." "Alas, wife! why should you wish to be emperor?" said the fisherman. "Husband," said she, "go to the fish; I say I will be emperor." "Ah, wife!" replied the fisherman, "the fish cannot make an emperor, and I should not like to ask for such a thing." "I am king," said Alice, "and you are my slave, so go directly!" So the fisherman was obliged to go; and he muttered as he went along, "This will come to no good, it is too much to ask, the fish will be tired at last, and then we shall repent of what we have done." He soon arrived at the sea, and the water was quite black and muddy, and a mighty whirlwind blew over it; but he went to the shore, and said,

> "O man of the sea!
> Come listen to me,
> For Alice my wife,
> The plague of my life,
> Hath sent me to beg a boon of thee!"

"What would she have now!" said the fish. "Ah!" said the fisherman, "she wants to be emperor." "Go home," said the fish; "she is emperor already."

So he went home again; and as he came near he saw his wife sitting on a very lofty throne made of solid gold, with a great crown on her head full two yards high, and on each side of her stood her guards and attendants in a row, each one smaller than the other, from the tallest giant down to a little dwarf no bigger than my finger. And before her stood princes, and dukes, and earls: and the fisherman went up to her and said, "Wife, are you emperor?" "Yes," said she, "I am emperor." "Ah!" said the man as he gazed upon her, "what a fine thing it is to be emperor!" "Husband," said she, "why should we stay at being emperor; I will be pope next." "O wife, wife!" said he, "how can you be pope? there is but one pope at a time in Christendom." "Husband," said she, "I will be pope this very day." "But," replied the husband, "the fish cannot make you pope." "What nonsense!" said she, "if he can make an emperor, he can make a pope, go and try him." So the fisherman went. But when he came to the shore the wind was raging, and the sea was tossed up and down like boiling water, and the ships were in the greatest distress and danced upon the waves most fearfully; in the middle of the sky there was a little blue, but towards the south it was all red as if a dreadful

storm was rising. At this the fisherman was terribly frightened, and trembled, so that his knees knocked together:
but he went to the shore and said,

"O man of the sea!
Come listen to me,
For Alice my wife,
The plague of my life,
Hath sent me to beg a boon of thee!"

"What does she want now?" said the fish. "Ah!"
said the fisherman, "my wife wants to be pope." "Go
home," said the fish, "she is pope already."

Then the fisherman went home, and found his wife
sitting on a throne that was two miles high; and she
had three great crowns on her head, and around stood
all the pomp and power of the Church; and on each side
were two rows of burning lights, of all sizes, the greatest
as large as the highest and biggest tower in the world,
and the least no larger than a small rush-light. "Wife,"
said the fisherman as he looked at all this grandeur, "are
you pope?" "Yes," said she, "I am pope." "Well,
wife," replied he, "it is a grand thing to be pope; and now
you must be content, for you can be nothing greater."
"I will consider of that," said the wife. Then they went
to bed: but Dame Alice could not sleep all night for
thinking what she should be next. At last morning came,
and the sun rose. "Ha!" thought she as she looked at it
through the window, "cannot I prevent the sun rising?"
At this she was very angry, and she wakened her husband,
and said, "Husband, go to the fish and tell him I want
to be lord of the sun and moon." The fisherman was
half asleep, but the thought frightened him so much, that
he started and fell out of bed. "Alas, wife!" said he,
"cannot you be content to be pope?" "No," said she, "I

am very uneasy, and cannot bear to see the sun and moon rise without my leave. Go to the fish directly."

Then the man went trembling for fear; and as he was going down to the shore a dreadful storm arose, so that the trees and the rocks shook; and the heavens became black, and the lightning played, and the thunder rolled; and you might have seen in the sea great black waves like mountains with a white crown of foam upon them; and the fisherman said,

> "O man of the sea!
> Come listen to me,
> For Alice my wife,
> The plague of my life,
> Hath sent me to beg a boon of thee!"

"What does she want now?" said the fish. "Ah!" said he, "she wants to be lord of the sun and moon." "Go home," said the fish, "to your ditch again!" And there they live to this very day.

The Tom-Tit and the Bear

ONE summer day, as the wolf and the bear were walking together in a wood, they heard a bird singing most delightfully. "Brother," said the bear, "what can that bird be that is singing so sweetly?" "O!" said the wolf, "that is his majesty the king of the birds, we must take care to show him all possible respect." (Now I should tell you that this bird was after all no other than the tom-tit.) "If that is the case," said the bear, "I should like to see the royal palace; so pray come along and show it to me." "Gently, my friend," said the wolf, "we cannot see it just yet, we must wait till the queen comes home."

Soon afterwards the queen came with food in her beak, and she and the king began to feed their young ones. "Now for it!" said the bear; and was about to follow them, to see what was to be seen. "Stop a little, master Bruin," said the wolf, "we must wait now till their majesties are gone again." So they marked the hole where they had seen the nest, and went away. But the bear, being very eager to see the royal palace, soon came back again, and peeping into the nest, saw five or six young birds lying at the bottom of it. "What nonsense!" said Bruin, "this is not a royal palace: I never saw such a filthy place in my life; and you are no royal children, you little base-born brats!" As soon as the young tom-tits heard this they were very angry, and screamed out "We are not base-born, you stupid bear! our father and mother are honest good

33

sort of people: and depend upon it you shall suffer for your insolence!" At this the wolf and the bear grew frightened, and ran away to their dens. But the young tom-tits kept crying and screaming; and when their father and mother came home and offered them food, they all said, "We will not touch a bit; no, not the leg of a fly, though we should die of hunger, till that rascal Bruin has been punished for calling us base-born brats." "Make yourselves easy, my darlings," said the old king, "you may be sure he shall meet with his deserts."

So he went out and stood before the bear's den, and cried out with a loud voice, "Bruin the bear! thou hast shamefully insulted our lawful children: we therefore hereby declare bloody and cruel war against thee and thine, which shall never cease until thou hast been punished as thou so richly deservest." Now when the bear heard this, he called together the ox, the ass, the stag, and all the beasts of the earth, in order to consult about the means of his defence. And the tom-tit also enlisted on his side all the birds of the air, both great and small, and a very large army of hornets, gnats, bees, and flies, and other insects.

As the time approached when the war was to begin, the tom-tit sent out spies to see who was the commander-in-chief of the enemy's forces; and the gnat, who was by far the cleverest spy of them all, flew backwards and forwards in the wood where the enemy's troops were, and at last hid himself under a leaf on a tree, close by which the orders of the day were given out. And the bear, who was standing so near the tree that the gnat could hear all he said, called to the fox and said, "Reynard, you are the cleverest of all the beasts; therefore you shall be our general and lead us to battle: but we must first agree upon some signal, by which we may know what you want us to do." "Behold," said the fox, "I have a fine, long, bushy tail, which is very like a plume of red feathers, and gives me a very warlike air: now remember, when you see me raise up my tail, you may be sure that the battle is won, and you have then nothing to do but to rush down upon the enemy with all your force. On the other hand, if I drop my tail, the day is lost, and you must run away as fast as you can." Now when the gnat had heard all this, she flew back to the tom-tit and told him everything that had passed.

At length the day came when the battle was to be fought; and as soon as it was light, behold! the army of beasts came rushing forward with such a fearful sound that the earth shook. And his majesty the tom-tit, with his troops, came flying along in warlike array, flapping and fluttering, and beating the air, so that it was quite frightful to hear; and both armies set themselves in order of battle upon the field. Now the tom-tit gave orders to a troop of hornets that at the first onset they should march straight towards Captain Reynard, and fixing themselves about his tail, should sting him with all their might and main. The hornets did as they were told: and when Reynard felt the first sting, he started aside and shook one of his legs, but still held up his tail with wonderful bravery; at the second sting he was forced to drop his tail for a moment; but when the third hornet had fixed itself, he could bear it no longer, but clapped his tail between his legs and scampered away as fast as he could. As soon as the beasts saw this, they thought of course all was lost, and scoured across the country in the greatest dismay, leaving the birds masters of the field.

And now the king and queen flew back in triumph to their children, and said, "Now, children, eat, drink, and be merry, for the victory is ours!" But the young birds said, "No: not till Bruin has humbly begged our pardon for calling us base-born."   So the king flew back to the bear's den, and cried out, "Thou villain bear! come forthwith to my abode, and humbly beseech my children to forgive thee the insult thou hast offered them; for, if thou wilt not do this, every bone in thy wretched body shall be broken to pieces."   So the bear was forced to crawl out of his den very sulkily, and do what the king bade him: and after that the young birds sat down together, and ate and drank and made merry till midnight.

The Twelve Dancing Princesses

THERE was a king who had twelve beautiful daughters. They slept in twelve beds all in one room; and when they went to bed, the doors were shut and locked up; but every morning their shoes were found to be quite worn through, as if they had been danced in all night; and yet nobody could find out how it happened, or where they had been.

Then the king made it known to all the land, that if any person could discover the secret, and find out where it was that the princesses danced in the night, he should have the one he liked best for his wife, and should be king after his death; but whoever tried and did not succeed, after three days and nights, should be put to death.

A king's son soon came. He was well entertained, and in the evening was taken to the chamber next to the one where the princesses lay in their twelve beds. There he was to sit and watch where they went to dance; and, in order that nothing might pass without his hearing it, the door of his chamber was left open. But the king's son soon fell asleep; and when he awoke in the morning he found that the princesses had all been dancing, for the soles of their shoes were full of holes. The same thing happened the second and third night: so the king ordered his head to be cut off. After him came several others; but they had all the same luck, and all lost their lives in the same manner.

Now it chanced that an old soldier, who had been wounded in battle and could fight no longer, passed through the country where this king reigned; and as he was travelling through a wood, he met an old woman, who asked him where he was going. "I hardly know where I am going, or what I had better do," said the soldier; "but I think I should like very well to find out where it is that the princesses dance, and then in time I might be a king." "Well," said the old dame, "that is no very hard task: only take care not to drink any of the wine which one of the princesses will bring to you in the evening; and as soon as she leaves you pretend to be fast asleep."

Then she gave him a cloak, and said, "As soon as you put that on you will become invisible, and you will then be able to follow the princesses wherever they go." When the soldier heard all this good counsel, he determined to try his luck: so he went to the king, and said he was willing to undertake the task.

He was as well received as the others had been, and the king ordered fine royal robes to be given him; and when the evening came he was led to the outer chamber. Just as he was going to lie down, the eldest of the princesses brought him a cup of wine; but the soldier threw it all away secretly, taking care not to drink a drop. Then he laid himself down on his bed, and in a little while began to snore very loud as if he was fast asleep. When the twelve princesses heard this they laughed heartily; and the eldest said, "This fellow too might have done a wiser thing than lose his life in this way!" Then they rose up and opened their drawers and boxes, and took out all their fine clothes, and dressed themselves at the glass, and skipped about as if they were eager to begin dancing. But the youngest said, "I don't know how it is, while you are so happy I feel very uneasy; I am sure some mischance will befall us."

"You simpleton," said the eldest, "you are always afraid; have you forgotten how many kings' sons have already watched us in vain?   And as for this soldier, even if I had not given him his sleeping draught, he would have slept soundly enough."

When they were all ready, they went and looked at the soldier; but he snored on, and did not stir hand or foot: so they thought they were quite safe; and the eldest went up to her own bed and clapped her hands, and the bed sunk into the floor and a trap-door flew open.   The soldier saw them going down through the trap-door one after another, the eldest leading the way; and thinking he had no time to lose, he jumped up, put on the cloak which the old woman had given him, and followed them; but in the middle of the stairs he trod on the gown of the youngest princess, and she cried out to her sisters, "All is not right; some one took hold of my gown."   "You silly creature!" said the eldest, "it is nothing but a nail in the wall."   Then down they all went, and at the bottom they found themselves in a most delightful grove of trees; and the leaves were all of silver, and glittered and sparkled beautifully.   The soldier wished to take away some token of the place; so he broke off a little branch, and there came a loud noise from the tree.   Then the youngest daughter said again, "I am sure all is not right—did not you hear that noise?   That never happened before."   But the eldest said, "It is only our princes, who are shouting for joy at our approach."

Then they came to another grove of trees, where all the leaves were of gold; and afterwards to a third, where the leaves were all glittering diamonds.   And the soldier broke a branch from each; and every time there was a loud noise, which made the youngest sister tremble with fear; but the eldest still said it was only the princes, who were crying for joy. So they went on till they came to a great lake; and at the side of the lake there lay twelve little boats with twelve handsome princes in them, who seemed to be waiting there for the princesses.

One of the princesses went into each boat, and the soldier stepped into the same boat with the youngest. As they were rowing over the lake, the prince who was in the boat with the youngest princess and the soldier said, "I do not know why it is, but though I am rowing with all my might we do not get on so fast as usual, and I am quite tired: the boat seems very heavy to-day." "It is only the heat of the weather," said the princess; "I feel it very warm too."

On the other side of the lake stood a fine illuminated castle, from which came the merry music of horns and trumpets. There they all landed, and went into the castle, and each prince danced with his princess; and the soldier, who was all the time invisible, danced with them too; and when any of the princesses had a cup of wine set by her, he drank it all up, so that when she put the cup to her mouth it was empty. All this, too, the youngest sister was terribly frightened, but the eldest always silenced her. They danced on till three o'clock in the morning, and then all their shoes were worn out, so that they were obliged to leave off. The princes rowed them back again over the lake; (but this time the soldier placed himself in the boat with the eldest princess;) and on the opposite shore they took leave of each other, the princesses promising to come again the next night.

When they came to the stairs, the soldier ran on before the princesses, and laid himself down; and as the twelve sisters slowly came up very much tired, they heard him snoring in his bed; so they said, "Now all is quite safe;" then they undressed themselves, put away their fine clothes, pulled off their shoes, and went to bed. In the morning the soldier said nothing about what had happened, but determined to see more of this strange adventure, and went again the second and third night; and everything happened just as before; the princesses danced each time till their shoes were worn to pieces, and then returned home. However, on the third night the soldier carried away one of the golden cups as a token of where he had been.

As soon as the time came when he was to declare the secret, he was taken before the king with the three branches and the golden cup; and the twelve princesses stood listening behind the door to hear what he would say. And when the king asked him "Where do my twelve daughters dance at night?" he answered, "With twelve princes in a castle underground." And then he told the king all that had happened, and showed him the three branches and the golden cup which he had brought with him. Then the king called for the princesses, and asked them whether what the soldier said was true: and when they saw that they were discovered, and that it was of no use to deny what had happened, they confessed it all. And the king asked the soldier which of them he would choose for his wife; and he answered, "I am not very young, so I will have the eldest."—And they were married that very day, and the soldier was chosen to be the king's heir.

Rose-Bud

or Sleeping Beauty

ONCE upon a time there lived a king and queen who had no children; and this they lamented very much. But one day as the queen was walking by the side of the river, a little fish lifted its head out of the water, and said, "Your wish shall be fulfilled, and you shall soon have a daughter." What the little fish had foretold soon came to pass; and the queen had a little girl that was so very beautiful that the king could not cease looking on it for joy, and determined to hold a great feast. So he invited not only his relations, friends and neighbours, but also all the fairies, that they might be kind and good to his little daughter. Now there were thirteen fairies in his kingdom, and he had only twelve golden dishes for them to eat out of, so that he was obliged to leave one of the fairies without an invitation. The rest came, and after the feast was over they gave all their best gifts to the little princess: one gave her virtue, another beauty, another riches, and so on till she had all that was excellent in the world. When eleven had done blessing her, the thirteenth, who had not been invited, and was very angry on that account, came in, and determined to take her revenge. So she cried out, "The king's daughter shall in her fifteenth year be wounded by a spindle, and fall down dead." Then the twelfth, who had not yet given her gift, came forward and said, that the bad wish must be fulfilled, but that she could

43

soften it, and that the king's daughter should not die, but fall asleep for a hundred years.

But the king hoped to save his dear child from the threatened evil, and ordered that all the spindles in the kingdom should be bought up and destroyed. All the fairies' gifts were in the meantime fulfilled; for the princess was so beautiful, and well-behaved, and amiable, and wise, that every one who knew her loved her. Now it happened that on the very day she was fifteen years old the king and queen were not at home, and she was left alone in the palace. So she roved about by herself, and looked at all the rooms and chambers, till at last she came to an old tower, to which there was a narrow staircase ending with a little door. In the door there was a golden key, and when she turned it the door sprang open, and there sat an old lady spinning away very busily. "Why, how now, good mother," said the princess, "what are you doing there?" "Spinning," said the old lady, and nodded her head. "How prettily that little thing turns round!" said the princess, and took the spindle and began to spin. But scarcely had she touched it, before the prophecy was fulfilled, and she fell down lifeless on the ground.

However, she was not dead, but had only fallen into a deep sleep; and the king and the queen, who just then came home, and all their court, fell asleep too; and the horses slept in the stables, and the dogs in the court, the pigeons on the house-top and the flies on the walls. Even the fire on the hearth left off blazing, and went to sleep; and the meat that was roasting stood still; and the cook, who was at that moment pulling the kitchen-boy by the hair to give him a box on the ear for something he had done amiss, let him go, and both fell asleep; and so everything stood still, and slept soundly.

A large hedge of thorns soon grew round the palace,

and every year it became higher and thicker, till at last the whole palace was surrounded and hid, so that not even the roof or the chimneys could be seen. But there went a report through all the land of the beautiful sleeping Rose-Bud (for so was the king's daughter called); so that from time to time several kings' sons came, and tried to break through the thicket into the palace. This they could never do; for the thorns and bushes laid hold of them as it were with hands, and there they stuck fast and died miserably.

After many many years there came a king's son into that land, and an old man told him the story of the thicket of thorns, and how a beautiful palace stood behind it, in which was a wondrous princess, called Rose-Bud, asleep with all her court. He told, too, how he had heard from his grandfather that many many princes had come, and had tried to break through the thicket, but had stuck fast and died. Then the young prince said, "All this shall not frighten me, I will go and see Rose-Bud." The old man tried to dissuade him, but he persisted in going.

Now that very day were the hundred years completed; and as the prince came to the thicket, he saw nothing but beautiful flowering shrubs, through which he passed with ease, and they closed after him as firm as ever. Then he came at last to the palace, and there in the court lay the dogs asleep, and the horses in the stables, and on the roof sat the pigeons fast asleep with their heads under their wings; and when he came into the palace, the flies slept on the walls, and the cook in the kitchen was still holding up her hand as if she would beat the boy, and the maid sat with a black fowl in her hand ready to be plucked.

Then he went on still further, and all was so still that he could hear every breath he drew; till at last he came to the old tower and opened the door of the little room in which Rose-Bud was; and there she lay fast asleep, and looked so beautiful that he could not take his eyes off, and he stooped down and gave her a kiss. But the moment he kissed her she opened her eyes and awoke, and smiled upon him. Then they went out together, and presently the king and queen also awoke, and all the court, and they gazed on each other with great wonder. And the horses got up and shook themselves, and the dogs jumped about and barked; the pigeons took their heads from under their wings, and looked about and fled into the fields; the flies on the walls buzzed away; the fire in the kitchen blazed up and cooked the dinner, and the roast meat turned round again; the cook gave the boy the box on his ear so that he cried out, and the maid went on plucking the fowl. And then was the wedding of the prince and Rose-Bud celebrated, and they lived happily together all their lives long.

Tom Thumb

THERE was once a poor woodman sitting by the fire in his cottage, and his wife sat by his side spinning. "How lonely it is," said he, "for you and me to sit here by ourselves without any children to play about and amuse us, while other people seem so happy and merry with their children!" "What you say is very true," said the wife, sighing and turning round her wheel, "how happy should I be if I had but one child! and if it were ever so small, nay, if it were no bigger than my thumb, I should be very happy, and love it dearly." Now it came to pass that this good woman's wish was fulfilled just as she desired; for, some time afterwards, she had a little boy who was quite healthy and strong, but not much bigger than my thumb. So they said, "Well, we cannot say we have not got what we wished for, and, little as he is, we will love him dearly;" and they called him Tom Thumb.

They gave him plenty of food, yet he never grew bigger, but remained just the same size as when he was born; still his eyes were sharp and sparkling, and he soon showed himself to be a clever little fellow, who always knew well what he was about. One day, as the woodman was getting ready to go into the wood to cut fuel, he said, "I wish I had some one to bring the cart after me, for I want to make haste." "Oh father!" cried Tom, "I will take care of that; the cart shall be in the wood by the time you want it." Then the woodman laughed, and said, "How can

that be? you cannot reach up to the horse's bridle."
"Never mind that, father," said Tom, "if my mother
will only harness the horse, I will get into his ear and tell
him which way to go." "Well," said the father, "we will
try for once."

When the time came, the mother harnessed the horse
to the cart, and put Tom into his ear; and as he sat there,
the little man told the beast how to go, crying out, "Go
on," and "Stop," as he wanted; so the horse went on just
as if the woodman had driven it himself into the wood.
It happened that, as the horse was going a little too fast,
and Tom was calling out "Gently! gently!" two strangers
came up. "What an odd thing that is!" said one, "there
is a cart going along, and I hear a carter talking to the
horse, but can see no one." "That is strange," said the
other; "let us follow the cart and see where it goes." So
they went on into the wood, till at last they came to the
place where the woodman was. Then Tom Thumb, seeing his father, cried out, "See, father, here I am, with the
cart, all right and safe; now take me down." So his father
took hold of the horse with one hand, and with the other
took his son out of the ear; then he put him down upon a
straw, where he sat as merry as you please. The two
strangers were all this time looking on, and did not know
what to say for wonder. At last one took the other aside
and said, "That little urchin will make our fortune if we
can get him and carry him about from town to town as a
show: we must buy him." So they went to the woodman
and asked him what he would take for the little man:
"He will be better off," said they, "with us than with
you." "I won't sell him at all," said the father, "my own
flesh and blood is dearer to me than all the silver and gold
in the world." But Tom, hearing of the bargain they
wanted to make, crept up his father's coat to his shoulder,

and whispered in his ear, "Take the money, father, and let them have me, I'll soon come back to you."

So the woodman at last agreed to sell Tom to the strangers for a large piece of gold. "Where do you like to sit?" said one of them. "Oh! put me on the rim of your hat, that will be a nice gallery for me; I can walk about there, and see the country as we go along." So they did as he wished; and when Tom had taken leave of his father, they took him away with them. They journeyed on till it began to be dusky, and then the little man said, "Let me get down, I'm tired." So the man took off his hat and set him down on a clod of earth in a ploughed field by the side of the road. But Tom ran about amongst the furrows, and at last slipt into an old mouse-hole. "Good night, masters," said he, "I'm off! mind and look sharp after me the next time." They ran directly to the place, and poked the ends of their sticks into the mouse-hole, but all in vain; Tom only crawled further and further in, and at last it became quite dark, so that they were obliged to go their way without their prize, as sulky as you please.

When Tom found they were gone, he came out of his hiding-place. "What dangerous walking it is," said he, "in this ploughed field! If I were to fall from one of these great clods, I should certainly break my neck." At last, by good luck, he found a large empty snail-shell. "This is lucky," said he, "I can sleep here very well," and in he crept. Just as he was falling asleep he heard two men passing, and one said to the other, "How shall we manage to steal that rich parson's silver and gold?" "I'll tell you," cried Tom. "What noise was that?" said the thief, frightened, "I am sure I heard some one speak." They stood still listening, and Tom said, "Take me with you, and I'll soon show you how to get the parson's money." "But where are you?" said they. "Look about on the ground," answered he, "and listen where the sound comes from." At last the thieves found him out, and lifted him up in their hands. "You little urchin!" said they, "what can you do for us?" "Why I can get between the iron window-bars of the parson's house, and throw you out whatever you want." "That's a good thought," said the thieves, "come along, we shall see what you can do."

When they came to the parson's house, Tom slipt through the window-bars into the room, and then called out as loud as he could bawl, "Will you have all that is here?" At this the thieves were frightened, and said, "Softly, softly! Speak low, that you may not awaken anybody." But Tom pretended not to understand them, and bawled out again, "How much will you have? Shall I throw it all out?" Now the cook lay in the next room, and hearing a noise she raised herself in her bed and listened. Meantime the thieves were frightened, and ran off to a little distance; but at last they plucked up courage, and said, "The little urchin is only trying to make fools of us." So they came back and whispered softly to him, saying, "Now let us have no more of your jokes, but throw out some of the money." Then Tom called out as loud as he could, "Very well: hold your hands, here it comes." The cook heard this quite plain, so she sprang out of bed and ran to open the door. The thieves ran off as if a wolf was at their tails; and the maid, having groped about and found nothing, went away for a light. By the time she returned, Tom had slipt off into the barn; and when the cook had looked about and searched every hole and corner, and found nobody, she went to bed, thinking she must have been dreaming with her eyes open. The little man crawled about in the hay-loft, and at last found a glorious place to finish his night's rest in; so he laid himself down, meaning to sleep till day-light, and then find his way home to his father and mother. But, alas! how cruelly was he disappointed! what crosses and sorrows happen in this world! The cook got up early before day-break to feed the cows: she went straight to the hay-loft, and carried away a large bundle of hay with the little man in the middle of it fast asleep. He still, however, slept on, and did not awake till he found himself in the mouth of the cow, who had taken him up with a mouthful of hay. "Good lack-a-day!" said he, "how did I manage to tumble into the mill?" But he soon found out where he really was, and was obliged to have all his wits about him in order that he might not get between the cow's teeth, and so be crushed to death. At last down he went into her stomach. "It is rather dark here," said he; "they forgot to build windows in this room to let the sun in: a candle would be no bad thing."

Though he made the best of his bad luck, he did not like his quarters at all; and the worst of it was, that more and more hay was always coming down, and the space in which he was became smaller and smaller. At last he cried out as loud as he could, "Don't bring me any more hay! Don't bring me any more hay!" The maid happened to be just then milking the cow, and hearing some one speak and seeing nobody, and yet being quite sure it was the same voice that she had heard in the night, she was so frightened that she fell off her stool and overset the milk-pail. She ran off as fast as she could to her master the parson, and said, "Sir, sir, the cow is talking!" But the parson said, "Woman, thou art surely mad!" However, he went with her into the cow-house to see what was the matter.—Scarcely had they set their foot on the threshold, when Tom called out, "Don't bring me any more hay!" Then the parson himself was frightened; and thinking the cow was surely bewitched, ordered that she should be killed directly. So the cow was killed, and the stomach, in which Tom lay, was thrown out upon a dunghill.

Tom soon set himself to work to get out, which was not a very easy task; but at last, just as he had made room to get his head out, a new misfortune befell him: a hungry wolf sprung out, and swallowed the whole stomach with Tom in it at a single gulp, and ran away. Tom, however, was not disheartened; and, thinking the wolf would not dislike having some chat with him as he was going along, he called out, "My good friend, I can show you a famous treat." "Where's that?" said the wolf. "In such and such a house," said Tom, describing his father's house, "you can crawl through the drain into the kitchen, and there you will find cakes, ham, beef, and everything your heart can desire." The wolf did not want to be asked twice; so that very night he went to the house and crawled through the drain into the kitchen, and ate and drank there to his heart's content. As soon as he was satisfied, he wanted to get away, but he had eaten so much that he could not get out the same way that he came in. This was just what Tom had reckoned upon; and he now began to set up a great shout, making all the noise he could. "Will you be quiet?" said the wolf: "you'll awaken everybody in the house." "What's that to me?" said the little man: "you have had your frolic, now I've a mind to be merry myself;" and he began again singing and shouting as loud as he could.

The woodman and his wife, being awakened by the noise, peeped through a crack in the door; but when they saw that the wolf was there, you may well suppose that they were terribly frightened; and the woodman ran for his axe, and gave his wife a scythe.—"Now do you stay behind," said the woodman; "and when I have knocked him on the head, do you rip up his belly for him with the scythe." Tom heard all this, and said, "Father, father! I am here, the wolf has swallowed me:" and his father said, "Heaven be praised! we have found our dear child again;" and he told his wife not to use the scythe, for fear she should hurt him. Then he aimed a great blow, and struck the wolf on the head, and killed him on the spot; and when he was dead they cut open his body and set Tommy free. "Ah!" said the father, "what fears we have had for you!" "Yes, father," answered he, "I have travelled all over the world, since we parted, in one way or other; and now I am very glad to get fresh air again." "Why, where have you been?" said his father. "I have been in a mouse-hole, in a snail-shell, down a cow's throat, and in the wolf's belly; and yet here I am again safe and sound." "Well," said they, "we will not sell you again for all the riches in the world." So they hugged and kissed their dear little son, and gave him plenty to eat and drink, and fetched new clothes for him, for his old ones were quite spoiled on his journey.

The Grateful Beasts

A CERTAIN man, who had lost almost all his money, resolved to set off with the little that was left him, and travel into the wide world. Then the first place he came to was a village, where the young people were running about crying and shouting. "What is the matter?" asked he. "See here," answered they, "we have got a mouse that we make dance to please us. Do look at him: what a droll sight it is! how he jumps about!" But the man pitied the poor little thing, and said, "Let the mouse go, and I will give you money." So he gave them some, and took the mouse and let him run; and he soon jumped into a hole that was close by, and was out of their reach.

Then he travelled on and came to another village, and there the children had got an ass that they made stand on its hind legs and tumble, at which they laughed and shouted, and gave the poor beast no rest. So the good man gave them also some money to let the poor ass alone.

At the next village he came to, the young people had got a bear that had been taught to dance, and they were plaguing the poor thing sadly. Then he gave them too some money to let the beast go, and the bear was very glad to get on his four feet, and seemed quite happy.

But the man had now given away all the money he had in the world, and had not a shilling in his pocket. Then said he to himself, "The king has heaps of gold in his treasury that he never uses; I cannot die of hunger, I hope

55

I shall be forgiven if I borrow a little, and when I get rich again I will repay it all."

Then he managed to get into the treasury, and took a very little money; but as he came out the king's guards saw him; so they said he was a thief, and took him to the Judge, and he was sentenced to be thrown into the water in a box. The lid of the box was full of holes to let in air, and a jug of water and a loaf of bread were given him.

Whilst he was swimming along in the water very sorrowfully, he heard something nibbling and biting at the lock; and all of a sudden it fell off, the lid flew open, and there stood his old friend the little mouse, who had done him this service. And then came the ass and the bear, and pulled the box ashore; and all helped him because he had been kind to them.

But now they did not know what to do next, and began to consult together; when on a sudden a wave threw on the shore a beautiful white stone that looked like an egg. Then the bear said, "That's a lucky thing: this is the wonderful stone, and whoever has it may have everything else that he wishes." So the man went and picked up the stone, and wished for a palace and a garden, and a stud of horses; and his wish was fulfilled as soon as he had made it. And there he lived in his castle and garden, with fine stables and horses; and all was so grand and beautiful, that he never could wonder and gaze at it enough.

After some time, some merchants passed by that way. "See," said they, "what a princely palace! The last time we were here, it was nothing but a desert waste." They were very curious to know how all this had happened; so they went in and asked the master of the palace how it had been so quickly raised. "I have done nothing myself," answered he, "it is the wonderful stone that did all."— "What a strange stone that must be!" said they: then he invited them in and showed it to them. They asked him whether he would sell it, and offered him all their goods for it; and the goods seemed so fine and costly, that he quite forgot that the stone would bring him in a moment a thousand better and richer things, and he agreed to make the bargain.

Scarcely was the stone, however, out of his hands before all his riches were gone, and he found himself sitting in his box in the water, with his jug of water and loaf of bread by his side. The grateful beasts, the mouse, the ass, and the bear, came directly to help him; but the mouse found she could not nibble off the lock this time, for it was a great deal stronger than before. Then the bear said, "We must find the wonderful stone again, or all our endeavours will be fruitless."

The merchants, meantime, had taken up their abode in the palace; so away went the three friends, and when they came near, the bear said, "Mouse, go in and look through the key-hole and see where the stone is kept: you are small, nobody will see you." The mouse did as she was told, but soon came back and said, "Bad news! I have looked in, and the stone hangs under the looking-glass by a red silk string, and on each side of it sits a great cat with fiery eyes to watch it."

Then the others took council together and said, "Go back again, and wait till the master of the palace is in bed asleep, then nip his nose and pull his hair." Away went the mouse, and did as they directed her; and the master jumped up very angry, and rubbed his nose, and cried, "Those rascally cats are good for nothing at all, they let the mice eat my very nose and pull the hair off my head." Then he hunted them out of the room; and so the mouse had the best of the game.

Next night as soon as the master was asleep, the mouse

crept in again, and nibbled at the red silken string to which the stone hung, till down it dropped, and she rolled it along to the door; but when it got there, the poor little mouse was quite tired; so she said to the ass, "Put in your foot, and lift it over the threshold." This was soon done: and they took up the stone, and set off for the water side. Then the ass said, "How shall we reach the box?" But the bear answered, "That is easily managed; I can swim very well, and do you, donkey, put your fore-feet over my shoulders;—mind and hold fast, and take the stone in your mouth: as for you, mouse, you can sit in my ear."

It was all settled thus, and away they swam. After a time, the bear began to brag and boast: "We are brave fellows, are not we, ass?" said he; "what do you think?" But the ass held his tongue, and said not a word. "Why don't you answer me?" said the bear, "you must be an ill-mannered brute not to speak when you're spoken to." When the ass heard this, he could hold no longer; so he opened his mouth, and dropped the wonderful stone. "I could not speak," said he; "did not you know I had the stone in my mouth? now 'tis lost, and that's your fault." "Do but hold your tongue and be quiet," said the bear; "and let us think what's to be done."

Then a council was held: and at last they called together all the frogs, their wives and families, relations and friends, and said, "A great enemy is coming to eat you all up; but never mind, bring us up plenty of stones, and we'll build a strong wall to guard you." The frogs hearing this were dreadfully frightened, and set to work, bringing up all the stones they could find. At last came a large fat frog pulling along the wonderful stone by the silken string: and when the bear saw it, he jumped for joy, and said, "Now we have found what we wanted." So he released the old frog from his load, and told him to tell his friends they might go about their business as soon as they pleased.

Then the three friends swam off again for the box; and the lid flew open, and they found that they were but just in time, for the bread was all eaten, and the jug almost empty. But as soon as the good man had the stone in his hand, he wished himself safe and sound in his palace again; and in a moment there he was, with his garden and his stables and his horses; and his three faithful friends dwelt with him, and they all spent their time happily and merrily as long as they lived.

Jorinda and Jorindel

THERE was once an old castle that stood in the middle of a large thick wood, and in the castle lived an old fairy. All the day long she flew about in the form of an owl, or crept about the country like a cat; but at night she always became an old woman again. When any youth came within a hundred paces of her castle, he became quite fixed, and could not move a step till she came and set him free: but when any pretty maiden came within that distance, she was changed into a bird; and the fairy put her into a cage and hung her up in a chamber in the castle. There were seven hundred of these cages hanging in the castle, and all with beautiful birds in them.

Now there was once a maiden whose name was Jorinda: she was prettier than all the pretty girls that ever were seen; and a shepherd whose name was Jorindel was very fond of her, and they were soon to be married. One day they went to walk in the wood, that they might be alone; and Jorindel said, "We must take care that we don't go too near to the castle." It was a beautiful evening; the last rays of the setting sun shone bright through the long stems of the trees upon the green underwood beneath, and the turtledoves sang plaintively from the tall birches.

Jorinda sat down to gaze upon the sun; Jorindel sat by her side; and both felt sad, they knew not why; but it seemed as if they were to be parted from one another for ever. They had wandered a long way; and when they

looked to see which way they should go home, they found
themselves at a loss to know what path to take.

The sun was setting fast, and already half of his circle
had disappeared behind the hill: Jorindel on a sudden
looked behind him, and as he saw through the bushes that
they had, without knowing it, sat down close under the old
walls of the castle, he shrank for fear, turned pale, and
trembled.   Jorinda was singing,

> The ring-dove sang from the willow spray,
>   Well-a-day! well-a-day!
> He mourn'd for the fate
> Of his lovely mate,
>   Well-a-day!

The song ceased suddenly.   Jorindel turned to see
the reason, and beheld his Jorinda changed into a nightingale; so that her song ended with a mournful *jug, jug*.
An owl with fiery eyes flew three times round them, and
three times screamed Tu whu! Tu whu! Tu whu!   Jorindel could not move: he stood fixed as a stone, and could
neither weep, nor speak, nor stir hand or foot.   And now
the sun went quite down; the gloomy night came; the owl
flew into a bush; and a moment after the old fairy came
forth pale and meagre, with staring eyes, and a nose and
chin that almost met one another.

She mumbled something to herself, seized the nightingale, and went away with it in her hand.   Poor Jorindel
saw the nightingale was gone,—but what could he do?
he could not speak, he could not move from the spot where
he stood.   At last the fairy came back, and sung with a
hoarse voice,

> Till the prisoner's fast,
> And her doom is cast,
>   There stay! Oh, stay!

When the charm is around her,
And the spell has bound her,
Hie away! away!

On a sudden Jorindel found himself free. Then he fell on his knees before the fairy, and prayed her to give him back his dear Jorinda: but she said he should never see her again, and went her way.

He prayed, he wept, he sorrowed, but **all in vain.** "Alas!" he said, "what will become of me?"

He could not return to his own home, so he went to a strange village, and employed himself in keeping sheep. Many a time did he walk round and round as near to the hated castle as he dared go. At last he dreamt one night that he found a beautiful purple flower, and in the middle of it lay a costly pearl; and he dreamt that he plucked the flower, and went with it in his hand into the castle, and that everything he touched with it was disenchanted, and that there he found his dear Jorinda again.

In the morning when he awoke, he began to search over hill and dale for this pretty flower; and eight long days he sought for it in vain: but on the ninth day early in the morning he found the beautiful purple flower; and in the middle of it was a large dew drop as big as a costly pearl.

Then he plucked the flower, and set out and travelled day and night till he came again to the castle. He walked nearer than a hundred paces to it, and yet he did not become fixed as before, but found that he could go close up to the door.

Jorindel was very glad to see this: he touched the door with the flower, and it sprang open, so that he went in through the court, and listened when he heard so many birds singing. At last he came to the chamber where the fairy sat, with the seven hundred birds singing in the seven hundred cages. And when she saw Jorindel she was very angry, and screamed with rage; but she could not come within two yards of him; for the flower he held in his hand protected him. He looked around at the birds, but alas! there were many many nightingales, and how then should he find his Jorinda? While he was thinking what to do, he observed that the fairy had taken down one of the cages, and was making her escape through the door. He ran or flew to her, touched the cage with the flower,—and his Jorinda stood before him. She threw her arms round his neck and looked as beautiful as ever, as beautiful as when they walked together in the wood.

Then he touched all the other birds with the flower, so that they resumed their old forms; and took his dear Jorinda home, where they lived happily together many years.

Hansel and Grettel

ONCE upon a time there dwelt on the outskirts of a large forest a poor woodcutter with his wife and two children; the boy was called Hansel and the girl Grettel. He had always little enough to live on, and once, when there was a great famine in the land, he could n't even provide them with daily bread. One night, as he was tossing about in bed, full of cares and worry, he sighed and said to his wife: "What 's to become of us? How are we to support our poor children, now that we have nothing more for ourselves?" "I 'll tell you what, husband," answered the woman; "early to-morrow morning we 'll take the children out into the thickest part of the wood; there we shall light a fire for them and give them each a piece of bread; then we 'll go on to our work and leave them alone. They won't be able to find their way home, and we shall thus be rid of them." "No, wife," said her husband, "that I won't do; how could I find it in my heart to leave my children alone in the wood? The wild beasts would soon come and tear them to pieces." "Oh! you fool," said she, "then we must all four die of hunger, and you may just as well go and plane the boards for our coffins;" and she left him no peace till he consented. "But I can't help feeling sorry for the poor children," added the husband.

The children, too, had not been able to sleep for hunger, and had heard what their stepmother had said to their father. Grettel wept bitterly and spoke to Hansel: "Now it 's all up with us." "No, no, Grettel," said Hansel, "don't fret yourself; I 'll be able to find a way of escape, no fear." And when the old people had fallen asleep he got up, slipped on his little coat, opened the back door, and stole out. The moon was shining clearly, and the white pebbles which lay in front of the house glittered like bits of silver. Hansel bent down and filled his pocket with as many of them as he could cram in. Then he went back and said to Grettel, " Be comforted, my dear little sister, and go to sleep: God will not desert us," and he lay down in bed again.

At daybreak, even before the sun was up, the woman came and woke the two children: " Get up, you lie-abeds, we 're all going to the forest to fetch wood." She gave them each a bit of bread and spoke: " There 's something for your luncheon, but don't you eat it up before, for it 's all you 'll get." Grettel took the bread under her apron, as Hansel had the stones in his pocket. Then they all set out together on the way to the forest. After they had walked for a little, Hansel stood still and looked back at the house, and this manœuvre he repeated again and again. His father observed him and spoke: " Hansel, what are you gazing at there, and why do you always remain behind? Take care, and don't lose your footing." " Oh! father," said Hansel, " I am looking back at my white kitten, which is sitting on the roof, waving me a farewell." The woman exclaimed: " What a donkey you are! That is n't your kitten, that 's the morning sun shining on the chimney." But Hansel had not looked back at his kitten, but had always dropped one of the white pebbles out of his pocket on to the path.

When they had reached the middle of the forest the father said: " Now, children, go and fetch a lot of wood, and I 'll light a fire that you may n't feel cold." Hansel and Grettel heaped up brushwood till they had made a pile nearly the size of a small hill. The brushwood was set fire to, and when the flames leaped high the woman said: " Now lie down at the fire, children, and rest yourselves: we are going into the forest to cut down wood;

when we 've finished we 'll come back and fetch you." Hansel
and Grettel sat down beside the fire, and at mid-day ate their
little bits of bread. They heard the strokes of the ax, so they
thought their father was quite near. But it was no ax they heard,
but a bough he had tied on to a dead tree, and that was blown
about by the wind. And when they had sat for a long time their
eyes closed with fatigue, and they fell fast asleep. When they
awoke at last it was pitch-dark. Grettel began to cry and said:
" How are we ever to get out of the wood?" But Hansel comforted her. "Wait a bit," he said, "till the moon is up, and then
we 'll find our way sure enough." And when the full moon had
risen he took his sister by the hand and followed the pebbles,
which shone like new threepenny bits and showed them the path.
They walked all through the night, and at daybreak reached
their father's house again. They knocked at the door, and when
the woman opened it she exclaimed: " You naughty children,
what a time you 've slept in the wood! We thought you were
never going to come back." But the father rejoiced, for his conscience had reproached him for leaving his children behind by
themselves.

Not long afterward there was again great dearth in the land,
and the children heard their mother address their father thus in
bed one night: " Everything is eaten up once more; we have
only half a loaf in the house, and when that 's done it 's all up
with us. The children must be got rid of; we 'll lead them
deeper into the wood this time, so that they won't be able to find
their way out again. There is no other way of saving ourselves."
The man's heart smote him heavily, and he thought, " Surely
it would be better to share the last bite with one's children!" But
his wife would n't listen to his arguments, and did nothing but
scold and reproach him. If a man yields once he 's done for, and
so, because he had given in the first time, he was forced to do so
the second.

But the children were awake and had heard the conversation. When the old people were asleep Hansel got up and wanted to go out and pick up pebbles again, as he had done the first time; but the woman had barred the door and Hansel could n't get out. But he consoled his little sister and said: "Don't cry, Grettel, and sleep peacefully, for God is sure to help us."

At early dawn the woman came and made the children get up. They received their bit of bread, but it was even smaller than the time before. On the way to the wood Hansel crumbled it in his pocket, and every few minutes he stood still and dropped a crumb on the ground. "Hansel, what are you stopping and looking about you for?" said the father. "I'm looking back at my little pigeon, which is sitting on the roof waving me a farewell," answered Hansel. "Fool!" said the wife; "that is n't your pigeon, it's the morning sun glittering on the chimney." But Hansel gradually threw all his crumbs on to the path. The woman led the children still deeper into the forest, further than they had ever been in their lives before. Then a big fire was lit again, and the mother said: "Just sit down there, children, and if you're tired you can sleep a bit; we're going into the forest to cut down wood, and in the evening when we're finished we'll come back to fetch you." At mid-day Grettel divided her bread with Hansel, for he had strewn his all along their path. Then they fell asleep, and evening passed away, but nobody came to the poor children. They did n't awake till it was pitch-dark, and Hansel comforted his sister, saying: "Only wait, Grettel, till the moon rises, then we shall see the bread-crumbs I scattered along the path; they will show us the way back to the house." When the moon appeared they got up, but they found no crumbs, for the thousands of birds that fly about the woods and fields had picked them all up. "Never mind," said Hansel to Grettel; "you'll see we'll still find a way out"; but all the same they did not. They wandered about the whole night, and the next day, from morning till evening, but they could not find a path out of the wood. They were very hungry, too, for they had nothing to eat but a few berries they found growing on the ground. And at last they were so tired that their legs refused to carry them any longer, so they lay down under a tree and fell fast asleep.

On the third morning after they had left their father's house they set about their wandering again, but only got deeper and deeper into the wood, and now they felt that if help did not come to them soon they must perish. At mid-day they saw a beautiful little snow-white bird sitting on a branch, which sang so sweetly that they stopped still and listened to it. And when its song was finished it flapped its wings and flew on in front of them. They followed it and came to a little house, on the roof of which it perched; and when they came quite near they saw that the cottage was made of bread and roofed with cakes, while the window was made of transparent sugar. "Now we'll set to," said Hansel, "and have a regular blow-out. I'll eat a bit of the roof, and you, Grettel, can eat some of the window, which you'll find a sweet morsel." Hansel stretched up his hand and broke off a little bit of the roof to see what it was like, and Grettel went to the casement and began to nibble at it. Thereupon a shrill voice called out from the room inside:

> "Nibble, nibble, little mouse,
> Who's nibbling my house?"

The children answered,

> "'T is Heaven's own child,
> The tempest wild,"

and went on eating, without putting themselves about. Hansel, who thoroughly appreciated the roof, tore down a big bit of it, while Grettel pushed out a whole round window-pane, and sat down the better to enjoy it. Suddenly the door opened and an ancient dame leaning on a staff hobbled out. Hansel and Grettel were so terrified that they let what they had in their hands fall. But the old woman shook her head and said: "Oh, ho! you dear children, who led you here? Just come in and stay with me; no ill shall befall you." She took them both by the hand and led them into the house, and laid a most sumptuous dinner before them — milk and sugared pancakes, with apples and nuts. After they had finished, two beautiful little white beds were prepared for them, and when Hansel and Grettel lay down in them they felt as if they had got into heaven.

The old woman had appeared to be most friendly, but she was really an old witch who had waylaid the children, and had only built the little bread house in order to lure them in. When any one came into her power she killed, cooked, and ate him, and held a regular feast-day for the occasion. Now, witches have red eyes and cannot see far, but, like beasts, they have a keen sense of smell and know when human beings pass by. When Hansel and Grettel fell into her hands she laughed maliciously and said jeeringly: "I've got them now; they sha'n't escape me." Early in the morning, before the children were awake, she arose, and when she saw them both sleeping so peacefully, with their round rosy cheeks, she muttered to herself: "That'll be a dainty bite." Then she seized Hansel with her bony hand and carried him into a little stable, and barred the door on him; he might scream as much as he liked, it did him no good. Then she went to Grettel, shook her till she awoke, and cried: "Get up, you lazy-bones; fetch water and cook something for your brother. When he's fat I'll eat him up." Grettel began to cry bitterly, but it was of no use: she had to do what the wicked witch bade her.

So the best food was cooked for poor Hansel, but Grettel got nothing but crab-shells. Every morning the old woman hobbled

out to the stable and cried: " Hansel, put out your finger, that
I may feel if you are getting fat." But Hansel always stretched
out a bone, and the old dame, whose eyes were dim, could n't see
it, and thinking always it was Hansel's finger, wondered why he
fattened so slowly. When four weeks passed and Hansel still
remained thin, she lost patience and determined to wait no longer.
" Hi! Grettel," she called to the girl, " be quick and get some
water. Hansel may be fat or thin, I 'm going to kill him to-
morrow and cook him." Oh! how the poor little sister sobbed
as she carried the water, and how the tears rolled down her
cheeks! " Kind Heaven help us now!" she cried; " if only the
wild beasts in the wood had eaten us, then at least we should have
died together." " Just hold your peace," said the old hag; " it
won't help you."

Early in the morning Grettel had to go out and hang up the
kettle full of water and light the fire. " First we 'll bake," said
the old dame; " I 've heated the oven already and kneaded the
dough." She pushed Grettel out to the oven, from which fiery
flames were already issuing. " Creep in," said the witch, " and
see if it 's properly heated, so that we can shove in the bread."
For when she had got Grettel in she meant to close the oven and
let the girl bake, that she might eat her up too. But Grettel perceived her intention and spoke: " I don't know how I 'm to do
it; how do I get in?" " You silly goose!" said the hag, " the
opening is big enough; see, I could get in myself "; and she
crawled toward it and poked her head into the oven. Then
Grettel gave her a shove that sent her right in, shut the iron door,
and drew the bolt. Gracious! how she yelled! it was quite hor-
rible; but Grettel fled, and the wretched old woman was left
to perish miserably.

Grettel flew straight to Hansel, opened the little stable door,
and cried: " Hansel, we are free; the old witch is dead." Then
Hansel sprang like a bird out of a cage when the door is opened.

How they rejoiced, and fell on each other's necks, and jumped for joy, and kissed one another! And as they had no longer any cause for fear, they went into the old hag's house, and there they found, in every corner of the room, boxes with pearls and precious stones. "These are even better than pebbles," said Hansel, and crammed his pockets full of them; and Grettel said, "I too will bring something home"; and she filled her apron full. "But now," said Hansel, "let's go and get well away from the witch's wood." When they had wandered about for some hours they came to a big lake. "We can't get over," said Hansel; "I see no bridge of any sort or kind." "Yes, and there's no ferry-boat either," answered Grettel; "but look, there swims a white duck; if I ask her she'll help us over"; and she called out:

> "Here are two children, mournful very,
> Seeing neither bridge nor ferry;
> Take us upon your white back,
> And row us over quack, quack!"

The duck swam toward them, and Hansel got on her back and bade his little sister sit beside him. "No," answered Grettel, "we should be too heavy a load for the duck: she shall carry us across separately." The good bird did this, and when they were landed safely on the other side and had gone on for awhile, the wood became more and more familiar to them, and at length they saw their father's house in the distance. Then they set off to run, and bounding into the room fell on their father's neck. The man had not passed a happy hour since he left them in the wood, but the woman had died. Grettel shook out her apron so that the pearls and precious stones rolled about the room, and Hansel threw down one handful after the other out of his pocket. Thus all their troubles were ended, and they all lived happily ever afterward.

My story is done. See! there runs a little mouse; any one who catches it may make himself a large fur cap out of it.

The Queen Bee

TWO king's sons once upon a time went out into the world to seek their fortunes; but they soon fell into a wasteful foolish way of living, so that they could not return home again. Then their young brother, who was a little insignificant dwarf, went out to seek for his brothers: but when he had found them they only laughed at him, to think that he, who was so young and simple, should try to travel through the world, when they, who were so much wiser, had been unable to get on. However, they all set out on their journey together, and came at last to an ant-hill. The two elder brothers would have pulled it down, in order to see how the poor ants in their fright would run about and carry off their eggs. But the little dwarf said, "Let the poor things enjoy themselves, I will not suffer you to trouble them."

So on they went, and came to a lake where many many ducks were swimming about. The two brothers wanted to catch two, and roast them. But the dwarf said, "Let the poor things enjoy themselves, you shall not kill them." Next they came to a bees' nest in a hollow tree, and there was so much honey that it ran down the trunk; and the two brothers wanted to light a fire under the tree and kill the bees, so as to get their honey. But the dwarf held them back, and said, "Let the pretty insects enjoy themselves, I cannot let you burn them."

At length the three brothers came to a castle: and as

they passed by the stables they saw fine horses standing there, but all were of marble, and no man was to be seen. Then they went through all the rooms, till they came to a door on which were three locks: but in the middle of the door there was a wicket, so that they could look into the next room. There they saw a little grey old man sitting at a table; and they called to him once or twice, but he did not hear: however, they called a third time, and then he rose and came out to them.

He said nothing, but took hold of them and led them to a beautiful table covered with all sorts of good things: and when they had eaten and drunk, he showed each of them to a bedchamber.

The next morning he came to the eldest and took him to a marble table, where were three tablets, containing an account of the means by which the castle might be disenchanted. The first tablet said—"In the wood, under the moss, lie the thousand pearls belonging to the king's daughter; they must all be found: and if one be missing by set of sun, he who seeks them will be turned into marble."

The eldest brother set out, and sought for the pearls the whole day; but the evening came, and he had not found the first hundred: so he was turned into stone as the tablet had foretold.

The next day the second brother undertook the task; but he succeeded no better than the first; for he could only find the second hundred of the pearls; and therefore he too was turned into stone.

At last came the little dwarf's turn; and he looked in the moss; but it was so hard to find the pearls, and the job was so tiresome!—so he sat down upon a stone and cried. And as he sat there, the king of the ants (whose life he had saved) came to help him, with five thousand ants; and it was not long before they had found all the pearls and lay them in a heap.

The second tablet said—"The key of the princess's bedchamber must be fished up out of the lake." And as the dwarf came to the brink of it, he saw the two ducks whose lives he had saved swimming about; and they dived down and soon brought up the key from the bottom.

The third task was the hardest. It was to choose out the youngest and the best of the king's three daughters. Now they were all beautiful, and all exactly alike: but he was told that the eldest had eaten a piece of sugar, the next some sweet syrup, and the youngest a spoonful of honey; so he was to guess which it was that had eaten the honey.

Then came the queen of the bees, who had been saved by the little dwarf from the fire, and she tried the lips of all three; but at last she sat upon the lips of the one that had eaten the honey; and so the dwarf knew which was the youngest. Thus the spell was broken, and all who had been turned into stones awoke, and took their proper forms. And the dwarf married the youngest and the best of the princesses, and was king after her father's death; but his two brothers married the other two sisters.

Frederick and Catherine

THERE was once a man called Frederick: he had a wife whose name was Catherine, and they had not long been married. One day Frederick said, "Kate! I am going to work in the fields; when I come back I shall be hungry, so let me have something nice cooked, and a good draught of ale." "Very well," said she, "it shall all be ready." When dinner-time drew nigh, Catherine took a nice steak, which was all the meat she had, and put it on the fire to fry. The steak soon began to look brown, and to crackle in the pan; and Catherine stood by with a fork and turned it: then she said to herself, "The steak is almost ready, I may as well go to the cellar for the ale." So she left the pan on the fire, and took a large jug and went into the cellar and tapped the ale cask. The beer ran into the jug, and Catherine stood looking on. At last it popped into her head, "The dog is not shut up—he may be running away with the steak; that's well thought of." So up she ran from the cellar; and sure enough the rascally cur had got the steak in his mouth, and was making off with it.

Away ran Catherine, and away ran the dog across the field: but he ran faster than she, and stuck close to the steak. "It's all gone, and 'what can't be cured must be endured,'" said Catherine. So she turned round; and as she had run a good way and was tired, she walked home leisurely to cool herself.

Now all this time the ale was running too, for Catherine had not turned the cock; and when the jug was full the liquor ran upon the floor till the cask was empty. When she got to the cellar stairs she saw what had happened. "My stars!" said she, "what shall I do to keep Frederick from seeing all this slopping about?" So she thought a while; and at last remembered that there was a sack of fine meal bought at the last fair, and that if she sprinkled this over the floor it would suck up the ale nicely. "What a lucky thing," said she, "that we kept that meal! we have now a good use for it." So away she went for it: but she managed to set it down just upon the great jug full of beer, and upset it; and thus all the ale that had been saved was set swimming on the floor also. "Ah! well," said she, "when one goes, another may as well follow." Then she strewed the meal all about the cellar, and was quite pleased with her cleverness, and said, "How very neat and clean it looks!"

At noon Frederick came home. "Now, wife," cried he, "what have you for dinner?" "O Frederick!" answered she, "I was cooking you a steak; but while I went down to draw the ale, the dog ran away with it; and while I ran after him, the ale all ran out; and when I went to dry up the ale with the sack of meal that we got at the fair, I upset the jug: but the cellar is now quite dry, and looks so clean!" "Kate, Kate," said he, "how could you do all this? Why did you leave the steak to fry, and the ale to run, and then spoil all the meal?" "Why, Frederick," said she, "I did not know I was doing wrong, you should have told me before."

The husband thought to himself, If my wife manages matters thus, I must look sharp myself. Now he had a good deal of gold in the house: so he said to Catherine, "What pretty yellow buttons these are! I shall put them into a box and bury them in the garden; but take care that you never go near or meddle with them." "No, Frederick," said she, "that I never will." As soon as he was gone, there came by some pedlars with earthenware plates and dishes, and they asked her whether she would buy. "Oh dear me, I should like to buy very much, but I have no money: if you had any use for yellow buttons, I might deal with you." "Yellow buttons!" said they: "let us have a look at them." "Go into the garden, and dig where I tell you, and you will find the yellow buttons: I dare not go myself." So the rogues went: and when they found what these yellow buttons were, they took them all away, and left her plenty of plates and dishes. Then she set them all about the house for a show: and when Frederick came back, he cried out, "Kate, what have you been doing?" "See," said she, "I have bought all these with your yellow buttons: but I did not touch them myself; the pedlars went themselves and dug them up." "Wife, wife," said Frederick, "what a pretty piece of work you have made! those yellow buttons were all my money: how came you to do such a thing?" "Why," answered she, "I did not know there was any harm in it; you should have told me."

Catherine stood musing for a while, and at last said to her husband, "Hark ye, Frederick, we will soon get the gold back: let us run after the thieves." "Well, we will try," answered he; "but take some butter and cheese with you, that we may have something to eat by the way." "Very well," said she; and they set out: and as Frederick walked the fastest, he left his wife some way behind. "It does not matter," thought she: "when we turn back, I shall be so much nearer home than he."

Presently she came to the top of a hill; down the side of which there was a road so narrow that the cart-wheels always chafed the trees on each side as they passed. "Ah, see now," said she, "how they have bruised and wounded those poor trees; they will never get well." So she took pity on them, and made use of the butter to grease them all, so that the wheels might not hurt them so much. While she was doing this kind office, one of her cheeses fell out of the basket, and rolled down the hill. Catherine looked, but could not see where it was gone; so she said, "Well, I suppose the other will go the same way and find you; he has younger legs than I have." Then she rolled the other cheese after it; and away it went, nobody knows where, down the hill. But she said she supposed they knew the road, and would follow her, and she could not stay there all day waiting for them.

At last she overtook Frederick, who desired her to give him something to eat. Then she gave him the dry bread. "Where are the butter and cheese?" said he. "Oh!" answered she, "I used the butter to grease those poor trees that the wheels chafed so: and one of the cheeses ran away, so I sent the other after it to find it, and I suppose they are both on the road together somewhere." "What a goose you are to do such silly things!" said the husband. "How can you say so?" said she; "I am sure you never told me not."

They ate the dry bread together; and Frederick said, "Kate, I hope you locked the door safe when you came away." "No," answered she, "you did not tell me." "Then go home, and do it now before we go any further," said Frederick, "and bring with you something to eat."

Catherine did as he told her, and thought to herself by the way, "Frederick wants something to eat; but I don't think he is very fond of butter and cheese: I'll bring him a bag of fine nuts, and the vinegar, for I have often seen him take some."

When she reached home, she bolted the back door, but the front door she took off the hinges, and said, "Frederick told me to lock the door, but surely it can nowhere be so safe as if I take it with me." So she took her time by the way: and when she overtook her husband she cried out, "There, Frederick, there is the door itself, now you may watch it as carefully as you please." "Alas! alas!" said he, "what a clever wife I have! I sent you to make the house fast, and you take the door away, so that everybody may go in and out as they please:—however, as you have brought the door, you shall carry it about with you for your pains." "Very well," answered she, "I'll carry the door; but I'll not carry the nuts and vinegar bottle also,—that would be too much of a load; so, if you please, I'll fasten them to the door."

Frederick of course made no objection to that plan, and they set off into the wood to look for the thieves; but they could not find them: and when it grew dark, they climbed up into a tree to spend the night there. Scarcely were they up, than who should come by but the very rogues they were looking for. They were in truth great rascals, and belonged to that class of people who find things before they are lost: they were tired; so they sat down and made a fire under the very tree where Frederick and Catherine were. Frederick slipped down on the other side, and picked up some stones. Then he climbed up again, and tried to hit the thieves on the head with them: but they only said, "It must be near morning, for the wind shakes the fir-apples down."

Catherine, who had the door on her shoulder, began to be very tired; but she thought it was the nuts upon it that were so heavy: so she said softly, "Frederick, I must let the nuts go." "No," answered he, "not now, they will discover us." "I can't help that, they must go." "Well

then, make haste and throw them down, if you will."
Then away rattled the nuts down among the boughs; and
one of the thieves cried, "Bless me it is hailing."

A little while after, Catherine thought the door was
still very heavy: so she whispered to Frederick, "I must
throw the vinegar down." "Pray don't," answered he,
"it will discover us." "I can't help that," said she, "go
it must." So she poured all the vinegar down; and the
thieves said, "What a heavy dew there is!"

At last it popped into Catherine's head that it was
the door itself that was so heavy all the time: so she whispered Frederick, "I must throw the door down soon."
But he begged and prayed her not to do so, for he was
sure it would betray them. "Here goes, however," said
she: and down went the door with such a clatter upon the
thieves, that they cried out "Murder!" and not knowing
what was coming, ran away as fast as they could, and left
all the gold. So when Frederick and Catherine came
down, there they found all their money safe and sound.

The Three Children of Fortune

ONCE upon a time a father sent for his three sons, and gave to the eldest a cock, to the second a scythe, and to the third a cat. "I am now old," said he, "my end is approaching, and I would fain provide for you before I die. Money I have none, and what I now give you seems of but little worth; yet it rests with yourselves alone to turn my gifts to good account. Only seek out for a land where what you have is as yet unknown, and your fortune is made."

After the death of the father, the eldest set out with his cock: but wherever he went, in every town he saw from afar off a cock sitting upon the church steeple, and turning round with the wind. In the villages he always heard plenty of them crowing, and his bird was therefore nothing new; so there did not seem much chance of his making his fortune. At length it happened that he came to an island where the people who lived there had never heard of a cock, and knew not even how to reckon the time. They knew, indeed, if it were morning or evening; but at night, if they lay awake, they had no means of knowing how time went. "Behold," said he to them, "what a noble animal this is! how like a knight he is! he carries a bright red crest upon his head, and spurs upon his heels; he crows three times every night, at stated hours, and at the third time the sun is about to rise. But this is not all; sometimes he screams in broad day-light, and then you must take warning, for the weather is surely about to change." This pleased the

83

natives mightily; they kept awake one whole night, and heard, to their great joy, how gloriously the cock called the hour, at two, four, and six o'clock. Then they asked him whether the bird was to be sold, and how much he would sell it for. "About as much gold as an ass can carry," said he. "A very fair price for such an animal," cried they with one voice; and agreed to give him what he asked.

When he returned home with his wealth, his brothers wondered greatly; and the second said, "I will now set forth likewise, and see if I can turn my scythe to as good an account." There did not seem, however, much likelihood of this; for go where he would, he was met by peasants who had as good a scythe on their shoulders as he had. But at last, as good luck would have it, he came to an island where the people had never heard of a scythe: there, as soon as the corn was ripe, they went into the fields and pulled it up; but this was very hard work, and a great deal of it was lost. The man then set to work with his scythe; and mowed down their whole crop so quickly, that the people stood staring open-mouthed with wonder. They were willing to give him what he asked for such a marvellous thing: but he only took a horse laden with as much gold as it could carry.

Now the third brother had a great longing to go and see what he could make of his cat. So he set out: and at first it happened to him as it had to the others, so long as he kept upon the mainland, he met with no success; there were plenty of cats everywhere, indeed too many, so that the young ones were for the most part, as soon as they came into the world, drowned in the water. At last he passed over to an island, where, as it chanced most luckily for him, nobody had ever seen a cat; and they were overrun with mice to such a degree, that the little wretches danced upon the tables and chairs, whether the master of the house were at home or not. The people complained loudly of this grievance; the king himself knew not how to rid himself of them in his palace; in every corner mice were squeaking, and they gnawed everything that their teeth could lay hold of. Here was a fine field for Puss— she soon began her chase, and had cleared two rooms in the twinkling of an eye; when the people besought their king to buy the wonderful animal, for the good of the public, at any price. The king willingly gave what was asked,—a mule laden with gold and jewels; and thus the third brother returned home with a richer prize than either of the others.

Meantime the cat feasted away upon the mice in the royal palace, and devoured so many that they were no longer in any great numbers. At length, quite spent and tired with her work, she became extremely thirsty; so she stood still, drew up her head, and cried, "Miau, Miau!" The king gathered together all his subjects when they heard this strange cry, and many ran shrieking in a great fright out of the palace. But the king held a council below as to what was best to be done; and it was at length fixed to send a herald to the cat, to warn her to leave the castle forthwith, or that force would be used to remove her. "For," said the counsellors, "we would far more willingly put up with the mice (since we are used to that evil), than get rid of them at the risk of our lives." A page accordingly went, and asked the cat whether she were willing to quit the castle. But Puss, whose thirst became every moment more and more pressing, answered nothing but "Miau! Miau!" which the page interpreted to mean "No! No!" and therefore carried this answer to the king. "Well," said the counsellors, "then we must try what force will do." So the guns were planted, and the palace was fired upon from all sides. When the fire reached the room where the cat was, she sprang out of the window and ran away; but the besiegers did not see her, and went on firing until the whole palace was burnt to the ground.

He dressed himself as a poor man, and came secretly to the king's court.

THE GOLDEN BIRD

Page 23

They said he was a thief, and took him to the Judge.

THE GRATEFUL BEASTS

Page 56

King Grisly-Beard

A GREAT king had a daughter who was very beautiful, but so proud and haughty and conceited, that none of the princes who came to ask her in marriage were good enough for her, and she only made sport of them.

Once upon a time the king held a great feast, and invited all her suitors; and they sat in a row according to their rank, kings and princes and dukes and earls. Then the princess came in and passed by them all, but she had something spiteful to say to every one. The first was too fat: "He's as round as a tub," said she. The next was too tall: "What a maypole!" said she. The next was too short: "What a dumpling!" said she. The fourth was too pale, and she called him "Wallface." The fifth was too red, so she called him "Cockscomb." The sixth was not straight enough, so she said he was like a green stick that had been laid to dry over a baker's oven. And thus she had some joke to crack upon every one: but she laughed more than all at a good king who was there. "Look at him," said she, "his beard is like an old mop, he shall be called Grisly-beard." So the king got the nickname of Grisly-beard.

But the old king was very angry when he saw how his daughter behaved, and how she ill-treated all his guests; and he vowed that, willing or unwilling, she should marry the first beggar that came to the door.

Two days after there came by a travelling musician,

who began to sing under the window, and beg alms: and when the king heard him, he said, "Let him come in." So they brought in a dirty-looking fellow; and when he had sung before the king and the princess, he begged a boon. Then the king said, "You have sung so well, that I will give you my daughter for your wife." The princess begged and prayed; but the king said, "I have sworn to give you to the first beggar and I will keep my word." So words and tears were of no avail; the parson was sent for, and she was married to the musician. When this was over, the king said, "Now get ready to go; you must not stay here; you must travel on with your husband."

Then the beggar departed, and took her with him; and they soon came to a great wood. "Pray," said she, "whose is this wood?" "It belongs to king Grisly-beard," answered he; "hadst thou taken him, all had been thine." "Ah! unlucky wretch that I am!" sighed she, "would that I had married king Grisly-beard!" Next they came to some fine meadows. "Whose are these beautiful green meadows?" said she. "They belong to king Grisly-beard; hadst thou taken him, they had all been thine." "Ah! unlucky wretch that I am!" said she, "would that I had married king Grisly-beard!"

Then they came to a great city. "Whose is this noble city?" said she. "It belongs to king Grisly-beard; hadst thou taken him, it had all been thine." "Ah! miserable wretch that I am!" sighed she, "why did I not marry king Grisly-beard?" "That is no business of mine," said the musician; "why should you wish for another husband? am not I good enough for you?"

At last they came to a small cottage. "What a paltry place!" said she; "to whom does that little dirty hole belong?" The musician answered, "That is your and my house, where we are to live." "Where are your servants?"

cried she. "What do we want with servants?" said he, "you must do for yourself whatever is to be done. Now make the fire, and put on water and cook my supper, for I am very tired." But the princess knew nothing of making fires and cooking, and the beggar was forced to help her. When they had eaten a very scanty meal they went to bed; but the musician called her up very early in the morning to clean the house. Thus they lived for two days: and when they had eaten up all there was in the cottage, the man said, "Wife, we can't go on thus, spending money and earning nothing. You must learn to weave baskets." Then he went out and cut willows and brought them home, and she began to weave; but it made her fingers very sore. "I see this work won't do," said he, "try and spin; perhaps you will do that better." So she sat down and tried to spin; but the threads cut her tender fingers till the blood ran. "See now," said the musician, "you are good for nothing, you can do no work;—what a bargain I have got! However, I'll try and set up a trade in pots and pans, and you shall stand in the market and sell them." "Alas!" sighed she, "when I stand in the market and any of my father's court pass by and see me there, how they will laugh at me!"

But the beggar did not care for that; and said she must work, if she did not wish to die of hunger. At first the trade went well; for many people, seeing such a beautiful woman, went to buy her wares, and paid their money without thinking of taking away the goods. They lived on this as long as it lasted, and then her husband bought a fresh lot of ware, and she sat herself down with it in the corner of the market; but a drunken soldier soon came by, and rode his horse against her stall and broke all her goods into a thousand pieces. Then she began to weep, and knew not what to do. "Ah! what will become of me!" said she;

"what will my husband say?" So she ran home and told him all. "Who would have thought you would have been so silly," said he, "as to put an earthenware stall in the corner of the market, where everybody passes?—But let us have no more crying; I see you are not fit for this sort of work: so I have been to the king's palace, and asked if they did not want a kitchen-maid, and they have promised to take you, and there you will have plenty to eat."

Thus the princess became a kitchen-maid, and helped the cook to do all the dirtiest work: she was allowed to carry home some of the meat that was left, and on this she and her husband lived.

She had not been there long, before she heard that the king's eldest son was passing by, going to be married; and she went to one of the windows and looked out. Everything was ready, and all the pomp and splendour of the court was there. Then she thought with an aching heart on her own sad fate, and bitterly grieved for the pride and folly which had brought her so low. And the servants gave her some of the rich meats, which she put into her basket to take home.

All on a sudden, as she was going out, in came the king's son in golden clothes: and when he saw a beautiful woman at the door, he took her by the hand, and said she should be his partner in the dance: but she trembled for fear, for she saw that it was king Grisly-beard, who was making sport of her. However, he kept fast hold and led her in; and the cover of the basket came off, so that the meats in it fell all about. Then everybody laughed and jeered at her; and she was so abashed that she wished herself a thousand feet deep in the earth. She sprang to the door to run away; but on the steps king Grisly-beard overtook and brought her back, and said, "Fear me not! I am the musician who has lived with you in the hut: I brought you there because I loved you. I am also the soldier who overset your stall. I have done all this only to cure you of pride, and to punish you for the ill-treatment you bestowed on me. Now all is over; you have learnt wisdom, your faults are gone, and it is time to celebrate our marriage feast!"

Then the chamberlains came and brought her the most beautiful robes; and her father and his whole court were there already, and congratulated her on her marriage. Joy was in every face. The feast was grand, and all were merry; and I wish you and I had been of the party.

The Adventures of Chanticleer and Partlet

1. How they went to the Mountains to eat Nuts.

"THE nuts are quite ripe now," said Chanticleer to his wife Partlet, "suppose we go together to the mountains, and eat as many as we can, before the squirrel takes them all away." "With all my heart," said Partlet, "let us go and make a holiday of it together." So they went to the mountains; and as it was a lovely day they stayed there till the evening. Now, whether it was that they had eaten so many nuts that they could not walk, or whether they were lazy and would not, I do not know: however, they took it into their heads that it did not become them to go home on foot. So Chanticleer began to build a little carriage of nut-shells: and when it was finished, Partlet jumped into it and sat down, and bid Chanticleer harness himself to it and draw her home. "That's a good joke!" said Chanticleer; "no, that will never do; I had rather by half walk home; I'll sit on the box and be coachman, if you like, but I'll not draw." While this was passing, a duck came quacking up, and cried out, "You thieving vagabonds, what business have you in my grounds? I'll give it you well for your insolence!" and upon that she fell upon Chanticleer most lustily. But Chanticleer was no coward, and returned the duck's blows with his sharp spurs so fiercely, that she soon began to cry out for mercy; which was only granted her upon condition that she would draw the carriage home for them. This she agreed to do; and

93

Chanticleer got upon the box, and drove, crying, "Now, duck, get on as fast as you can." And away they went at a pretty good pace.

After they had travelled along a little way, they met a needle and a pin walking together along the road: and the needle cried out, "Stop! stop!" and said it was so dark that they could hardly find their way, and such dirty walking they could not get on at all: he told them that he and his friend, the pin, had been at a public house a few miles off, and had sat drinking till they had forgotten how late it was; he begged therefore that the travellers would be so kind as to give them a lift in their carriage. Chanticleer, observing that they were but thin fellows, and not likely to take up much room, told them they might ride, but made them promise not to dirty the wheels of the carriage in getting in, nor to tread on Partlet's toes.

Late at night they arrived at an inn; and as it was bad travelling in the dark, and the duck seemed much tired, and waddled about a good deal from one side to the other, they made up their minds to fix their quarters there: but the landlord at first was unwilling, and said his house was full, thinking they might not be very respectable company: however, they spoke civilly to him, and gave him the egg which Partlet had laid by the way, and said they would give him the duck, who was in the habit of laying one every day: so at last he let them come in, and they bespoke a handsome supper, and spent the evening very jollily.

Early in the morning, before it was quite light, and when nobody was stirring in the inn, Chanticleer awakened his wife, and, fetching the egg, they pecked a hole in it, ate it up, and threw the shells into the fire-place: they then went to the pin and needle, who were fast asleep, and, seizing them by their heads, stuck one into the landlord's easy-chair, and the other into his handkerchief; and having done this, they crept away as softly as possible. However, the duck, who slept in the open air in the yard, heard them coming, and jumping into the brook which ran close by the inn, soon swam out of their reach.

An hour or two afterwards the landlord got up, and took his handkerchief to wipe his face, but the pin ran into him and pricked him: then he walked into the kitchen to light his pipe at the fire, but when he stirred it up the egg-shells flew into his eyes, and almost blinded him. "Bless me!" said he, "all the world seems to have a design against my head this morning:" and so saying, he threw himself sulkily into his easy-chair; but, oh dear! the needle ran into him; and this time the pain was not in his head. He now flew into a very great passion, and, suspecting the company who had come in the night before, he went to look after them, but they were all off; so he swore that he never again would take in such a troop of vagabonds, who ate a great deal, paid no reckoning, and gave him nothing for his trouble but their apish tricks.

2. How Chanticleer and Partlet went to visit Mr. Korbes.

Another day, Chanticleer and Partlet wished to ride out together; so Chanticleer built a handsome carriage with four red wheels, and harnessed six mice to it; and then he and Partlett got into the carriage, and away they drove. Soon afterwards a cat met them, and said, "Where are you going?" And Chanticleer replied,

> "All on our way
> A visit to pay
> To Mr. Korbes, the fox, to-day."

Then the cat said, "Take me with you." Chanticleer

said, "With all my heart: get up behind, and be sure you do not fall off."

> "Take care of this handsome coach of mine,
> Nor dirty my pretty red wheels so fine!
> Now, mice, be ready,
> And, wheels, run steady!
> For we are going a visit to pay
> To Mr. Korbes, the fox, to-day."

Soon after came up a mill-stone, an egg, a duck, and a pin; and Chanticleer gave them all leave to get into the carriage and go with them.

When they arrived at Mr. Korbes's house, he was not at home; so the mice drew the carriage into the coach-house, Chanticleer and Partlet flew upon a beam, the cat sat down in the fire-place, the duck got into the washing cistern, the pin stuck himself into the bed pillow, the mill-stone laid himself over the house door, and the egg rolled herself up in the towel.

When Mr. Korbes came home, he went to the fire-place to make a fire; but the cat threw all the ashes in his eyes: so he ran to the kitchen to wash himself; but there the duck splashed all the water in his face; and when he tried to wipe himself, the egg broke to pieces in the towel all over his face and eyes. Then he was very angry, and went without his supper to bed; but when he laid his head on the pillow, the pin ran into his cheek: at this he became quite furious, and, jumping up, would have run out of the house; but when he came to the door, the mill-stone fell down on his head, and killed him on the spot.

3. How Partlet died and was buried, and how Chanticleer died of grief.

Another day Chanticleer and Partlet agreed to go again to the mountains to eat nuts; and it was settled that all the nuts which they found should be shared equally between them. Now Partlet found a very large nut; but she said nothing about it to Chanticleer, and kept it all to herself: however, it was so big that she could not swallow it, and it stuck in her throat. Then she was in a great fright, and cried out to Chanticleer, "Pray run as fast as you can, and fetch me some water, or I shall be choked." Chanticleer ran as fast as he could to the river, and said, "River, give me some water, for Partlet lies on the mountain, and will be choked by a great nut." The river said, "Run first to the bride, and ask her for a silken cord, to draw up the water." Chanticleer ran to the bride, and said, "Bride, you must give me a silken cord, for then the river will give me water, and the water I will carry to Partlet, who lies on the mountain, and will be choked by a great nut." But the bride said, "Run first, and bring me my garland that is hanging on a willow in the garden." Then Chanticleer ran to the garden, and took the garland from the bough where it hung, and brought it to the bride; and then the bride gave him the silken cord, and he took the silken cord to the river, and the river gave him water, and he carried the water to Partlet; but in the meantime she was choked by the great nut, and lay quite dead, and never moved any more.

Then Chanticleer was very sorry, and cried bitterly; and all the beasts came and wept with him over poor Partlet. And six mice built a little hearse to carry her to her grave; and when it was ready they harnessed themselves before it, and Chanticleer drove them. On the way they met the fox. "Where are you going, Chanticleer?" said he. "To bury my Partlet," said the other. "May I go with you?" said the fox. "Yes; but you must get up behind, or my horses will not be able to draw you." Then the fox got up behind; and presently the wolf, the bear, the goat, and all the beasts of the wood, came and climbed upon the hearse.

So on they went till they came to a rapid stream. "How shall we get over?" said Chanticleer. Then said a straw, "I will lay myself across, and you may pass over upon me." But as the mice were going over, the straw slipped away and fell into the water, and the six mice all fell in and were drowned. What was to be done? Then a large log of wood came and said, "I am big enough; I will lay myself across the stream, and you shall pass over upon me." So he laid himself down; but they managed so clumsily, that the log of wood fell in and was carried away by the stream. Then a stone, who saw what had happened, came up and kindly offered to help poor Chanticleer by laying himself across the stream; and this time he got safely to the other side with the hearse, and managed to get Partlet out of it; but the fox and the other mourners, who were sitting behind, were too heavy, and fell back into the water and were all carried away by the stream and drowned.

Thus Chanticleer was left alone with his dead Partlet; and having dug a grave for her, he laid her in it, and made a little hillock over her. Then he sat down by the grave, and wept and mourned, till at last he died too: and so all were dead.

Snow-Drop

or Snow-White

IT was in the middle of winter, when the broad flakes of
snow were falling around, that a certain queen sat
working at a window, the frame of which was made of
fine black ebony; and as she was looking out upon the
snow, she pricked her finger, and three drops of blood fell
upon it. Then she gazed thoughtfully upon the red drops
which sprinkled the white snow, and said, "Would that
my little daughter may be as white as that snow, as red as
the blood, and as black as the ebony window-frame!" And
so the little girl grew up: her skin was as white as snow,
her cheeks as rosy as the blood, and her hair as black as
ebony; and she was called Snow-drop.

But this queen died; and the king soon married another wife, who was very beautiful, but so proud that she
could not bear to think that any one could surpass her.
She had a magical looking-glass, to which she used to go
and gaze upon herself in it, and say,

> "Tell me, glass, tell me true!
> Of all the ladies in the land,
> Who is the fairest? tell me who?"

And the glass answered,

> "Thou, queen, art fairest in the land."

But Snow-drop grew more and more beautiful; and
when she was seven years old, she was as bright as the day,

99

and fairer than the queen herself. Then the glass one day answered the queen, when she went to consult it as usual,

"Thou, queen, may'st fair and beauteous be,
But Snow-drop is lovelier far than thee!"

When she heard this, she turned pale with rage and envy; and called to one of her servants and said, "Take Snow-drop away into the wide wood, that I may never see her more." Then the servant led her away; but his heart melted when she begged him to spare her life, and he said, "I will not hurt thee, thou pretty child." So he left her by herself; and though he thought it most likely that the wild beasts would tear her in pieces, he felt as if a great weight were taken off his heart when he had made up his mind not to kill her, but leave her to her fate.

Then poor Snow-drop wandered along through the wood in great fear; and the wild beasts roared about her, but none did her any harm. In the evening she came to a little cottage, and went in there to rest herself, for her little feet would carry her no further. Every thing was spruce and neat in the cottage: on the table was spread a white cloth, and there were seven little plates with seven little loaves, and seven little glasses with wine in them; and knives and forks laid in order; and by the wall stood seven little beds. Then, as she was very hungry, she picked a little piece off each loaf, and drank a very little wine out of each glass; and after that she thought she would lie down and rest. So she tried all the little beds; and one was too long, and another was too short, till at last the seventh suited her; and there she laid herself down, and went to sleep.

Presently in came the masters of the cottage, who were seven little dwarfs that lived among the mountains, and dug and searched about for gold. They lighted up their seven lamps, and saw directly that all was not right. The first said, "Who has been sitting on my stool?" The second, "Who has been eating off my plate?" The third, "Who has been picking my bread?" The fourth, "Who has been meddling with my spoon?" The fifth, "Who has been handling my fork?" The sixth, "Who has been cutting with my knife?" The seventh, "Who has been drinking my wine?" Then the first looked round and said, "Who has been lying on my bed?" And the rest came running to him, and every one cried out that somebody had been upon his bed. But the seventh saw Snow-drop, and called all his brethren to come and see her; and they cried out with wonder and astonishment, and brought their lamps to look at her, and said, "Good heavens! what a lovely child she is!" And they were delighted to see her, and took care not to wake her; and the seventh dwarf slept an hour with each of the other dwarfs in turn, till the night was gone.

In the morning, Snow-drop told them all her story; and they pitied her, and said if she would keep all things in order, and cook and wash, and knit and spin for them, she might stay where she was, and they would take good care of her. Then they went out all day long to their work, seeking for gold and silver in the mountains; and Snow-drop remained at home: and they warned her, and said, "The queen will soon find out where you are, so take care and let no one in."

But the queen, now that she thought Snow-drop was dead, believed that she was certainly the handsomest lady in the land; and she went to her glass and said,

"Tell me, glass, tell me true!
Of all the ladies in the land,
Who is fairest? tell me who?"

And the glass answered,

"Thou, queen, art the fairest in all this land;
But over the hills, in the greenwood shade,
Where the seven dwarfs their dwelling have made,
There Snow-drop is hiding her head; and she
Is lovelier far, O queen! than thee."

Then the queen was very much alarmed; for she knew that the glass always spoke the truth, and was sure that the servant had betrayed her. And she could not bear to think that any one lived who was more beautiful than she was; so she disguised herself as an old pedlar, and went her way over the hills to the place where the dwarfs dwelt. Then she knocked at the door, and cried "Fine wares to sell!" Snow-drop looked out at the window, and said "Good-day, good-woman; what have you to sell?" "Good wares, fine wares," said she; "laces and bobbins of all colours." "I will let the old lady in; she seems to be a very good sort of body," thought Snow-drop; so she ran down, and unbolted the door. "Bless me!" said the old woman, "how badly your stays are laced! Let me lace them up with one of my nice new laces." Snow-drop did not dream of any mischief; so she stood up before the old woman; but she set to work so nimbly, and pulled the lace so tight, that Snow-drop lost her breath, and fell down as if she were dead. "There's an end of all thy beauty," said the spiteful queen, and went away home.

In the evening the seven dwarfs returned; and I need not say how grieved they were to see their faithful Snow-drop stretched upon the ground motionless, as if she were quite dead. However, they lifted her up, and when they found what was the matter, they cut the lace; and in a little time she began to breathe, and soon came to life again. Then they said, "The old woman was the queen herself; take care another time, and let no one in when we are away."

When the queen got home, she went straight to her glass, and spoke to it as usual; but to her great surprise it still said,

"Thou, queen, art the fairest in all this land;
But over the hills, in the greenwood shade,
Where the seven dwarfs their dwelling have made,
There Snow-drop is hiding her head; and she
Is lovelier far, O queen! than thee."

Then the blood ran cold in her heart with spite and malice to see that Snow-drop still lived; and she dressed herself up again in a disguise, but very different from the one she wore before, and took with her a poisoned comb. When she reached the dwarfs' cottage, she knocked at the door, and cried "Fine wares to sell!" But Snow-drop said, "I dare not let any one in." Then the queen said, "Only look at my beautiful combs;" and gave her the poisoned one. And it looked so pretty that she took it up and put it into her hair to try it; but the moment it touched her head the poison was so powerful that she fell down senseless. "There you may lie," said the queen, and went her way. But by good luck the dwarfs returned very early that evening; and when they saw Snow-drop lying on the ground, they thought what had happened, and soon found the poisoned comb. And when they took it away, she recovered, and told them all that had passed; and they warned her once more not to open the door to any one.

Meantime the queen went home to her glass, and trembled with rage when she received exactly the same answer as before; and she said, "Snow-drop shall die, if it costs me my life." So she went secretly into a chamber, and prepared a poisoned apple: the outside looked very rosy and tempting, but whoever tasted it was sure to die. Then she dressed herself up as a peasant's wife, and travelled over the hills to the dwarfs' cottage, and knocked at the door; but Snow-drop put her head out of the window and said, "I dare not let any one in, for the dwarfs have told me not." "Do as you please," said the old woman, "but at any rate take this pretty apple; I will make you a present of it." "No," said Snow-drop, "I dare not take it." "You silly girl!" answered the other, "what are you afraid of? do you think it is poisoned? Come! do you eat one part, and I will eat the other." Now the apple was so prepared that one side was good, though the other side was poisoned. Then Snow-drop was very much tempted to taste, for the apple looked exceedingly nice; and when she saw the old woman eat, she could refrain no longer. But she had scarcely put the piece into her mouth, when she fell down dead upon the ground. "This time nothing will save thee," said the queen; and she went home to her glass, and at last it said,

"Thou, queen, art the fairest of all the fair."

And then her envious heart was glad, and as happy as such a heart could be.

When evening came, and the dwarfs returned home, they found Snow-drop lying on the ground: no breath passed her lips, and they were afraid that she was quite dead. They lifted her up, and combed her hair, and washed her face with wine and water; but all was in vain, for the little girl seemed quite dead. So they laid her down upon a bier, and all seven watched and bewailed her three whole days; and then they proposed to bury her: but her cheeks were still rosy, and her face looked just as it did while she was alive; so they said, "We will never bury her in the cold ground." And they made a coffin of glass, so that they might still look at her, and wrote her name upon it, in golden letters, and that she was a king's daughter. And the coffin was placed upon the hill, and one of the dwarfs always sat by it and watched. And the birds of the air came too, and bemoaned Snow-drop: first of all came an owl, and then a raven, but at last came a dove.

And thus Snow-drop lay for a long long time, and still only looked as though she were asleep; for she was even now as white as snow, and as red as blood, and as black as ebony. At last a prince came and called at the dwarfs' house; and he saw Snow-drop, and read what was written in golden letters. Then he offered the dwarfs money, and earnestly prayed them to let him take her away; but they said, "We will not part with her for all the gold in the world." At last however they had pity on him, and gave him the coffin: but the moment he lifted it up to carry it home with him, the piece of apple fell from between her lips, and Snow-drop awoke, and said, "Where am I?" And the prince answered, "Thou art safe with me." Then he told her all that had happened, and said, "I love you better than all the world: come with me to my father's palace, and you shall be my wife." And Snow-drop consented, and went home with the prince; and everything was prepared with great pomp and splendour for their wedding.

To the feast was invited, among the rest, Snow-drop's old enemy the queen; and as she was dressing herself in fine rich clothes, she looked in the glass, and said,

> "Tell me, glass, tell me true!
> Of all the ladies in the land,
> Who is fairest? tell me who?"

And the glass answered,

> "Thou, lady, art loveliest *here*, I ween;
> But lovelier far is the new-made queen."

When she heard this, she started with rage; but her envy and curiosity were so great, that she could not help setting out to see the bride. And when she arrived, and saw that it was no other than Snow-drop, who, as she thought, had been dead a long while, she choked with passion, and fell ill and died; but Snow-drop and the prince lived and reigned happily over that land many many years.

The Elves and the Shoemaker

THERE was once a shoemaker who worked very hard and was very honest; but still he could not earn enough to live upon, and at last all he had in the world was gone, except just leather enough to make one pair of shoes. Then he cut them all ready to make up the next day, meaning to get up early in the morning to work. His conscience was clear and his heart light amidst all his troubles; so he went peaceably to bed, left all his cares to heaven, and fell asleep. In the morning, after he had said his prayers, he set himself down to his work, when, to his great wonder, there stood the shoes, all ready made, upon the table. The good man knew not what to say or think of this strange event. He looked at the workmanship; there was not one false stitch in the whole job; and all was so neat and true, that it was a complete masterpiece.

That same day a customer came in, and the shoes pleased him so well that he willingly paid a price higher than usual for them; and the poor shoemaker with the money bought leather enough to make two pairs more. In the evening he cut out the work, and went to bed early that he might get up and begin betimes next day: but he was saved all the trouble, for when he got up in the morning the work was finished ready to his hand. Presently in came buyers, who paid him handsomely for his goods, so that he bought leather enough for four pairs more. He cut out the work again overnight, and found it finished in the morning as before; and so it went on for some time: what was got ready in the evening was always done by day-break, and the good man soon became thriving and prosperous again.

One evening about Christmas time, as he and his wife were sitting over the fire chatting together, he said to her, "I should like to sit up and watch to-night, that we may see who it is that comes and does my work for me." The wife liked the thought; so they left a light burning, and hid themselves in the corner of the room behind a curtain that was hung up there, and watched what should happen.

As soon as it was midnight, there came two little naked dwarfs; and they sat themselves upon the shoemaker's bench, took up all the work that was cut out, and began to ply with their little fingers, stitching and rapping and tapping away at such a rate, that the shoemaker was all amazement, and could not take his eyes off for a moment. And on they went till the job was quite finished, and the shoes stood ready for use upon the table. This was long before day-break; and then they bustled away as quick as lightning.

The next day the wife said to the shoemaker, "These little wights have made us rich, and we ought to be thankful to them, and do them a good office in return. I am quite vexed to see them run about as they do; they have nothing upon their backs to keep off the cold. I'll tell you what, I will make each of them a shirt, and a coat and waistcoat, and a pair of pantaloons into the bargain; do you make each of them a little pair of shoes."

The thought pleased the good shoemaker very much; and one evening, when all the things were ready, they laid them on the table instead of the work that they used to cut out, and then went and hid themselves to watch what the little elves would do. About midnight they came in, and were going to sit down to their work as usual; but when they saw the clothes lying for them, they laughed and were greatly delighted. Then they dressed themselves in the twinkling of an eye, and danced and capered and sprang about as merry as could be, till at last they danced out at the door over the green; and the shoemaker saw them no more: but everything went well with him from that time forward, as long as he lived.

The Turnip

THERE were two brothers who were both soldiers; the one was rich, and the other poor. The poor man thought he would try to better himself; so, pulling off his red coat, he became a gardener, and dug his ground well, and sowed turnips.

When the seed came up, there was one plant bigger than all the rest; and it kept getting larger and larger, and seemed as if it would never cease growing; so that it might have been called the prince of turnips, for there never was such a one seen before, and never will again. At last it was so big that it filled a cart, and two oxen could hardly draw it; and the gardener knew not what in the world to do with it, nor whether it would be a blessing or a curse to him. One day he said to himself, "What shall I do with it? if I sell it, it will bring no more than another; and for eating, the little turnips are better than this; the best thing perhaps is to carry it and give it to the king as a mark of respect."

Then he yoked his oxen, and drew the turnip to the Court, and gave it to the king. "What a wonderful thing!" said the king; "I have seen many strange things, but such a monster as this I never saw. Where did you get the seed? or is it only your good luck? If so, you are a true child of fortune." "Ah, no!" answered the gardener, "I am no child of fortune; I am a poor soldier, who never could get enough to live upon; so I laid aside my red coat, and set to work, tilling the ground. I have a brother, who is rich, and your majesty knows him well, and all the world knows him; but because I am poor, everybody forgets me."

The king then took pity on him, and said, "You shall be poor no longer. I will give you so much that you shall be even richer than your brother." Then he gave him gold and lands and flocks, and made him so rich that his brother's fortune could not at all be compared with his.

When the brother heard of all this, and how a turnip had made the gardener so rich, he envied him sorely, and bethought himself how he could contrive to get the same good fortune for himself. However, he determined to manage more cleverly than his brother, and got together a rich present of gold and fine horses for the king; and thought he must have a much larger gift in return: for if his brother had received so much for only a turnip, what must his present be worth?

The king took the gift very graciously, and said he knew not what to give in return more valuable and wonderful than the great turnip; so the soldier was forced to put it into a cart, and drag it home with him. When he reached home, he knew not upon whom to vent his rage and spite; and at length wicked thoughts came into his head, and he resolved to kill his brother.

So he hired some villains to murder him; and having shown them where to lie in ambush, he went to his brother, and said, "Dear brother, I have found a hidden treasure; let us go and dig it up, and share it between us." The other had no suspicions of his roguery: so they went out together, and as they were travelling along, the murderers rushed out upon him, bound him, and were going to hang him on a tree.

But whilst they were getting all ready, they heard the trampling of a horse at a distance, which so frightened them that they pushed their prisoner neck and shoulders together into a sack, and swung him up by a cord to the tree, where they left him dangling, and ran away. Meantime he worked and worked away, till he made a hole large enough to put out his head.

When the horseman came up, he proved to be a student, a merry fellow, who was journeying along on his nag, and singing as he went. As soon as the man in the sack saw him passing under the tree, he cried out, "Good morning! good morning to thee, my friend!" The student looked about everywhere; and seeing no one, and not knowing where the voice came from, cried out, "Who calls me?"

Then the man in the tree answered, "Lift up thine eyes, for behold here I sit in the sack of wisdom; here have I, in a short time, learned great and wondrous things. Compared to this seat, all the learning of the schools is as empty air. A little longer, and I shall know all that man can know, and shall come forth wiser than the wisest of mankind. Here I discern the signs and motions of the heavens and the stars; the laws that control the winds; the number of the sands on the sea-shore; the healing of the sick; the virtues of all simples, of birds, and of precious stones. Wert thou but once here, my friend, thou wouldst feel and own the power of knowledge."

The student listened to all this and wondered much; at last he said, "Blessed be the day and hour when I found you; cannot you contrive to let me into the sack for a little while?" Then the other answered, as if very unwillingly, "A little space I may allow thee to sit here, if thou wilt reward me well and entreat me kindly; but thou must tarry yet an hour below, till I have learnt some little matters that are yet unknown to me."

So the student sat himself down and waited a while;

but the time hung heavy upon him, and he begged earnestly that he might ascend forthwith, for his thirst of knowledge was great. Then the other pretended to give way, and said, "Thou must let the sack of wisdom descend, by untying yonder cord, and then thou shalt enter." So the student let him down, opened the sack, and set him free. "Now then," cried he, "let me ascend quickly." As he began to put himself into the sack heels first, "Wait a while," said the gardener, "that is not the way." Then he pushed him in head first, tied up the sack, and soon swung up the searcher after wisdom dangling in the air. "How is it with thee, friend?" said he, "dost thou not feel that wisdom comes unto thee? Rest there in peace, till thou art a wiser man than thou wert."

So saying, he trotted off on the student's nag, and left the poor fellow to gather wisdom till somebody should come and let him down.

Old Sultan

A SHEPHERD had a faithful dog, called Sultan, who was grown very old, and had lost all his teeth. And one day when the shepherd and his wife were standing together before the house, the shepherd said, "I will shoot old Sultan to-morrow morning, for he is of no use now." But his wife said, "Pray let the poor faithful creature live; he has served us well a great many years, and we ought to give him a livelihood for the rest of his days." "But what can we do with him?" said the shepherd, "he has not a tooth in his head, and the thieves don't care for him at all; to be sure he has served us, but then he did it to earn his livelihood; to-morrow shall be his last day, depend upon it."

Poor Sultan, who was lying close by them, heard all that the shepherd and his wife said to one another, and was very much frightened to think to-morrow would be his last day; so in the evening he went to his good friend the wolf, who lived in the wood, and told him all his sorrows, and how his master meant to kill him in the morning. "Make yourself easy," said the wolf, "I will give you some good advice. Your master, you know, goes out every morning very early with his wife into the field; and they take their little child with them, and lay it down behind the hedge in the shade while they are at work. Now do you lie down close by the child, and pretend to be watching it, and I will come out of the wood and run away with it: you must

115

run after me as fast as you can, and I will let it drop; then you may carry it back, and they will think you have saved their child, and will be so thankful to you that they will take care of you as long as you live." The dog liked this plan very well; and accordingly so it was managed. The wolf ran with the child a little way; the shepherd and his wife screamed out; but Sultan soon overtook him, and carried the poor little thing back to his master and mistress. Then the shepherd patted him on the head, and said, "Old Sulton has saved our child from the wolf, and therefore he shall live and be well taken care of, and have plenty to eat. Wife, go home, and give him a good dinner, and let him have my old cushion to sleep on as long as he lives." So from this time forward Sultan had all that he could wish for.

Soon afterwards the wolf came and wished him joy, and said, "Now, my good fellow, you must tell no tales, but turn your head the other way when I want to taste one of the old shepherd's fine fat sheep." "No," said Sultan; "I will be true to my master." However, the wolf thought he was in joke, and came one night to get a dainty morsel. But Sultan had told his master what the wolf meant to do; so he laid wait for him behind the barn-door, and when the wolf was busy looking out for a good fat sheep, he had a stout cudgel laid about his back, that combed his locks for him finely.

Then the wolf was very angry, and called Sultan "an old rogue," and swore he would have his revenge. So the next morning the wolf sent the boar to challenge Sultan to come into the wood to fight the matter out. Now Sultan had nobody he could ask to be his second but the shepherd's old three-legged cat; so he took her with him, and as the poor thing limped along with some trouble, she stuck up her tail straight in the air.

The wolf and the wild boar were first on the ground; and when they espied their enemies coming, and saw the cat's long tail standing straight in the air, they thought she was carrying a sword for Sultan to fight with; and every time she limped, they thought she was picking up a stone to throw at them; so they said they should not like this way of fighting, and the boar lay down behind a bush, and the wolf jumped up into a tree. Sultan and the cat soon came up, and looked about, and wondered that no one was there. The boar, however, had not quite hidden himself, for his ears stuck out of the bush; and when he shook one of them a little, the cat, seeing something move, and thinking it was a mouse, sprang upon it, and bit and scratched it, so that the boar jumped up and grunted, and ran away, roaring out, "Look up in the tree, there sits the one who is to blame." So they looked up, and espied the wolf sitting amongst the branches; and they called him a cowardly rascal, and would not suffer him to come down till he was heartily ashamed of himself, and had promised to be good friends again with old Sultan.

Then the beggar departed, and took her with him.

KING GRISLY-BEARD

Page 88

There he saw a large pile of gold lying on the floor.

THE KING OF
THE GOLDEN MOUNTAIN

Page 132

The Lady and the Lion

A MERCHANT, who had three daughters, was once setting out upon a journey; but before he went he asked each daughter what gift he should bring back for her. The eldest wished for pearls; the second for jewels; but the third said, "Dear father, bring me a rose." Now it was no easy task to find a rose, for it was the middle of winter; yet, as she was the fairest daughter, and was very fond of flowers, her father said he would try what he could do. So he kissed all three, and bid them good-bye. And when the time came for his return, he had bought pearls and jewels for the two eldest, but he had sought everywhere in vain for the rose; and when he went into any garden and inquired for such a thing, the people laughed at him, and asked him whether he thought roses grew in snow. This grieved him very much, for his third daughter was his dearest child; and as he was journeying home, thinking what he should bring her, he came to a fine castle; and around the castle was a garden, in half of which it appeared to be summer time, and in the other half winter. On one side the finest flowers were in full bloom, and on the other everything looked desolate and buried in snow. "A lucky hit!" said he as he called to his servant, and told him to go to a beautiful bed of roses that was there, and bring him away one of the flowers. This done, they were riding away well pleased, when a fierce lion sprung up, and roared out, "Whoever dares to steal my roses

119

shall be eaten up alive." Then the man said, "I knew not that the garden belonged to you; can nothing save my life?" "No!" said the lion, "nothing, unless you promise to give me whatever meets you first on your return home; if you agree to this, I will give you your life, and the rose too for your daughter." But the man was unwilling to do so, and said, "It may be my youngest daughter, who loves me most, and always runs to meet me when I go home." Then the servant was greatly frightened, and said, "It may perhaps be only a cat or a dog." And at last the man yielded with a heavy heart, and took the rose; and promised the lion whatever should meet him first on his return.

And as he came near home, it was his youngest and dearest daughter that met him; she came running and kissed him, and welcomed him home; and when she saw that he had brought her the rose, she rejoiced still more. But her father began to be very melancholy, and to weep, saying, "Alas! my dearest child! I have bought this flower dear, for I have promised to give you to a wild lion, and when he has you, he will tear you in pieces, and eat you." And he told her all that had happened; and said she should not go, let what would happen.

But she comforted him, and said, "Dear father, what you have promised must be fulfilled; I will go to the lion, and soothe him, that he may let me return again safe home."

The next morning she asked the way she was to go, and took leave of her father, and went forth with a bold heart into the wood. But the lion was an enchanted prince, and by day he and all his court were lions, but in the evening they took their proper forms again. And when the lady came to the castle, he welcomed her so courteously that she consented to marry him. The wedding-feast was held, and they lived happily together a long time. The prince was only to be seen as soon as evening came, and then he held his court; but every morning he left his bride, and went away by himself, she knew not whither, till night came again.

After some time he said to her, "To-morrow there will be a great feast in your father's house, for your eldest sister is to be married; and, if you wish to go to visit her, my lions shall lead you thither." Then she rejoiced much at the thoughts of seeing her father once more, and set out with the lions; and every one was overjoyed to see her, for they had thought her dead long since. But she told them how happy she was; and stayed till the feast was over, and then went back to the wood.

Her second sister was soon after married; and when she was invited to the wedding, she said to the prince, "I will not go alone this time; you must go with me." But he would not, and said that would be a very hazardous thing, for if the least ray of the torch-light should fall upon him, his enchantment would become still worse, for he should be changed into a dove, and be obliged to wander about the world for seven long years. However, she gave him no rest, and said she would take care no light should fall upon him. So at last they set out together, and took with them their little child too; and she chose a large hall with thick walls, for him to sit in while the wedding torches were lighted; but unluckily no one observed that there was a crack in the door. Then the wedding was held with great pomp; but as the train came from the church, and passed with the torches before the hall, a very small ray of light fell upon the prince. In a moment he disappeared; and when his wife came in, and sought him, she found only a white dove. Then he said to her, "Seven years must I fly up and down over the face of the earth; but every now and then I will let fall a white feather, that shall show you the way I am going; follow it, and at last you may overtake and set me free."

This said, he flew out at the door, and she followed; and every now and then a white feather fell, and showed her the way she was to journey. Thus she went roving on through the wide world, and looked neither to the right hand nor to the left, nor took any rest for seven years. Then she began to rejoice, and thought to herself that the time was fast coming when all her troubles should cease; yet repose was still far off: for one day as she was travelling on, she missed the white feather, and when she lifted up her eyes she could nowhere see the dove. "Now," thought she to herself, "no human aid can be of use to me;" so she went to the sun, and said, "Thou shinest everywhere, on the mountain's top, and the valley's depth: hast thou anywhere seen a white dove?" "No," said the sun, "I have not seen it; but I will give thee a casket—open it when thy hour of need comes." So she thanked the sun, and went on her way till eventide; and when the moon arose, she cried unto it, and said, "Thou shinest through all the night, over field and grove: hast thou nowhere seen a white dove?" "No," said the moon, "I cannot help thee; but I will give thee an egg—break it when need comes." Then she thanked the moon, and went on till the night-wind blew; and she raised up her voice to it, and said, "Thou blowest through every tree and under every leaf: hast thou not seen the white dove?" "No," said the night-wind; "but I will ask three other winds; perhaps they have seen it." Then the east wind and the west wind came, and said they too had not seen it; but the south wind said, "I have seen the white dove; he has fled to the Red Sea, and is changed once more into a lion, for the seven years are passed away; and there he is fighting with a dragon, and the dragon is an enchanted princess, who seeks to separate him from you." Then the night-wind said, "I will give thee counsel: go to the Red Sea; on the right shore stand many rods; number them, and when thou comest to the eleventh, break it off and smite the dragon with it; and so the lion will have the victory, and both of them will appear to you in their human forms. Then instantly set out with thy beloved prince, and journey home over sea and land."

So our poor wanderer went forth, and found all as the night-wind had said; and she plucked the eleventh rod, and smote the dragon, and immediately the lion became a prince and the dragon a princess again. But she forgot the counsel which the night-wind had given; and the false princess watched her opportunity, and took the prince by the arm, and carried him away.

Thus the unfortunate traveller was again forsaken and forlorn; but she took courage and said, "As far as the wind blows, and so long as the cock crows, I will journey on till I find him once again." She went on for a long long way, till at length she came to the castle whither the princess had carried the prince; and there was a feast prepared, and she heard that the wedding was about to be held. "Heaven aid me now!" said she; and she took the casket that the sun had given her, and found that within it lay a dress as dazzling as the sun itself. So she put it on, and went into the palace; and all the people gazed upon her; and the dress pleased the bride so much that she asked whether it was to be sold: "Not for gold and silver," answered she; "but for flesh and blood." The princess asked what she meant; and she said, "Let me speak with the bridegroom this night in his chamber, and I will give thee the dress." At last the princess agreed; but she told her chamberlain to give the prince a sleeping-draught, that he might not hear or see her. When evening came, and the prince had fallen asleep, she was led into his chamber, and she sat herself down at his feet and said, "I have followed thee seven years; I have been to the sun, the moon, and the night-wind, to seek thee; and at last I have helped thee to overcome the dragon.   Wilt thou then forget me quite?"   But the prince slept so soundly that her voice only passed over him, and seemed like the murmuring of the wind among the fir-trees.

Then she was led away, and forced to give up the golden dress; and when she saw that there was no help for her, she went out into a meadow and sat herself down and wept.   But as she sat she bethought herself of the egg that the moon had given her; and when she broke it, there ran out a hen and twelve chickens of pure gold, that played about, and then nestled under the old one's wings, so as to form the most beautiful sight in the world.   And she rose up, and drove them before her till the bride saw them from her window, and was so pleased that she came forth, and asked her if she would sell the brood.   "Not for gold or silver; but for flesh and blood: let me again this evening speak with the bridegroom in his chamber."

Then the princess thought to betray her as before, and agreed to what she asked; but when the prince went to his chamber, he asked the chamberlain why the wind had murmured so in the night.   And the chamberlain told him all; how he had given him a sleeping-draught, and a poor maiden had come and spoken to him in his chamber, and was to come again that night.   Then the prince took care to throw away the sleeping-draught; and when she came and began again to tell him what woes had befallen her, and how faithful and true to him she had been, he knew his beloved wife's voice, and sprung up, and said, "You have awakened me as from a dream; for the strange princess had thrown a spell around me, so that I had altogether forgotten you: but heaven hath sent you to me in a lucky hour."

And they stole away out of the palace by night secretly, (for they feared the princess,) and journeyed home; and there they found their child, now grown comely and fair, and lived happily together to the end of their days.

Red Riding Hood

THERE was once a sweet little maiden, who was loved by all who knew her; but she was especially dear to her Grandmother, who did not know how to make enough of the child. Once she gave her a little red velvet cloak. It was so becoming, and she liked it so much, that she would never wear anything else; and so she got the name of Red Riding Hood.

One day her Mother said to her: "Come here, Red Riding Hood, take this cake and bottle of wine to Grandmother; she is weak and ill, and it will do her good. Go quickly, before it gets hot, and don't loiter by the way, or run, or you will fall down and break the bottle, and there will be no wine for Grandmother. When you get there, don't forget to say 'Good-morning' prettily, without staring about you."

"I will do just as you tell me," Red Riding Hood promised her Mother.

Her Grandmother lived away in the woods a good half-hour from the village. When she got to the wood, she met a Wolf; but Red Riding Hood did not know what a wicked animal he was, so she was not a bit afraid of him.

"Good-morning, Red Riding Hood," he said.

"Good-morning, Wolf," she answered.

"Whither away so early, Red Riding Hood?"

"To Grandmother's."

"What have you got in your basket?"

"Cake and wine; we baked yesterday, so I'm taking a cake to Grannie; she wants something to make her well."

"Where does your Grandmother live, Red Riding Hood?"

"A good quarter of an hour further into the wood. Her house stands under three big oak trees, near a hedge of nut trees which you must know," said Red Riding Hood.

The Wolf thought: "This tender little creature will be a plump morsel; she will be nicer than the old woman. I must be cunning, and snap them both up."

He walked along with Red Riding Hood for a while, then he said: "Look at the pretty flowers, Red Riding Hood. Why don't you look about you? I don't believe you even hear the birds sing. You are just as solemn as if you were going to school: everything else is so gay out here in the woods."

Red Riding Hood raised her eyes, and when she saw the sunlight dancing through the trees, and all the bright flowers, she thought: "I'm sure Grannie would be pleased if I took her a bunch of fresh flowers. It is still quite early. I shall have plenty of time to pick them."

So she left the path, and wandered off among the trees to pick the flowers. Each time she picked one, she always saw another prettier one further on. So she went deeper and deeper into the forest.

In the meantime the Wolf went straight off to the Grandmother's cottage, and knocked at the door.

"Who is there?"

"Red Riding Hood, bringing you a cake and some wine. Open the door!"

"Press the latch!" cried the old woman. "I am too weak to get up."

The Wolf pressed the latch, and the door sprang open. He went straight in and up to the bed without saying a word, and ate up the poor old woman.   Then he put on her nightdress and nightcap, got into bed and drew the curtains.

Red Riding Hood ran about picking flowers till she could carry no more, and then she remembered her Grandmother again.   She was astonished when she got to the house to find the door open, and when she entered the room everything seemed so strange.

She felt quite frightened, but she did not know why. " Generally I like coming to see Grandmother so much," she thought.   She cried: " Good-morning, Grandmother," but she received no answer.

Then she went up to the bed and drew the curtain back. There lay her Grandmother but she had drawn her cap down over her face, and she looked very odd.

" Oh, Grandmother, what big ears you have got," she said.

" The better to hear with, my dear."

" Grandmother, what big eyes you have got."

" The better to see with, my dear."

" What big hands you have got, Grandmother."

" The better to catch hold of you with, my dear."

" But Grandmother, what big teeth you have got."

" The better to eat you with, my dear."

Hardly had the Wolf said this, than he made a spring out of bed, and devoured poor little Red Riding Hood.   When the Wolf had satisfied himself, he went back to bed and he was soon snoring loudly.

A Huntsman went past the house, and thought, " How loudly the old lady is snoring; I must see if there is anything the matter with her."

So he went into the house, and up to the bed, where he found the Wolf fast asleep.   " Do I find you here, you old sinner? " he said.   " Long enough have I sought you."

He raised his gun to shoot, when it just occurred to him

that perhaps the Wolf had eaten up the old lady, and that she might still be saved. So he took a knife and began cutting open the sleeping Wolf. At the first cut he saw the little red cloak, and after a few more slashes, the little girl sprang out, and cried: " Oh, how frightened I was, it was so dark inside the Wolf!" Next the old Grandmother came out, alive, but hardly able to breathe.

Red Riding Hood brought some big stones with which they filled the Wolf, so that when he woke and tried to spring away, they dragged him back, and he fell down dead.

They were all quite happy now. The Huntsman skinned the Wolf, and took the skin home. The Grandmother ate the cake and drank the wine which Red Riding Hood had brought, and she soon felt quite strong. Red Riding Hood thought: " I will never again wander off into the forest as long as I live, if my Mother forbids it.

The King of the Golden Mountain

A CERTAIN merchant had two children, a son and daughter, both very young, and scarcely able to run alone. He had two richly laden ships then making a voyage upon the seas, in which he had embarked all his property, in the hope of making great gains, when the news came that they were lost. Thus from being a rich man he became very poor, so that nothing was left him but one small plot of land; and, to relieve his mind a little of his trouble, he often went out to walk there.

One day, as he was roving along, a little rough-looking dwarf stood before him, and asked him why he was so sorrowful, and what it was that he took so deeply to heart. But the merchant replied, "If you could do me any good, I would tell you." "Who knows but I may?" said the little man; "tell me what is the matter, and perhaps I can be of some service." Then the merchant told him how all his wealth was gone to the bottom of the sea, and how he had nothing left except that little plot of land. "Oh! trouble not yourself about that," said the dwarf; "only promise to bring me here, twelve years hence, whatever meets you first on your return home, and I will give you as much gold as you please." The merchant thought this was no great request; that it would most likely be his dog, or something of that sort, but forgot his little child: so he agreed to the bargain, and signed and sealed the engagement to do what was required.

But as he drew near home, his little boy was so pleased to see him, that he crept behind him and laid fast hold of his legs. Then the father started with fear, and saw what it was that he had bound himself to do; but as no gold was come, he consoled himself by thinking that it was only a joke that the dwarf was playing him.

About a month afterwards he went upstairs into an old lumber room to look for some old iron, that he might sell it and raise a little money; and there he saw a large pile of gold lying on the floor. At the sight of this he was greatly delighted, went into trade again, and became a greater merchant than before.

Meantime his son grew up, and as the end of the twelve years drew near, the merchant became very anxious and thoughtful; so that care and sorrow were written upon his face. The son one day asked what was the matter: but his father refused to tell for some time; at last however he said that he had, without knowing it, sold him to a little ugly-looking dwarf for a great quantity of gold; and that the twelve years were coming round when he must perform his agreement. Then the son said, "Father, give yourself very little trouble about that; depend upon it I shall be too much for the little man."

When the time came, they went out together to the appointed place; and the son drew a circle on the ground, and set himself and his father in the middle. The little dwarf soon came, and said to the merchant, "Have you brought me what you promised?" The old man was silent, but his son answered, "What do you want here?" The dwarf said, "I come to talk with your father, not with you." "You have deceived and betrayed my father," said the son; "give him up his bond." "No," replied the other, "I will not yield up my rights." Upon this a long dispute arose; and at last it was agreed that the son should be put into an open boat, that lay on the side of a piece of water hard by, and that the father should push him off with his own hand; so that he should be turned adrift. Then he took leave of his father, and set himself in the boat; and as it was pushed off it heaved, and fell on one side into the water: so the merchant thought that his son was lost, and went home very sorrowful.

But the boat went safely on, and did not sink; and the young man sat securely within, till at length it ran ashore upon an unknown land. As he jumped upon the shore, he saw before him a beautiful castle, but empty and desolate within, for it was enchanted. At last, however, he found a white snake in one of the chambers.

Now the white snake was an enchanted princess; and she rejoiced greatly to see him, and said, "Art thou at last come to be my deliverer? Twelve long years have I waited for thee, for thou alone canst save me. This night twelve men will come: their faces will be black, and they will be hung round with chains. They will ask what thou dost here; but be silent, give no answer, and let them do what they will—beat and torment thee. Suffer all, only speak not a word, and at twelve o'clock they must depart. The second night twelve others will come; and the third night twenty-four, who will even cut off thy head; but at the twelfth hour of that night their power is gone, and I shall be free, and will come and bring thee the water of life, and will wash thee with it, and restore thee to life and health." And all came to pass as she had said; the merchant's son spoke not a word, and the third night the princess appeared, and fell on his neck and kissed him; joy and gladness burst forth throughout the castle; the wedding was celebrated, and he was king of the Golden Mountain.

They lived together very happily, and the queen had a son. Eight years had passed over their heads when the

king thought of his father: and his heart was moved, and
he longed to see him once again. But the queen opposed
his going, and said, "I know well that misfortunes will
come." However, he gave her no rest till she consented.
At his departure she presented him with a wishing-ring,
and said, "Take this ring, and put it on your finger; whatever you wish it will bring you: only promise that you will
not make use of it to bring me hence to your father's."
Then he promised what she asked, and put the ring on
his finger, and wished himself near the town where his
father lived. He found himself at the gates in a moment; but the guards would not let him enter, because he
was so strangely clad. So he went up to a neighbouring
mountain where a shepherd dwelt, and borrowed his old
frock, and thus passed unobserved into the town. When
he came to his father's house, he said he was his son; but the
merchant would not believe him, and said he had had but
one son, who he knew was long since dead: and as he was
only dressed like a poor shepherd, he would not even
offer him anything to eat. The king however persisted
that he was his son, and said, "Is there no mark by which
you would know if I am really your son?" "Yes," observed his mother, "our son has a mark like a raspberry
under the right arm." Then he showed them the mark,
and they were satisfied that what he had said was true.
He next told them how he was king of the Golden Mountain, and was married to a princess, and had a son seven
years old. But the merchant said, "That can never be
true; he must be a fine king truly who travels about in a
shepherd's frock." At this the son was very angry; and,
forgetting his promise, turned his ring, and wished for his
queen and son. In an instant they stood before him; but
the queen wept, and said he had broken his word, and misfortune would follow. He did all he could to soothe her,

and she at last appeared to be appeased; but she was not so in reality, and only meditated how she should take her revenge.

One day he took her to walk with him out of the town, and showed her the spot where the boat was turned adrift upon the wide waters. Then he sat himself down, and said, "I am very much tired; sit by me, I will rest my head in your lap, and sleep a while." As soon as he had fallen asleep, however, she drew the ring from his finger, and crept softly away, and wished herself and her son at home in their kingdom. And when the king awoke, he found himself alone, and saw that the ring was gone from his finger. "I can never return to my father's house," said he; "they would say I am a sorcerer: I will journey forth into the world till I come again to my kingdom."

So saying, he set out and travelled till he came to a mountain, where three giants were sharing their inheritance; and as they saw him pass, they cried out and said, "Little men have sharp wits; he shall divide the inheritance between us." Now it consisted of a sword that cut off an enemy's head whenever the wearer gave the words "Heads off!"—a cloak that made the owner invisible, or gave him any form he pleased; and a pair of boots that transported the person who put them on wherever he wished. The king said they must first let him try these wonderful things, that he might know how to set a value upon them. Then they gave him the cloak, and he wished himself a fly, and in a moment he was a fly. "The cloak is very well," said he; "now give me the sword." "No," said they, "not unless you promise not to say 'Heads off!' for if you do, we are all dead men." So they gave it him on condition that he tried its virtue only on a tree. He next asked for the boots also; and the moment he had all three in his possession he wished himself at the Golden

Mountain; and there he was in an instant. So the giants were left behind with no inheritance to divide or quarrel about.

As he came near to the castle he heard the sound of merry music; and the people around told him that his queen was about to celebrate her marriage with another prince. Then he threw his cloak around him, and passed through the castle, and placed himself by the side of his queen, where no one saw him. But when anything to eat was put upon her plate, he took it away and ate it himself; and when a glass of wine was handed to her, he took and drank it: and thus, though they kept on serving her with meat and drink, her plate continued always empty.

Upon this, fear and remorse came over her, and she went into her chamber and wept; and he followed her there. "Alas!" said she to herself, "did not my deliverer come? why then doth enchantment still surround me?"

"Thou traitress!" said he, "thy deliverer indeed came, and now is near thee: has he deserved this of thee?" And he went out and dismissed the company, and said the wedding was at an end, for that he was returned to his kingdom: but the princes and nobles and counsellors mocked at him. However, he would enter into no parley with them, but only demanded whether they would depart in peace, or not. Then they turned and tried to seize him; but he drew his sword, and, with a word, the traitors' heads fell before him; and he was once more king of the Golden Mountain.

The Golden Goose

THERE was a man who had three sons. The youngest was called Dummling, and was on all occasions despised and ill-treated by the whole family. It happened that the eldest took it into his head one day to go into the wood to cut fuel; and his mother gave him a delicious pasty and a bottle of wine to take with him, that he might refresh himself at his work. As he went into the wood, a little old man bid him good day, and said, "Give me a little piece of meat from your plate, and a little wine out of your bottle; I am very hungry and thirsty." But this clever young man said, "Give you my meat and wine! No, I thank you; I should not have enough left for myself;" and away he went. He soon began to cut down a tree; but he had not worked long before he missed his stroke, and cut himself, and was obliged to go home to have the wound dressed. Now it was the little old man that caused him this mischief.

Next went out the second son to work; and his mother gave him too a pasty and a bottle of wine. And the same little old man met him also, and asked him for something to eat and drink. But he too thought himself vastly clever, and said, "Whatever you get, I shall lose; so go your way!" The little man took care that he should have his reward; and the second stroke that he aimed against a tree, hit him on the leg; so that he too was forced to go home.

Then Dummling said, "Father, I should like to go and cut wood too." But his father answered, "Your brothers have both lamed themselves; you had better stay at home, for you know nothing of the business." But Dummling was very pressing; and at last his father said, "Go your way; you will be wiser when you have suffered for your folly." And his mother gave him only some dry bread, and a bottle of sour beer; but when he went into the wood, he met the little old man, who said, "Give me some meat and drink, for I am very hungry and thirsty." Dummling said, "I have only dry bread and sour beer; if that will suit you, we will sit down and eat it together." So they sat down; and when the lad pulled out his bread, behold it was turned into a capital pasty, and his sour beer became delightful wine. They ate and drank heartily; and when they had done, the little man said, "As you have a kind heart, and have been willing to share everything with me, I will send a blessing upon you. There stands an old tree; cut it down, and you will find something at the root." Then he took his leave, and went his way.

Dummling set to work, and cut down the tree; and when it fell, he found in a hollow under the roots a goose with feathers of pure gold. He took it up, and went on to an inn, where he proposed to sleep for the night. The landlord had three daughters; and when they saw the goose, they were very curious to examine what this wonderful bird could be, and wished very much to pluck one of the feathers out of its tail. At last the eldest said, "I must and will have a feather." So she waited till his back was turned, and then seized the goose by the wing; but to her great surprise there she stuck, for neither hand nor finger could she get away again. Presently in came the second sister, and thought to have a feather too; but the moment she touched her sister, there she too hung fast.

At last came the third, and wanted a feather; but the other two cried out, "Keep away! for heaven's sake, keep away!" However, she did not understand what they meant. "If they are there," thought she, "I may as well be there too." So she went up to them; but the moment she touched her sisters she stuck fast, and hung to the goose as they did. And so they kept company with the goose all night.

The next morning Dummling carried off the goose under his arm; and took no notice of the three girls, but went out with them sticking fast behind; and wherever he travelled, they too were obliged to follow, whether they would or no, as fast as their legs could carry them.

In the middle of a field the parson met them; and when he saw the train, he said, "Are you not ashamed of yourselves, you bold girls, to run after the young man in that way over the fields? is that proper behaviour?" Then he took the youngest by the hand to lead her away; but the moment he touched her he too hung fast, and followed in the train. Presently up came the clerk; and when he saw his master the parson running after the three girls, he wondered greatly, and said, "Hollo! hollo! your reverence! whither so fast? there is a christening to-day." Then he ran up, and took him by the gown, and in a moment he was fast too. As the five were thus trudging along, one behind another, they met two labourers with their mattocks coming from work; and the parson cried out to them to set him free. But scarcely had they touched him, when they too fell into the ranks, and so made seven, all running after Dummling and his goose.

At last they arrived at a city, where reigned a king who had an only daughter. The princess was of so thoughtful and serious a turn of mind that no one could make her laugh; and the king had proclaimed to all the world, that whoever could make her laugh should have her for his wife.

When the young man heard this, he went to her with his goose and all its train; and as soon as she saw the seven all hanging together, and running about, treading on each other's heels, she could not help bursting into a long and loud laugh. Then Dummling claimed her for his wife; the wedding was celebrated, and he was heir to the kingdom, and lived long and happily with his wife.

Mrs. Fox

THERE was once a sly old fox with nine tails, who was very curious to know whether his wife was true to him: so he stretched himself out under a bench, and pretended to be as dead as a mouse.

Then Mrs. Fox went up into her own room and locked the door: but her maid, the cat, sat at the kitchen fire cooking; and soon after it became known that the old fox was dead, some one knocked at the door, saying,

> "Miss Pussy! Miss Pussy! how fare you to-day?
> Are you sleeping or watching the time away?"

Then the cat went and opened the door, and there stood a young fox; so she said to him,

> "No, no, Master Fox, I don't sleep in the day,
> I'm making some capital white wine whey.
> Will your honour be pleased to dinner to stay?"

"No, I thank you," said the fox; "but how is poor Mrs. Fox?" Then the cat answered,

> "She sits all alone in her chamber upstairs,
> And bewails her misfortune with floods of tears:
> She weeps till her beautiful eyes are red;
> For, alas! alas! Mr. Fox is dead."

"Go to her," said the other, "and say that there is a young fox come, who wishes to marry her."

Then up went the cat,—trippety trap,
And knocked at the door,—tippety tap;
"Is good Mrs. Fox within?" said she.
"Alas! my dear, what want you with me?"
"There waits a suitor below at the gate."

Then said Mrs. Fox,

"How looks he, my dear? is he tall and straight?
Has he nine good tails?   There must be nine,
Or he never shall be a suitor of mine."

"Ah!" said the cat, "he has but one."   "Then I will never have him," answered Mrs. Fox.

So the cat went down, and sent this suitor about his business.   Soon after, some one else knocked at the door; it was another fox that had two tails, but he was not better welcomed than the first.   After this came several others, till at last one came that had really nine tails just like the old fox.

When the widow heard this, she jumped up and said,

"Now, Pussy, my dear, open windows and doors,
And bid all our friends at our wedding to meet;
And as for that nasty old master of ours,
Throw him out of the window, Puss, into the street."

But when the wedding feast was all ready, up sprung the old gentleman on a sudden, and taking a club drove the whole company, together with Mrs. Fox, out of doors.

After some time, however, the old fox really died; and soon afterwards a wolf came to pay his respects, and knocked at the door.

Wolf. Good day, Mrs. Cat, with your whiskers so trim;
 How comes it you're sitting alone so prim?
 What's that you are cooking so nicely, I pray?
Cat. Oh, that's bread and milk for my dinner to-day.
 Will your worship be pleased to stay and dine,
 Or shall I fetch you a glass of wine?

"No, I thank you: Mrs. Fox is not at home, I suppose?"

Cat. She sits all alone,
 Her griefs to bemoan;
 For, alas! alas! Mr. Fox is gone.
Wolf. Ah! dear Mrs. Puss! that's a loss indeed:
 D'ye think she'd take *me* for a husband instead?
Cat. Indeed, Mr. Wolf, I don't know but she **may**,
 If you'll sit down a moment, I'll step up and see.

So she gave him a chair, and shaking her ears,
She very obligingly tripped it upstairs.
She knocked at the door with the rings on her toes,
And said, "Mrs. Fox, you're within, I suppose?"
"Oh yes," said the widow, "pray come in, my **dear**,
And tell me whose voice in the kitchen I hear."
"It's a wolf," said the cat, "with a nice smooth **skin**,
Who was passing this way, and just stepped in
To see (as old Mr. Fox is dead)
If you like to take him for a husband instead."

"But," said Mrs. Fox, "has he red feet and a sharp snout?" "No," said the cat. "Then he won't do for me." Soon after the wolf was sent about his business, there came a dog, then a goat, and after that a bear, a lion, and all the beasts, one after another. But they all wanted something that old Mr. Fox had, and the cat was ordered to send them all away. At last came a young fox, and Mrs. Fox said, "Has he four red feet and a sharp snout?" "Yes," said the cat.

"Then, Puss, make the parlour look clean and neat,
And throw the old gentleman into the street;
A stupid old rascal! I'm glad that he's dead,
Now I've got such a charming young fox instead."
So the wedding was held, and the merry bells rung,
And the friends and relations they danced and they sung,
And feasted and drank, I can't tell how long.

Brother and Sister

HANSEL one day took his sister Grettel by the hand, and said, "Since our poor mother died we have had no happy days; for our new mother beats us all day long, and when we go near her, she pushes us away. We have nothing but hard crusts to eat; and the little dog that lies by the fire is better off than we; for he sometimes has a nice piece of meat thrown to him. Heaven have mercy upon us! Oh, if our poor mother knew how we are used! Come, we will go and travel over the wide world." They went the whole day walking over the fields, till in the evening they came to a great wood; and then they were so tired and hungry that they sat down in a hollow tree and went to sleep.

In the morning when they awoke, the sun had risen high above the trees, and shone warm upon the hollow tree. Then Hansel said, "Sister, I am very thirsty; if I could find a brook, I would go and drink, and fetch you some water too. Listen, I think I hear the sound of one." Then Hansel rose up and took Grettel by the hand and went in search of the brook. But their cruel step-mother was a fairy, and had followed them into the wood to work them mischief: and when they had found a brook that ran sparkling over the pebbles, Hansel wanted to drink; but Grettel thought she heard the brook, as it babbled along, say, "Whoever drinks here will be turned into a tiger."

Then she cried out, "Ah, brother! do not drink, or you will be turned into a wild beast and tear me to pieces." Then Hansel yielded, although he was parched with thirst. "I will wait," said he, "for the next brook." But when they came to the next, Grettel listened again, and thought she heard "Whoever drinks here will become a wolf." Then she cried out, "Brother, brother, do not drink, or you will become a wolf and eat me." So he did not drink, but said, "I will wait for the next brook; there I must drink, say what you will, I am so thirsty."

As they came to the third brook, Grettel listened, and heard "Whoever drinks here will become a fawn." "Ah, brother!" said she, "do not drink, or you will be turned into a fawn and run away from me." But Hansel had already stooped down upon his knees, and the moment he put his lips into the water he was turned into a fawn.

Grettel wept bitterly over the poor creature, and the tears too rolled down his eyes as he laid himself beside her. Then she said, "Rest in peace, dear fawn, I will never never leave thee." So she took off her golden necklace and put it round his neck, and plucked some rushes and plaited them into a soft string to fasten to it; and led the poor little thing by her side further into the wood.

After they had travelled a long way, they came at last to a little cottage; and Grettel, having looked in and seen that it was quite empty, thought to herself, "We can stay and live here." Then she went and gathered leaves and moss to make a soft bed for the fawn: and every morning she went out and plucked nuts, roots, and berries for herself, and sweet shrubs and tender grass for her companion; and it ate out of her hand, and was pleased, and played and frisked about her. In the evening, when Grettel was tired, and had said her prayers, she laid her head upon the fawn for her pillow, and slept: and if poor Hansel could but have his right form again, they thought they should lead a very happy life.

They lived thus a long while in the wood by themselves, till it chanced that the king of that country came to hold a great hunt there. And when the fawn heard all around the echoing of the horns, and the baying of dogs, and the merry shouts of the huntsmen, he wished very much to go and see what was going on. "Ah, sister! sister!" said he, "let me go out into the wood, I can stay no longer." And he begged so long, that she at last agreed to let him go. "But," said she, "be sure to come to me in the evening: I shall shut up the door to keep out those wild huntsmen; and if you tap at it, and say 'Sister, let me in,' I shall know you; but if you don't speak, I shall keep the door fast." Then away sprang the fawn, and frisked and bounded along in the open air. The king and his huntsmen saw the beautiful creature, and followed but could not overtake him; for when they thought they were sure of their prize, he sprung over the bushes and was out of sight in a moment.

As it grew dark he came running home to the hut, and tapped, and said "Sister, sister, let me in." Then she opened the little door, and in he jumped and slept soundly all night on his soft bed.

Next morning the hunt began again; and when he heard the huntsmen's horns, he said, "Sister, open the door for me, I must go again." Then she let him out, and said "Come back in the evening, and remember what you are to say." When the king and the huntsmen saw the fawn with the golden collar again, they gave him chase; but he was too quick for them. The chase lasted the whole day; but at last the huntsmen nearly surrounded him, and one of them wounded him in the foot, so that he became sadly lame and could hardly crawl home. The man who had wounded him followed close behind, and hid himself, and heard the little fawn say, "Sister, sister, let me in:" upon which the door opened and soon shut again. The huntsman marked all well, and went to the king and told him what he had seen and heard; then the king said, "To-morrow we will have another chase."

Grettel was very much frightened when she saw that her dear little fawn was wounded; but she washed the blood away and put some healing herbs on it, and said, "Now go to bed, dear fawn, and you will soon be well again." The wound was so small, that in the morning there was nothing to be seen of it; and when the horn blew, the little creature said, "I can't stay here, I must go and look on; I will take care that none of them shall catch me." But Grettel said, "I am sure they will kill you this time, I will not let you go." "I shall die of vexation," answered he, "if you keep me here; when I hear the horns, I feel as if I could fly." Then Grettel was forced to let him go; so she opened the door with a heavy heart, and he bounded out gaily into the wood.

When the king saw him, he said to his huntsman, "Now chase him all day long till you catch him; but let none of you do him any harm." The sun set, however, without their being able to overtake him, and the king called away the huntsmen, and said to the one who had watched, "Now come and show me the little hut." So they went to the door and tapped, and said, "Sister, sister, let me in." Then the door opened and the king went in, and there stood a maiden more lovely than any he had ever seen. Grettel was frightened to see that it was not her fawn, but a king with a golden crown, that was come into her hut: however, he spoke kindly to her, and took her hand, and said, "Will you come with me to my castle and be my wife?" "Yes," said the maiden; "but my fawn must go with me, I cannot part with that." "Well," said the king, "he shall come and live with you all your life, and want for nothing." Just at that moment in sprung the little fawn; and his sister tied the string to his neck, and they left the hut in the wood together.

Then he king took Grettel to his palace, and celebrated the marriage in great state. And she told the king all her story; and he sent for the fairy and punished her: and the fawn was changed into Hansel again, and he and his sister loved one another, and lived happily together all their days.

The Giant with the Three Golden Hairs

THERE was once a poor man who had an only son born to him. The child was born under a lucky star; and those who told his fortune said that in his fourteenth year he would marry the king's daughter. It so happened that the king of that land soon after the child's birth passed through the village in disguise, and asked whether there was any news. "Yes," said the people, "a child has just been born, that they say is to be a lucky one, and when he is fourteen years old, he is fated to marry the king's daughter." This did not please the king; so he went to the poor child's parents and asked them whether they would sell him their son? "No," said they; but the stranger begged very hard and offered a great deal of money, and they had scarcely bread to eat, so at last they consented, thinking to themselves, he is a luck's child, he can come to no harm.

The king took the child, put it into a box, and rode away; but when he came to a deep stream, he threw it into the current, and said to himself, "That young gentleman will never be my daughter's husband." The box however floated down the stream; some kind spirit watched over it so that no water reached the child, and at last about two miles from the king's capital it stopt at the dam of a mill. The miller soon saw it, and took a long pole, and drew it towards the shore, and finding it heavy, thought there was gold inside; but when he opened it, he found a pretty little boy, that smiled upon him merrily. Now the miller and his wife had no children, and therefore rejoiced to see their prize, saying, "Heaven has sent it to us;" so they treated it very kindly, and brought it up with such care that every one admired and loved it.

About thirteen years passed over their heads, when the king came by accident to the mill, and asked the miller if that was his son. "No," said he, "I found him when a babe in a box in the mill-dam." "How long ago?" asked the king. "Some thirteen years," replied the miller. "He is a fine fellow," said the king, "can you spare him to carry a letter to the queen? it will please me very much, and I will give him two pieces of gold for his trouble." "As your majesty pleases," answered the miller.

Now the king had soon guessed that this was the child whom he had tried to drown; and he wrote a letter by him to the queen, saying, "As soon as the bearer of this arrives, let him be killed and immediately buried, so that all may be over before I return."

The young man set out with this letter, but missed his way, and came in the evening to a dark wood. Through the gloom he perceived a light at a distance, towards which he directed his course, and found that it proceeded from a little cottage. There was no one within except an old woman, who was frightened at seeing him, and said, "Why do you come hither, and whither are you going?" "I am going to the queen, to whom I was to have delivered a letter; but I have lost my way, and shall be glad if you will give me a night's rest." "You are very unlucky," said she, "for this is a robbers' hut, and if the band returns while you are here it may be worse for you." "I am so tired, however," replied he, "that I must take my chance, for I can go no further;" so he laid the letter on the table, stretched himself out upon a bench, and fell asleep.

When the robbers came home and saw him, they asked the old woman who the strange lad was. "I have given him shelter for charity," said she; "he had a letter to carry to the queen, and lost his way." The robbers took up the letter, broke it open and read the directions which it contained to murder the bearer. Then their leader tore it, and wrote a fresh one desiring the queen, as soon as the young man arrived, to marry him to the king's daughter. Meantime they let him sleep on till morning broke, and then showed him the right way to the queen's palace; where, as soon as she had read the letter, she had all possible preparations made for the wedding; and as the young man was very beautiful, the princess took him willingly for her husband.

After a while the king returned; and when he saw the prediction fulfilled, and that this child of fortune was, notwithstanding all his cunning, married to his daughter, he inquired eagerly how this had happened, and what were the orders which he had given. "Dear husband," said the queen, "here is your letter, read it for yourself." The king took it, and seeing that an exchange had been made, asked his son-in-law what he had done with the letter which he had given him to carry. "I know nothing of it," answered he; "it must have been taken away in the night while I slept." Then the king was very wroth, and said, "No man shall have my daughter who does not descend into the wonderful cave and bring me three golden hairs from the head of the giant king who reigns there; do this and you shall have my consent." "I will soon manage that," said the youth;—so he took leave of his wife and set out on his journey.

At the first city that he came to, the guard of the gate stopt him, and asked what trade he followed and what he knew. "I know everything," said he. "If that be so," replied they, "you are just the man we want; be so good as to tell us why our fountain in the market-place is dry and will give no water; find out the cause of that, and we will give you two asses loaded with gold." "With all my heart," said he, "when I come back."

Then he journeyed on and came to another city, and there the guard also asked him what trade he followed, and what he understood. "I know everything," answered he. "Then pray do us a piece of service," said they, "tell us why a tree which used to bear us golden apples, now does not even produce a leaf." "Most willingly," answered he, "as I come back."

At last his way led him to the side of a great lake of water over which he must pass. The ferryman soon began to ask, as the others had done, what was his trade, and what he knew. "Everything," said he. "Then," said the other, "pray inform me why I am bound for ever to ferry over this water, and have never been able to get my liberty; I will reward you handsomely." "I will tell you all about it," said the young man, "as I come home."

When he had passed the water, he came to the wonderful cave, which looked terribly black and gloomy. But the wizard king was not at home, and his grandmother sat at the door in her easy chair. "What do you seek?" said she. "Three golden hairs from the giant's head," answered he. "You run a great risk," said she, "when he returns home; yet I will try what I can do for you." Then she changed him into an ant, and told him to hide himself in the folds of her cloak. "Very well," said he: "but I want also to know why the city fountain is dry, why the tree that bore golden apples is now leafless, and what it is that binds the ferryman to his post." "Those are three puzzling questions," said the old dame; "but lie quiet and listen to what the giant says when I pull the golden hairs."

Presently night set in and the old gentleman returned home. As soon as he entered he began to snuff up the air, and cried, "All is not right here: I smell man's flesh." Then he searched all round in vain, and the old dame scolded, and said, "Why should you turn every thing topsy-turvy? I have just set all in order." Upon this he laid his head in her lap and soon fell asleep. As soon as he began to snore, she seized one of the golden hairs and pulled it out. "Mercy!" cried he, starting up, "what are you about?" "I had a dream that disturbed me," said she, "and in my trouble I seized your hair: I dreamt that the fountain in the market-place of the city was become dry and would give no water; what can be the cause?" "Ah! if they could find that out, they would be glad," said the giant: "under a stone in the fountain sits a toad; when they kill him, it will flow again."

This said, he fell asleep, and the old lady pulled out another hair. "What would you be at?" cried he in a rage. "Don't be angry," said she, "I did it in my sleep; I dreamt that in a great kingdom there was a beautiful tree that used to bear golden apples, and now has not even a leaf upon it; what is the reason of that?" "Aha!" said the giant, "they would like very well to know that secret: at the root of the tree a mouse is gnawing; if they were to kill him, the tree would bear golden apples again; if not, it will soon die. Now let me sleep in peace; if you wake me again, you shall rue it."

Then he fell once more asleep; and when she heard him snore she pulled out the third golden hair, and the giant jumped up and threatened her sorely; but she soothed him, and said, "It was a strange dream: methought I saw a ferryman who was fated to ply backwards and forwards over a lake, and could never be set at liberty; what is the charm that binds him?" "A silly fool!" said the giant; "if he were to give the rudder into the hand of any passenger, he would find himself at liberty, and the other would be obliged to take his place. Now let me sleep."

In the morning the giant arose and went out; and the old woman gave the young man the three golden hairs, reminded him of the answers to his three questions, and sent him on his way.

He soon came to the ferryman, who knew him again, and asked for the answer which he had promised him. "Ferry me over first," said he, "and then I will tell you." When the boat arrived on the other side, he told him to give the rudder to any of his passengers, and then he might run away as soon as he pleased. The next place he came to was the city where the barren tree stood: "Kill the mouse," said he, "that gnaws the root, and you will have golden apples again." They gave him a rich present, and he journeyed on to the city where the fountain had dried up, and the guard demanded his answer to their question. So he told them how to cure the mischief, and they thanked him and gave him the two asses laden with gold.

And now at last this child of fortune reached home, and his wife rejoiced greatly to see him, and to hear how well everything had gone with him. He gave the three golden hairs to the king, who could no longer raise any objection to him, and when he saw all the treasure, cried out in a transport of joy, "Dear son, where did you find all this gold?" "By the side of a lake," said the youth, "where there is plenty more to be had." "Pray, tell me," said the king, "that I may go and get some too." "As much as you please," replied the other; "you will see the ferryman on the lake, let him carry you across, and there you will see gold as plentiful as sand upon the shore."

Away went the greedy king; and when he came to the

lake, he beckoned to the ferryman, who took him into his boat, and as soon as he was there gave the rudder into his hand, and sprung ashore, leaving the old king to ferry away as a reward for his sins.

"And is his majesty plying there to this day?" You may be sure of that, for nobody will trouble himself to take the rudder out of his hands.

The Frog-Prince

ONE fine evening a young princess went into a wood, and sat down by the side of a cool spring of water. She had a golden ball in her hand, which was her favourite play-thing, and she amused herself with tossing it into the air and catching it again as it fell. After a time she threw it up so high that when she stretched out her hand to catch it, the ball bounded away and rolled along upon the ground, till at last it fell into the spring. The princess looked into the spring after her ball; but it was very deep, so deep that she could not see the bottom of it. Then she began to lament her loss, and said, "Alas! if I could only get my ball again, I would give all my fine clothes and jewels, and everything that I have in the world." Whilst she was speaking a frog put its head out of the water, and said, "Princess, why do you weep so bitterly?" "Alas!" said she, "what can you do for me, you nasty frog? My golden ball has fallen into the spring." The frog said, "I want not your pearls and jewels and fine clothes; but if you will love me and let me live with you, and eat from your little golden plate, and sleep upon your little bed, I will bring you your ball again." "What nonsense," thought the princess, "this silly frog is talking! He can never get out of the well: however, he may be able to get my ball for me; and therefore I will promise him what he asks." So she said to the frog, "Well, if you will bring me my ball, I promise to do all you require." Then the frog put his head down, and dived deep under the water; and after a little while he came up again with the ball in his mouth, and threw it on the ground.   As soon as the young princess saw her ball, she ran to pick it up, and was so overjoyed to have it in her hand again, that she never thought of the frog, but ran home with it as fast as she could.   The frog called after her, "Stay, princess, and take me with you as you promised;" but she did not stop to hear a word.

The next day, just as the princess had sat down to dinner, she heard a strange noise, tap-tap, as if somebody was coming up the marble-staircase; and soon afterwards something knocked gently at the door, and said,

> "Open the door, my princess dear,
> Open the door to thy true love here!
> And mind the words that thou and I said
> By the fountain cool in the greenwood shade."

Then the princess ran to the door and opened it, and there she saw the frog, whom she had quite forgotten; she was terribly frightened, and shutting the door as fast as she could, came back to her seat.   The king her father asked her what had frightened her.   "There is a nasty frog," said she, "at the door, who lifted my ball out of the spring this morning: I promised him that he should live with me here, thinking that he could never get out of the spring; but there he is at the door and wants to come in!"   While she was speaking the frog knocked again at the door, and said,

> "Open the door, my princess dear,
> Open the door to thy true love here!
> And mind the words that thou and I said
> By the fountain cool in the greenwood shade."

The king said to the young princess, "As you have made

a promise, you must keep it; so go and let him in." She
did so, and the frog hopped into the room, and came up
close to the table. "Pray lift me upon a chair," said he
to the princess, "and let me sit next to you." As soon as
she had done this, the frog said, "Put your plate closer to
me that I may eat out of it." This she did, and when he
had eaten as much as he could, he said, "Now I am tired;
carry me upstairs and put me into your little bed." And
the princess took him up in her hand and put him upon
the pillow of her own little bed, where he slept all night
long. As soon as it was light he jumped up, hopped
downstairs, and went out of the house. "Now," thought
the princess, "he is gone, and I shall be troubled with him
no more."

But she was mistaken; for when night came again, she
heard the same tapping at the door, and when she opened
it, the frog came in and slept upon her pillow as before
till the morning broke: and the third night he did the same;
but when the princess awoke on the following morning, she
was astonished to see, instead of the frog, a handsome
prince gazing on her with the most beautiful eyes that ever
were seen, and standing at the head of her bed.

He told her that he had been enchanted by a malicious
fairy, who had changed him into the form of a frog, in
which he was fated to remain till some princess should take
him out of the spring and let him sleep upon her bed for
three nights. "You," said the prince, "have broken this
cruel charm, and now I have nothing to wish for but that
you should go with me into my father's kingdom, where
I will marry you, and love you as long as you live."

The young princess, you may be sure, was not long in
giving her consent; and as they spoke a splendid carriage
drove up with eight beautiful horses decked with plumes
of feathers and golden harness, and behind rode the

prince's servant, the faithful Henry, who had bewailed the misfortune of his dear master so long and bitterly that his heart had well nigh burst. Then all set out full of joy for the prince's kingdom; where they arrived safely, and lived happily a great many years.

The Fox and the Horse

A FARMER had a horse that had been an excellent faithful servant to him: but he was now grown too old to work; so the farmer would give him nothing more to eat, and said, "I want you no longer, so take yourself off out of my stable; I shall not take you back again until you are stronger than a lion." Then he opened the door and turned him adrift.

The poor horse was very melancholy, and wandered up and down in the wood, seeking some little shelter from the cold wind and rain. Presently a fox met him: "What's the matter, my friend?" said he, "why do you hang down your head and look so lonely and woe-begone?" "Ah!" replied the horse, "justice and avarice never dwell in one house; my master has forgotten all that I have done for him so many years, and because I can no longer work he has turned me adrift, and says unless I become stronger than a lion he will not take me back again; what chance can I have of that? he knows I have none, or he would not talk so."

However, the fox bid him be of good cheer, and said, "I will help you; lie down there, stretch yourself out quite stiff, and pretend to be dead." The horse did as he was told, and the fox went straight to the lion who lived in a cave close by, and said to him, "A little way off lies a dead horse; come with me and you may make an excellent meal of his carcase." The lion was greatly pleased, and set off immediately; and when they came to the horse, the fox said, "You will not be able to eat him comfortably here; I'll tell you what—I will tie you fast to his tail, and then you can draw him to your den, and eat him at your leisure."

This advice pleased the lion, so he laid himself down quietly for the fox to make him fast to the horse. But the fox managed to tie his legs together and bound all so hard and fast that with all his strength he could not set himself free. When the work was done, the fox clapped the horse on the shoulder, and said, "Jip! Dobbin! Jip!" Then up he sprang, and moved off, dragging the lion behind him. The beast began to roar and bellow, till all the birds of the wood flew away for fright; but the horse let him sing on, and made his way quietly over the fields to his master's house.

"Here he is, master," said he, "I have got the better of him:" and when the farmer saw his old servant, his heart relented, and he said, "Thou shalt stay in thy stable and be well taken care of." And so the poor old horse had plenty to eat, and lived—till he died.

Rumpel-Stilts-Kin

IN a certain kingdom once lived a poor miller who had a very beautiful daughter. She was moreover exceedingly shrewd and clever; and the miller was so vain and proud of her, that he one day told the king of the land that his daughter could spin gold out of straw. Now this king was very fond of money; and when he heard the miller's boast, his avarice was excited, and he ordered the girl to be brought before him. Then he led her to a chamber where there was a great quantity of straw, gave her a spinning-wheel, and said, "All this must be spun into gold before morning, as you value your life." It was in vain that the poor maiden declared that she could do no such thing, the chamber was locked and she remained alone.

She sat down in one corner of the room and began to lament over her hard fate, when on a sudden the door opened, and a droll-looking little man hobbled in, and said, "Good morrow to you, my good lass, what are you weeping for?" "Alas!" answered she, "I must spin this straw into gold, and I know not how." "What will you give me," said the little man, "to do it for you?" "My necklace," replied the maiden. He took her at her word, and sat himself down to the wheel; round about it went merrily, and presently the work was done and the gold all spun.

When the king came and saw this, he was greatly astonished and pleased; but his heart grew still more greedy of gain, and he shut up the poor miller's daughter again with a fresh task. Then she knew not what to do, and sat down once more to weep; but the little man presently opened the door, and said, "What will you give me to do your task?" "The ring on my finger," replied she. So her little friend took the ring, and began to work at the wheel, till by the morning all was finished again.

The king was vastly delighted to see all this glittering treasure; but still he was not satisfied, and took the miller's daughter into a yet larger room, and said, "All this must be spun to-night; and if you succeed, you shall be my queen." As soon as she was alone the dwarf came in, and said, "What will you give me to spin gold for you this third time?" I have nothing left," said she. "Then promise me," said the little man, "your first little child when you are queen." "That may never be," thought the miller's daughter; and as she knew no other way to get her task done, she promised him what he asked, and he spun once more the whole heap of gold. The king came in the morning, and finding all he wanted, married her, and so the miller's daughter really became queen.

At the birth of her first little child the queen rejoiced very much, and forgot the little man and her promise; but one day he came into her chamber and reminded her of it. Then she grieved sorely at her misfortune, and offered him all the treasures of the kingdom in exchange; but in vain, till at last her tears softened him, and he said, "I will give you three days' grace, and if during that time you tell me my name, you shall keep your child."

Now the queen lay awake all night, thinking of all the odd names that she had ever heard, and dispatched messengers all over the land to inquire after new ones. The next day the little man came, and she began with Timothy, Benjamin, Jeremiah, and all the names she could remember; but to all of them he said, "That's not my name."

The second day she began with all the comical names she could hear of, Bandy-legs, Hunch-back, Crook-shanks, and so on, but the little gentleman still said to every one of them, "That's not my name."

The third day came back one of the messengers, and said, "I can hear of no one other name; but yesterday, as I was climbing a high hill among the trees of the forest where the fox and the hare bid each other good night, I saw a little hut, and before the hut burnt a fire, and round about the fire danced a funny little man upon one leg, and sung—

> "Merrily the feast I'll make,
> To-day I'll brew, to-morrow bake;
> Merrily I'll dance and sing,
> For next day will a stranger bring:
> Little does my lady dream
> Rumpel-Stilts-Kin is my name!"

When the queen heard this, she jumped for joy, and as soon as her little visitor came, and said "Now, lady, what is my name?" "Is it John?" asked she. "No!" "Is it Tom?" "No!"

> "Can your name be Rumpel-stilts-kin?"

"Some witch told you that! Some witch told you that!" cried the little man, and dashed his right foot in a rage so deep into the floor, that he was forced to lay hold of it with both hands to pull it out. Then he made the best of his way off, while everybody laughed at him for having had all his trouble for nothing.

The Goose-Girl

A N old queen, whose husband had been dead some years, had a beautiful daughter. When she grew up, she was betrothed to a prince who lived a great way off; and as the time drew near for her to be married, she got ready to set off on her journey to his country. Then the queen her mother packed up a great many costly things; jewels, and gold, and silver; trinkets, fine dresses, and in short everything that became a royal bride; for she loved her child very dearly: and she gave her a waiting-maid to ride with her, and give her into the bridegroom's hands; and each had a horse for the journey. Now the princess's horse was called Falada, and could speak.

When the time came for them to set out, the old queen went into her bed-chamber, and took a little knife, and cut off a lock of her hair, and gave it to her daughter, and said, "Take care of it, dear child; for it is a charm that may be of use to you on the road." Then they took a sorrowful leave of each other, and the princess put the lock of her mother's hair into her bosom, got upon her horse, and set off on her journey to her bridegroom's kingdom. One day, as they were riding along by the side of a brook, the princess began to feel very thirsty, and said to her maid, "Pray get down and fetch me some water in my golden cup out of yonder brook, for I want to drink." "Nay," said the maid, "if you are thirsty, get down yourself, and lie down by the water and drink; I shall not be your waiting-maid any longer." Then she was so thirsty that she got down, and knelt over the little brook, and drank, for she was frightened, and dared not bring out her golden cup; and then she wept, and said, "Alas! what will become of me?" And the lock of hair answered her, and said,

"Alas! alas! if thy mother knew it,
Sadly, sadly her heart would rue it."

But the princess was very humble and meek, so she said nothing to her maid's ill behaviour, but got upon her horse again.

Then all rode further on their journey, till the day grew so warm, and the sun so scorching, that the bride began to feel very thirsty again; and at last when they came to a river she forgot her maid's rude speech, and said, "Pray get down and fetch me some water to drink in my golden cup." But the maid answered her, and even spoke more haughtily than before, "Drink if you will, but I shall not be your waiting-maid." Then the princess was so thirsty that she got off her horse, and lay down, and held her head over the running stream, and cried, and said, "What will become of me?" And the lock of hair answered her again,

"Alas! alas! if thy mother knew it,
Sadly, sadly her heart would rue it."

And as she leaned down to drink, the lock of hair fell from her bosom, and floated away with the water, without her seeing it, she was so frightened. But her maid saw it, and was very glad, for she knew the charm, and saw that the poor bride would be in her power, now that she had lost the hair. So when the bride had done, and would have got upon Falada again, the maid said, "I shall ride upon Falada, and you may have my horse instead:" so she was forced to give up her horse, and soon afterwards to take off her royal clothes, and put on her maid's shabby ones.

At last, as they drew near the end of their journey, this treacherous servant threatened to kill her mistress if she ever told any one what had happened. But Falada saw it all, and marked it well. Then the waiting-maid got upon Falada, and the real bride was set upon the other horse, and they went on in this way till at last they came to the royal court. There was great joy at their coming, and the prince flew to meet them, and lifted the maid from her horse, thinking she was the one who was to be his wife; and she was led upstairs to the royal chamber, but the true princess was told to stay in the court below.

But the old king happened to be looking out of the window, and saw her in the yard below; and as she looked very pretty, and too delicate for a waiting-maid, he went into the royal chamber to ask the bride who it was she had brought with her, that was thus left standing in the court below. "I brought her with me for the sake of her company on the road," said she; "pray give the girl some work to do, that she may not be idle." The old king could not for some time think of any work for her to do; but at last he said, "I have a lad who takes care of my geese; she may go and help him." Now the name of this lad, that the real bride was to help in watching the king's geese, was Curdken.

Soon after, the false bride said to the prince, "Dear husband, pray do me one piece of kindness." "That I will," said the prince. "Then tell one of your slaughterers to cut off the head of the horse I rode upon, for it was very unruly, and plagued me sadly on the road;" but the truth was, she was very much afraid lest Falada should speak, and tell all she had done to the princess. She carried her point, and the faithful Falada was killed: but when the true princess heard of it, she wept, and begged the man to nail up Falada's head against a large dark gate of the city, through which she had to pass every morning and evening, that there she might still see him sometimes. Then the slaughterer said he would do as she wished; and cut off the head, and nailed it fast under the dark gate.

Early the next morning, as she and Curdken went out through the gate, she said sorrowfully,

> "Falada, Falada, there thou art hanging!"

and the head answered,

> "Bride, bride, there thou art ganging!
> Alas! alas! if thy mother knew it,
> Sadly, sadly her heart would rue it."

Then they went out of the city, and drove the geese on. And when she came to the meadow, she sat down upon a bank there, and let down her waving locks of hair, which were all of pure silver; and when Curdken saw it glitter in the sun, he ran up, and would have pulled some of the locks out; but she cried,

> "Blow, breezes, blow!
> Let Curdken's hat go!
> Blow, breezes, blow!
> Let him after it go!
> O'er hills, dales, and rocks,
> Away be it whirl'd,
> Till the silvery locks
> Are all comb'd and curl'd!"

Then there came a wind, so strong that it blew off Curdken's hat; and away it flew over the hills, and he after it;

till, by the time he came back, she had done combing and curling her hair, and put it up again safe. Then he was very angry and sulky, and would not speak to her at all; but they watched the geese until it grew dark in the evening, and then drove them homewards.

The next morning, as they were going through the dark gate, the poor girl looked up at Falada's head, and cried,

"Falada, Falada, there thou art hanging!"

and it answered,

"Bride, bride, there thou art ganging!
Alas! alas! if thy mother knew it,
Sadly, sadly her heart would rue it."

Then she drove on the geese, and sat down again in the meadow, and began to comb out her hair as before; and Curdken ran up to her, and wanted to take hold of it; but she cried out quickly,

"Blow, breezes, blow!
Let Curdken's hat go!
Blow, breezes, blow!
Let him after it go!
O'er hills, dales, and rocks,
Away be it whirl'd,
Till the silvery locks
Are all comb'd and curl'd!"

Then the wind came and blew his hat, and off it flew a great way, over the hills and far away, so that he had to run after it; and when he came back, she had done up her hair again, and all was safe. So they watched the geese till it grew dark.

In the evening, after they came home, Curdken went

to the old king, and said, "I cannot have that strange girl to help me to keep the geese any longer." "Why?" said the king. "Because she does nothing but tease me all day long." Then the king made him tell him all that had passed. And Curdken said, "When we go in the morning through the dark gate with our flock of geese, she weeps, and talks with the head of a horse that hangs upon the wall, and says,

> 'Falada, Falada, there thou art hanging!'

and the head answers,

> 'Bride, bride, there thou art ganging!
> Alas! alas! if thy mother knew it,
> Sadly, sadly her heart would rue it.' "

And Curdken went on telling the king what had happened upon the meadow where the geese fed; and how his hat was blown away, and he was forced to run after it, and leave his flock. But the old king told him to go out again as usual the next day: and when morning came, he placed himself behind the dark gate, and heard how she spoke to Falada, and how Falada answered; and then he went into the field, and hid himself in a bush by the meadow's side, and soon saw with his own eyes how they drove the flock of geese, and how, after a little time, she let down her hair that glittered in the sun; and then he heard her say,

> "Blow, breezes, blow!
> Let Curdken's hat go!
> Blow, breezes, blow!
> Let him after it go!
> O'er hills, dales, and rocks,
> Away be it whirl'd,
> Till the silvery locks
> Are all comb'd and curl'd!"

And soon came a gale of wind, and carried away Curd-ken's hat, while the girl went on combing and curling her hair. All this the old king saw: so he went home without being seen; and when the little goose-girl came back in the evening, he called her aside, and asked her why she did so: but she burst into tears, and said, "That I must not tell you or any man, or I shall lose my life."

But the old king begged so hard, that she had no peace till she had told him all, word for word: and it was very lucky for her that she did so, for the king ordered royal clothes to be put upon her, and gazed on her with wonder, she was so beautiful. Then he called his son, and told him, that he had only the false bride, for that she was merely a waiting-maid, while the true one stood by. And the young king rejoiced when he saw her beauty, and heard how meek and patient she had been; and, without saying anything, ordered a great feast to be got ready for all his court. The bridegroom sat at the top, with the false princess on one side, and the true one on the other; but nobody knew her, for she was quite dazzling to their eyes, and was not at all like the little goose-girl, now that she had her brilliant dress.

When they had eaten and drank, and were very merry, the old king told all the story, as one that he had once heard of, and asked the true waiting-maid what she thought ought to be done to any one who would behave thus. "Nothing better," said this false bride, "than that she should be thrown into a cask stuck round with sharp nails, and that two white horses should be put to it, and should drag it from street to street till she is dead." "Thou art she!" said the old king, "and since thou hast judged thy-self, it shall be so done to thee." And the young king was married to his true wife, and they reigned over the king-dom in peace and happiness all their lives.

Faithful John

AN old king fell sick; and when he found his end drawing near, he said, "Let Faithful John come to me." Now Faithful John was the servant that he was fondest of, and was so called because he had been true to his master all his life long. Then when he came to the bed-side, the king said, "My faithful John, I feel that my end draws nigh, and I have now no cares save for my son, who is still young, and stands in need of good counsel. I have no friend to leave him but you; if you do not pledge yourself to teach him all he should know, and to be a father to him, I shall not shut my eyes in peace." Then John said, "I will never leave him, but will serve him faithfully, even though it should cost me my life." And the king said, "I shall now die in peace: after my death, show him the whole palace; all the rooms and vaults, and all the treasures and stores which lie there: but take care how you show him one room,—I mean the one where hangs the picture of the daughter of the king of the golden roof. If he sees it, he will fall deeply in love with her, and will then be plunged into great dangers on her account: guard him in this peril." And when Faithful John had once more pledged his word to the old king, he laid his head on his pillow, and died in peace.

Now when the old king had been carried to his grave, Faithful John told the young king what had passed upon his death-bed, and said, "I will keep my word truly, and be faithful to you as I was always to your father, though it should cost me my life." And the young king wept, and said, "Neither will I ever forget your faithfulness."

The days of mourning passed away, and then Faithful John said to his master, "It is now time that you should see your heritage; I will show you your father's palace." Then he led him about every where, up and down, and let him see all the riches and all the costly rooms; only one room, where the picture stood, he did not open. Now the picture was so placed, that the moment the door opened, you could see it; and it was so beautifully done, that one would think it breathed and had life, and that there was nothing more lovely in the whole world. When the young king saw that Faithful John always went by this door, he said, "Why do you not open that room?" There is something inside," he answered, "which would frighten you." But the king said, "I have seen the whole palace, and I must also know what is in there;" and he went and began to force open the door: but Faithful John held him back, and said, "I gave my word to your father before his death, that I would take heed how I showed you what stands in that room, lest it should lead you and me into great trouble." "The greatest trouble to me," said the young king, "will be not to go in and see the room; I shall have no peace by day or by night until I do; so I shall not go hence until you open it."

Then Faithful John saw that with all he could do or say the young king would have his way; so, with a heavy heart and many foreboding sighs, he sought for the key out of his great bunch; and he opened the door of the room, and entered in first, so as to stand between the king and the picture, hoping he might not see it: but he raised himself upon tiptoes, and looked over John's shoulders; and as soon as he saw the likeness of the lady, so beautiful and shining with gold, he fell down upon the floor senseless. Then Faithful John lifted him up in his arms, and carried him to his bed, and was full of care, and thought to himself, "This trouble has come upon us; O Heaven! what will come of it?"

At last the king came to himself again; but the first thing that he said was, "Whose is that beautiful picture?" "It is the picture of the daughter of the king of the golden roof," said Faithful John. But the king went on, saying, "My love towards her is so great, that if all the leaves on the trees were tongues, they could not speak it; I care not to risk my life to win her; you are my faithful friend, you must aid me."

Then John thought for a long time what was now to be done; and at length said to the king, "All that she has about her is of gold: the tables, stools, cups, dishes, and all the things in her house are of gold; and she is always seeking new treasures. Now in your stores there is much gold; let it be worked up into every kind of vessel, and into all sorts of birds, wild beasts, and wonderful animals; then we will take it, and try our fortune." So the king ordered all the goldsmiths to be sought for; and they worked day and night, until at last the most beautiful things were made: and Faithful John had a ship loaded with them, and put on a merchant's dress, and the king did the same, that they might not be known.

When all was ready, they put out to sea, and sailed till they came to the coast of the land where the king of the golden roof reigned. Faithful John told the king to stay in the ship, and wait for him; "for perhaps," said he, "I may be able to bring away the king's daughter with me: therefore take care that everything be in order; let the golden vessels and ornaments be brought forth, and the whole ship be decked out with them." And he chose out something of each of the golden things to put into his basket, and got ashore, and went towards the king's palace. And when he came to the castle yard, there stood by the well side a beautiful maiden, who had two golden pails in her hand, drawing water. And as she drew up the water, which was glittering with gold, she turned herself round, and saw the stranger, and asked him who he was. Then he drew near, and said, "I am a merchant," and opened his basket, and let her look into it; and she cried out, "Oh! what beautiful things!" and set down her pails, and looked at one after the other. Then she said, "The king's daughter must see all these; she is so fond of such things, that she will buy all of you." So she took him by the hand, and led him in; for she was one of the waiting-maids of the daughter of the king.

When the princess saw the wares, she was greatly pleased, and said, "They are so beautiful that I will buy them all." But Faithful John said, "I am only the servant of a rich merchant; what I have here is nothing to what he has lying in yonder ship: there he has the finest and most costly things that ever were made in gold." The princess wanted to have them all brought ashore; but he said, "That would take up many days, there are such a number; and more rooms would be wanted to place them in than there are in the greatest house." But her wish to see them grew still greater, and at last she said, "Take me to the ship, I will go myself, and look at your master's wares."

Then Faithful John led her joyfully to the ship, and the king, when he saw her, thought that his heart would leap out of his breast; and it was with the greatest trouble that he kept himself still. So she got into the ship, and the king led her down; but Faithful John staid behind with the steersman, and ordered the ship to put off: "Spread all your sail," cried he, "that she may fly over the waves like a bird through the air."

And the king showed the princess the golden wares, each one singly; the dishes, cups, basins, and the wild and wonderful beasts; so that many hours flew away, and she looked at everything with delight, and was not aware that the ship was sailing away. And after she had looked at the last, she thanked the merchant, and said she would go home; but when she came upon the deck, she saw that the ship was sailing far away from land upon the deep sea, and that it flew along at full sail. "Alas!" she cried out in her fright, "I am betrayed; I am carried off, and have fallen into the power of a roving trader; I would sooner have died." But then the king took her by the hand, and said, "I am not a merchant, I am a king, and of as noble birth as you. I have taken you away by stealth, but I did so because of the very great love I have for you; for the first time that I saw your face, I fell on the ground in a swoon." When the daughter of the king of the golden roof heard all, she was comforted, and her heart soon turned towards him, and she was willing to become his wife.

But it so happened, that whilst they were sailing on the deep sea, Faithful John, as he sat on the prow of the ship playing on his flute, saw three ravens flying in the air towards him. Then he left off playing, and listened to what they said to each other, for he understood their tongue. The first said, "There he goes! he is bearing away the daughter of the king of the golden roof; let him go!" "Nay," said the second, "there he goes, but he has not got her yet." And the third said, "There he goes; he surely has her, for she is sitting by his side in the ship." Then the first began again, and cried out, "What boots it to him? See you not that when they come to land, a horse of a foxy-red colour will spring towards him; and then he will try to get upon it, and if he does, it will spring away with him into the air, so that he will never see his love again." "True! true!" said the second, "but is there no help?" "Oh! yes, yes!" said the first; "if he who sits upon the horse takes the dagger which is stuck in the saddle and strikes him dead, the young king is saved: but who knows that? and who will tell him, that he who thus saves the king's life will turn to stone from the toes of his feet to his knee?" Then the second said, "True! true! but I know more still; though the horse be dead, the king loses his bride: when they go together into the palace, there lies the bridal dress on the couch, and looks as if it were woven of gold and silver, but it is all brimstone and pitch; and if he puts it on, it will burn him, marrow and bones." "Alas! alas! is there no help?" said the third. "Oh! yes, yes!" said the second, "if some one draws near and throws it into the fire, the young king will be saved. But what boots that? who knows and will tell him, that, if he does, his body from the knee to the heart will be turned to stone?" "More! more! I know more," said the third: "were the dress burnt, still the king loses his bride. After the wedding, when the dance begins, and the young queen dances on, she will turn pale, and fall as though she were dead; and if some one does not draw near and lift her up, and take from her right breast three drops of blood, she will surely die. But if any one knew this, he would tell him, that if he does do so, his body will turn to stone, from the crown of his head to the tip of his toe."

Then the ravens flapped their wings, and flew on; but Faithful John, who had understood it all, from that time was sorrowful, and did not tell his master what he had heard; for he saw that if he told him, he must himself lay down his life to save him: at last he said to himself,

"I will be faithful to my word, and save my master, if it costs me my life."

Now when they came to land, it happened just as the ravens had foretold; for there sprung out a fine foxy-red horse. "See," said the king, "he shall bear me to my palace:" and he tried to mount, but Faithful John leaped before him, and swung himself quickly upon it, drew the dagger, and smote the horse dead. Then the other servants of the king, who were jealous of Faithful John, cried out, "What a shame to kill the fine beast that was to take the king to his palace!" But the king said, "Let him alone, it is my Faithful John; who knows but he did it for some good end?"

Then they went on to the castle, and there stood a couch in one room, and a fine dress lay upon it, that shone with gold and silver; and the young king went up to it to take hold of it, but Faithful John cast it in the fire, and burnt it. And the other servants began again to grumble, and said, "See, now he is burning the wedding dress." But the king said, "Who knows what he does it for? let him alone! he is my faithful servant John."

Then the wedding feast was held, and the dance began, and the bride also came in; but Faithful John took good heed, and looked in her face; and on a sudden she turned pale, and fell as though she were dead upon the ground. But he sprung towards her quickly, lifted her up, and took her and laid her upon a couch, and drew three drops of blood from her right breast. And she breathed again, and came to herself. But the young king had seen all, and did not know why Faithful John had done it; so he was angry at his boldness, and said, "Throw him into prison."

The next morning Faithful John was led forth, and stood upon the gallows, and said, "May I speak out before I die?" and when the king answered "It shall be granted thee," he said, "I am wrongly judged, for I have always been faithful and true:" and then he told what he had heard the ravens say upon the sea, and how he meant to save his master, and had therefore done all these things.

When he had told all, the king called out, "O my most faithful John! pardon! pardon! take him down!" But Faithful John had fallen down lifeless at the last word he spoke, and lay as a stone: and the king and the queen mourned over him; and the king said, "Oh, how ill have I rewarded thy truth!" And he ordered the stone figure to be taken up, and placed in his own room near to his bed; and as often as he looked at it he wept, and said, "Oh that I could bring thee back to life again, my Faithful John!"

After a time, the queen had two little sons, who grew up, and were her great joy. One day, when she was at church, the two children staid with their father; and as they played about, he looked at the stone figure, and sighed, and cried out, "Oh that I could bring thee back to life, my Faithful John!" Then the stone began to speak, and said, "O king! thou canst bring me back to life if thou wilt give up for my sake what is dearest to thee." But the king said, "All that I have in the world would I give up for thee." "Then," said the stone, "cut off the heads of thy children, sprinkle their blood over me, and I shall live again." Then the king was greatly shocked: but he thought how Faithful John had died for his sake, and because of his great truth towards him; and rose up and drew his sword to cut off his children's heads and sprinkle the stone with their blood; but the moment he drew his sword Faithful John was alive again, and stood before his face, and said, "Your truth is rewarded." And the children sprang about and played as if nothing had happened.

Then the king was full of joy: and when he saw the

queen coming, to try her, he put Faithful John and the two children in a large closet; and when she came in he said to her, "Have you been at church?" "Yes," said she, "but I could not help thinking of Faithful John, who was so true to us." "Dear wife," said the king, "we can bring him back to life again, but it will cost us both our little sons, and we must give them up for his sake." When the queen heard this, she turned pale and was frightened in her heart; but she said, "Let it be so; we owe him all, for his great faith and truth." Then he rejoiced because she thought as he had thought, and went in and opened the closet, and brought out the children and Faithful John, and said, "Heaven be praised! he is ours again, and we have our sons safe too." So he told her the whole story; and all lived happily together the rest of their lives.

The Blue Light

A SOLDIER had served a king his master many years, till at last he was turned off without pay **or** reward. How he should get his living he did not know: so he set out and journeyed homeward all day in a very downcast mood, until in the evening he came to the edge of **a** deep wood. The road leading that way, he pushed forward, but had not gone far before he saw a light glimmering through the trees, towards which he bent his weary steps; and soon came to a hut where no one lived but an old witch. The poor fellow begged for a night's lodging and something to eat and drink; but she would listen to nothing: however, he was not easily got rid of; and at last she said, "I think I will take pity on you this once; but if I do, you must dig over all my garden for me in the morning." The soldier agreed very willingly to anything she asked, and he became her guest.

The next day he kept his word and dug the garden very neatly. The job lasted all day; and in the evening, when his mistress would have sent him away, he said, "I am so tired with my work that I must beg you to let me stay over the night." The old lady vowed at first she would not do any such thing; but after a great deal of talk he carried his point, agreeing to chop up a whole cart-load of wood for her the next day.

This task too was duly ended; but not till towards night; and then he found himself so tired, that he begged a third night's rest: and this too was given, but only on his pledging his word that he next day would fetch the witch the blue light that burnt at the bottom of the well.

When morning came she led him to the well's mouth, tied him to a long rope, and let him down. At the bottom sure enough he found the blue light as the witch had said, and at once made the signal for her to draw him up again. But when she had pulled him up so near to the top that she could reach him with her hands, she said, "Give me the light, I will take care of it,"—meaning to play him a trick, by taking it for herself and letting him fall again to the bottom of the well. But the soldier saw through her wicked thoughts, and said, "No, I shall not give you the light till I find myself safe and sound out of the well." At this she became very angry, and dashed him, with the light she had longed for many a year, down to the bottom. And there lay the poor soldier for a while in despair, on the damp mud below, and feared that his end was nigh. But his pipe happened to be in his pocket still half full, and he thought to himself, "I may as well make an end of smoking you out; it is the last pleasure I shall have in this world." So he lit it at the blue light, and began to smoke.

Up rose a cloud of smoke, and on a sudden a little black dwarf was seen making his way through the midst of it, "What do you want with me, soldier?" said he. "I have no business with you," answered he. But the dwarf said, "I am bound to serve you in everything, as lord and master of the blue light." "Then first of all be so good as to help me out of this well." No sooner said than done: the dwarf took him by the hand and drew him up, and the blue light of course with him. "Now do me another piece of kindness," said the soldier; "pray let that old lady take my place in the well." When the dwarf had done this, and lodged the witch safely at the bottom, they began to ransack her treasures; and the soldier made bold to carry off as much of her gold and silver as he well could. Then the dwarf said, "if you should chance at any time to want me, you have nothing to do but to light your pipe at the blue light, and I will soon be with you."

The soldier was not a little pleased at his good luck, and went to the best inn in the first town he came to, and ordered some fine clothes to be made, and a handsome room to be got ready for him. When all was ready, he called his little man to him, and said, "The king sent me away penniless, and left me to hunger and want: I have a mind to show him that it is my turn to be master now; so bring me his daughter here this evening, that she may wait upon me, and do what I bid her." "That is rather a dangerous task," said the dwarf. But away he went, took the princess out of her bed, fast asleep as she was, and brought her to the soldier.

Very early in the morning he carried her back: and as soon as she saw her father, she said, "I had a strange dream last night: I thought I was carried away through the air to a soldier's house, and there I waited upon him as his servant." Then the king wondered greatly at such a story; but told her to make a hole in her pocket and fill it with peas, so that if it were really as she said, and the whole was not a dream, the peas might fall out in the streets as she passed through, and leave a clue to tell whither she had been taken. She did so; but the dwarf had heard the king's plot; and when evening came, and the soldier said he must bring him the princess again, he strewed peas over several of the streets, so that the few that fell from her pocket were not known from the others; and the people amused themselves all the next day picking up peas, and wondering where so many came from.

When the princess told her father what had happened to her the second time, he said, "Take one of your shoes with you, and hide it in the room you are taken to." The dwarf heard this also; and when the soldier told him to bring the king's daughter again, he said, "I cannot save you this time; it will be an unlucky thing for you if you are found out—as I think you will." But the soldier would have his own way. "Then you must take care and make the best of your way out of the city gate very early in the morning," said the dwarf. The princess kept one shoe on as her father bid her, and hid it in the soldier's room: and when she got back to her father, he ordered it to be sought for all over the town; and at last it was found where she had hid it. The soldier had run away, it is true; but he had been too slow, and was soon caught and thrown into a strong prison, and loaded with chains:—what was worse, in the hurry of his flight, he had left behind him his great treasure the blue light and all his gold, and had nothing left in his pocket but one poor ducat.

As he was standing very sorrowful at the prison grating, he saw one of his comrades, and calling out to him said, "If you will bring me a little bundle I left in the inn, I will give you a ducat." His comrade thought this very good pay for such a job: so he went away, and soon came back bringing the blue light and the gold. Then the prisoner soon lit his pipe: up rose the smoke, and with it came his old friend the little dwarf. "Do not fear, master," said he: "keep up your heart at your trial, and leave everything to take its course;—only mind to take the blue light with you." The trial soon came on; the matter was sifted to the bottom; the prisoner found guilty, and his doom passed:—he was ordered to be hung forthwith on the gallows-tree.

But as he was led out, he said he had one favour to

beg of the king. "What is it?" said his majesty. "That you will deign to let me smoke one pipe on the road." "Two, if you like," said the king. Then he lit his pipe at the blue light, and the black dwarf was before him in a moment. "Be so good as to kill, slay, or put to flight all these people," said the soldier: "and as for the king, you may cut him into three pieces." Then the dwarf began to lay about him, and soon got rid of the crowd around: but the king begged hard for mercy; and, to save his life, agreed to let the soldier have the princess for his wife, and to leave the kingdom to him when he died.

Ashputtel

or Cinderella

THE wife of a rich man fell sick: and when she felt that her end drew nigh, she called her only daughter to her bed-side, and said, "Always be a good girl, and I will look down from heaven and watch over you." Soon afterwards she shut her eyes and died, and was buried in the garden; and the little girl went every day to her grave and wept, and was always good and kind to all about her. And the snow spread a beautiful white covering over the grave; but by the time the sun had melted it away again, her father had married another wife. This new wife had two daughters of her own, that she brought home with her: they were fair in face, but foul at heart, and it was now a sorry time for the poor little girl. "What does the good-for-nothing thing want in the parlour?" said they; "they who would eat bread should first earn it; away with the kitchen maid!" Then they took away her fine clothes, and gave her an old gray frock to put on, and laughed at her and turned her into the kitchen.

There she was forced to do hard work; to rise early before day-light, to bring the water, to make the fire, to cook and to wash. Besides that, the sisters plagued her in all sorts of ways and laughed at her. In the evening when she was tired she had no bed to lie down on, but was made to lie by the hearth among the ashes; and then, as she was of course always dusty and dirty, they called her Ashputtel.

It happened once that the father was going to the fair, and asked his wife's daughters what he should bring them. "Fine clothes," said the first: "Pearls and diamonds," cried the second. "Now, child," said he to his own daughter, "what will you have?" "The first sprig, dear father, that rubs against your hat on your way home," said she. Then he bought for the two first the fine clothes and pearls and diamonds they had asked for: and on his way home as he rode through a green copse, a sprig of hazel brushed against him, and almost pushed off his hat: so he broke it off and brought it away; and when he got home he gave it to his daughter. Then she took it and went to her mother's grave and planted it there, and cried so much that it was watered with her tears; and there it grew and became a fine tree. Three times every day she went to it and wept; and soon a little bird came and built its nest upon the tree, and talked with her, and watched over her, and brought her whatever she wished for.

Now it happened that the king of the land held a feast which was to last three days, and out of those who came to it his son was to choose a bride for himself: and Ashputtel's two sisters were asked to come. So they called her up, and said, "Now, comb our hair, brush our shoes, and tie our sashes for us, for we are going to dance at the king's feast." Then she did as she was told, but when all was done she could not help crying, for she thought to herself, she should have liked to go to the dance too; and at last she begged her mother very hard to let her go. "You! Ashputtel?" said she; "you who have nothing to wear, no clothes at all, and who cannot even dance—you want to go to the ball?" And when she kept on begging,— to get rid of her, she said at last, "I will throw this basinful of peas into the ash heap, and if you have picked them all

out in two hours' time you shall go to the feast too." Then
she threw the peas into the ashes: but the little maiden
ran out at the back door into the garden, and cried out—

> "Hither, hither, through the sky,
> Turtle-doves and linnets, fly!
> Blackbird, thrush, and chaffinch gay,
> Hither, hither, haste away!
> One and all, come help me quick,
> Haste ye, haste ye,—pick, pick, pick!"

Then first came two white doves flying in at the
kitchen window; and next came two turtle-doves; and
after them all the little birds under heaven came chirping
and fluttering in, and flew down into the ashes: and the
little doves stooped their heads down and set to work, pick,
pick, pick; and then the others began to pick, pick, pick;
and picked out all the good grain and put it in a dish, and
left the ashes. At the end of one hour the work was done,
and all flew out again at the windows. Then she brought
the dish to her mother, overjoyed at the thought that now
she should go to the wedding. But she said, "No, no! you
slut, you have no clothes and cannot dance, you shall not
go." And when Ashputtel begged very hard to go, she
said, "If you can in one hour's time pick two of those
dishes of peas out of the ashes, you shall go too." And
thus she thought she should at last get rid of her. So
she shook two dishes of peas into the ashes; but the little
maiden went out into the garden at the back of the house,
and cried out as before—

> "Hither, hither, through the sky,
> Turtle-doves and linnets, fly!
> Blackbird, thrush, and chaffinch gay,
> Hither, hither, haste away!
> One and all, come help me quick,
> Haste ye, haste ye,—pick, pick, pick!"

Then first came two white doves in at the kitchen window; and next came the turtle-doves; and after them all the little birds under heaven came chirping and hopping about, and flew down about the ashes: and the little doves put their heads down and set to work, pick, pick, pick; and then the others began pick, pick, pick; and they put all the good grain into the dishes, and left all the ashes. Before half an hour's time all was done, and out they flew again. And then Ashputtel took the dishes to her mother, rejoicing to think that she should now go to the ball. But her mother said, "It is all of no use, you cannot go; you have no clothes, and cannot dance, and you would only put us to shame:" and off she went with her two daughters to the feast.

Now when all were gone, and nobody left at home, Ashputtel went sorrowfully and sat down under the hazel-tree, and cried out—

"Shake, shake, hazel-tree,
Gold and silver over me!"

Then her friend the bird flew out of the tree and brought a gold and silver dress for her, and slippers of spangled silk: and she put them on, and followed her sisters to the feast. But they did not know her, and thought it must be some strange princess, she looked so fine and beautiful in her rich clothes: and they never once thought of Ashputtel, but took for granted that she was safe at home in the dirt.

The king's son soon came up to her, and took her by the hand and danced with her and no one else: and he never left her hand; but when any one else came to ask her to dance, he said, "This lady is dancing with me." Thus they danced till a late hour of the night; and then she wanted to go home: and the king's son said, "I shall go and take care of you to your home;" for he wanted to see where the beautiful maid lived. But she slipped away from him unawares, and ran off towards home, and the prince followed her; but she jumped up into the pigeon-house and shut the door. Then he waited till her father came home, and told him that the unknown maiden who had been at the feast had hid herself in the pigeon-house. But when they had broken open the door they found no one within; and as they came back into the house, Ashputtel lay, as she always did, in her dirty frock by the ashes, and her dim little lamp burnt in the chimney: for she had run as quickly as she could through the pigeon-house and on to the hazel-tree, and had there taken off her beautiful clothes, and laid them beneath the tree, that the bird might carry them away, and had seated herself amid the ashes again in her little gray frock.

The next day when the feast was again held, and her father, mother, and sisters were gone, Ashputtel went to the hazel-tree, and said—

"Shake, shake, hazel-tree,
Gold and silver over me!"

And the bird came and brought a still finer dress than the one she had worn the day before. And when she came in it to the ball, every one wondered at her beauty: but the king's son, who was waiting for her, took her by the hand, and danced with her; and when any one asked her to dance, he said as before, "This lady is dancing with me." When night came she wanted to go home; and the king's son followed her as before, that he might see into what house she went: but she sprung away from him all at once into the garden behind her father's house. In this garden stood a fine large pear-tree full of ripe fruit; and

Ashputtel not knowing where to hide herself jumped up into it without being seen. Then the king's son could not find out where she was gone, but waited till her father came home, and said to him, "The unknown lady who danced with me has slipt away, and I think she must have sprung into the pear-tree." The father thought to himself, "Can it be Ashputtel?" So he ordered an axe to be brought; and they cut down the tree, but found no one upon it. And when they came back into the kitchen, there lay Ashputtel in the ashes as usual; for she had slipped down on the other side of the tree, and carried her beautiful clothes back to the bird at the hazel-tree, and then put on her little gray frock.

The third day, when her father and mother and sisters were gone, she went again into the garden, and said—

> "Shake, shake, hazel-tree,
> Gold and silver over me !"

Then her kind friend the bird brought a dress still finer than the former one, and slippers which were all of gold: so that when she came to the feast no one knew what to say for wonder at her beauty: and the king's son danced with her alone; and when any one else asked her to dance, he said, "This lady is my partner." Now when night came she wanted to go home; and the king's son would go with her, and said to himself, "I will not lose her this time;" but however she managed to slip away from him, though in such a hurry that she dropped her left golden slipper upon the stairs.

So the prince took the shoe, and went the next day to the king his father, and said, "I will take for my wife the lady that this golden slipper fits." Then both the sisters were overjoyed to hear this; for they had beautiful feet, and had no doubt that they could wear the golden slipper. The eldest went first into the room where the slipper was and wanted to try it on, and the mother stood by. But her great toe could not go into it, and the shoe was altogether much too small for her. Then the mother gave her a knife, and said, "Never mind, cut it off; when you are queen you will not care about toes, you will not want to go on foot." So the silly girl cut her great toe off, and squeezed the shoe on, and went to the king's son. Then he took her for his bride, and set her beside him on his horse and rode away with her.

But in their way home they had to pass by the hazel-tree that Ashputtel had planted, and there sat a little dove on the branch singing—

> "Back again! back again! look to the shoe!
> The shoe is too small, and not made for you!
> Prince! prince! look again for thy bride,
> For she's not the true one that sits by thy side."

Then the prince got down and looked at her foot, and saw by the blood that streamed from it what a trick she had played him. So he turned his horse round and brought the false bride back to her home, and said, "This is not the right bride; let the other sister try and put on the slipper." Then she went into the room and got her foot into the shoe, all but the heel, which was too large. But her mother squeezed it in till the blood came, and took her to the king's son; and he set her as his bride by his side on his horse, and rode away with her.

But when they came to the hazel-tree the little dove sate there still, and sang—

> "Back again! back again! look to the shoe!
> The shoe is too small, and not made for you!
> Prince! prince! look again for thy bride,
> For she's not the true one that sits by thy side."

Then he looked down and saw that the blood streamed so from the shoe that her white stockings were quite red. So he turned his horse and brought her back again also. "This is not the true bride," said he to the father; "have you no other daughters?" "No," said he; "there is only a little dirty Ashputtel here, the child of my first wife; I am sure she cannot be the bride." However, the prince told him to send her. But the mother said, "No, no, she is much too dirty, she will not dare to show herself:" however, the prince would have her come. And she first washed her face and hands, and then went in and curtsied to him, and he reached her the golden slipper. Then she took her clumsy shoe off her left foot, and put on the golden slipper; and it fitted her as if it had been made for her. And when he drew near and looked at her face he knew her, and said, "This is the right bride." But the mother and both the sisters were frightened and turned pale with anger as he took Ashputtel on his horse, and rode away with her. And when they came to the hazel-tree, the white dove sang—

> "Home! home! look at the shoe!
> Princess! the shoe was made for you!
> Prince! prince! take home thy bride,
> For she is the true one that sits by thy side!"

And when the dove had done its song, it came flying and perched upon her right shoulder, and so went home with her.

The Young Giant and the Tailor

A HUSBANDMAN had once a son, who was born no bigger than my thumb, and for many years did not grow a hair's breadth taller. One day as the father was going to plough in the field, the little fellow said, "Father, let me go too." "No," said his father; "stay where you are, you can do no good out of doors, and if you go perhaps I may lose you." Then little Thumbling fell a-crying: and his father, to quiet him, at last said he might go. So he put him in his pocket, and when he was in the field pulled him out and set him upon a newly made furrow, that he might look about. While he was sitting there, a great giant came striding over the hill. "Do you see that tall steeple-man?" said the father: "he will run away with you." (Now he only said this to frighten the little boy if he should be naughty.) But the giant had long legs, and with two or three strides he really came close to the furrow, and picked up little Thumbling to look at him; and taking a liking to the little chap went off with him. The father stood by all the time, but could not say a word for fright; for he thought his child was really lost, and that he should never see him again.

But the giant took care of him at his house in the woods, and laid him in his bosom and fed him with the same food that he lived on himself. So Thumbling, instead of being a little dwarf, became like the giant—tall

201

and stout and strong: so that at the end of two years when the old giant took him into the wood to try him, and said, "Pull up that birch-tree for yourself to walk with;" the lad was so strong that he tore it up by the root. The giant thought he should make him a still stronger man than this: so after taking care of him two years more, he took him into the wood to try his strength again. This time he took hold of one of the thickest oaks, and pulled it up as if it were mere sport to him. Then the old giant said, "Well done, my man, you will do now." So he carried him back to the field where he first found him.

His father happened to be just then ploughing as the young giant went up to him, saying, "Look here, father, see who I am;—don't you see I am your son?" But the husbandman was frightened, and cried out, "No, no, you are not my son; begone about your business." "Indeed, I am your son; let me plough a little, I can plough as well as you." "No, go your ways," said the father, but as he was afraid of the tall man, he at last let go the plough and sat down on the ground beside it. Then the youth laid hold of the ploughshare, and though he only pushed with one hand, he drove it deep into the earth. The ploughman cried out, "If you must plough, pray do not push so hard; you are doing more harm than good;" but he took off the horses, and said, "Father, go home and tell my mother to get ready a good dinner; I'll go round the field meanwhile." So he went on driving the plough without any horses, till he had done two mornings' work by himself; then he harrowed it, and when all was over, took up plough, harrow, horses and all, and carried them home like a bundle of straw.

When he reached the house he sat himself down on the bench, saying, "Now, mother, is dinner ready?" "Yes," said she, for she dared not deny him; so she brought two large dishes full, enough to have lasted herself and her husband eight days; however, he soon ate it all up, and said that was but a taste. "I see very well, father, that I shan't get enough to eat at your house; so if you will give me an iron walking-stick, so strong that I cannot break it against my knees, I will go away again." The husbandman very gladly put his two horses to the cart and drove them to the forge, and brought back a bar of iron as long and as thick as his two horses could draw; but the lad laid it against his knee; and snap! it went like a broken beanstalk. "I see, father," said he, "you can get no stick that will do for me, so I'll go and try my luck by myself."

Then away he went, and turned blacksmith, and travelled till he came to a village where lived a miserly smith, who earned a good deal of money, but kept all he got to himself, and gave nothing away to anybody. The first thing he did was to step into the smithy, and ask if the smith did not want a journeyman. "Aye," said the cunning fellow, (as he looked at him and thought what a stout chap he was, and how lustily he would work and earn his bread,) "what wages do you ask?" "I want no pay," said he; "but every fortnight when the other workmen are paid, you shall let me give you two strokes over the shoulders to amuse myself." The old smith thought to himself he could bear this very well, and reckoned on saving a great deal of money; so the bargain was soon struck.

The next morning the new workman was about to begin to work; but at the first stroke that he hit, when his master brought him the iron red hot, he shivered it in pieces, and the anvil sunk so deep into the earth, that he could not get it out again. This made the old fellow very angry; "Halloo!" cried he, "I can't have you for a workman, you are too clumsy; we must put an end to our bargain." "Very well," said the other, "but you must pay for what I have done, so let me give you only one little stroke, and then the bargain is all over." So saying, he gave him a thump that tossed him over a load of hay that stood near. Then he took the thickest bar of iron on the forge for a walking-stick, and went on his way.

When he had journeyed some way, he came to a farm-house, and asked the farmer if he wanted a foreman. The farmer said, "Yes," and the same wages were agreed for as before with the blacksmith. The next morning the workmen were all to go into the wood; but the giant was found to be fast asleep in his bed when the rest were all up and ready to start. "Come, get up," said one of them to him, "it is high time to be stirring; you must go with us." "Go your way," muttered he sulkily, "I shall have done my work and get home long before you." So he lay in bed two hours longer, and at last got up and cooked and ate his breakfast, and then at his leisure harnessed his horses to go to the wood. Just before the wood was a hollow, through which all must pass; so he drove the cart on first, and built up behind him such a mound of faggots and briars that no horse could pass. This done, he drove on, and as he was going into the wood met the others coming out on their road home; "Drive away," said he, "I shall be home before you still." However, he only went a very little way into the wood and tore up one of the largest timber trees, put it into his cart, and turned about homewards. When he came to the pile of faggots, he found all the others standing there, not being able to pass by. "So," said he, "you see if you had staid with me, you would have been home just as soon, and might have slept an hour or two longer." Then he took his tree on one shoulder, and his cart on the other, and pushed through as easily as though he were laden with feathers, and when he reached the yard showed the tree to the farmer, and asked if it was not a famous walking-stick. "Wife," said the farmer, "this man is worth something; if he sleeps longer, still he works better than the rest."

Time rolled on, and he had served the farmer his whole year; so when his fellow-labourers were paid, he said he also had a right to take his wages. But great dread came upon the farmer, at the thought of the blows he was to have, so he begged him to give up the old bargain, and take his whole farm and stock instead. "Not I," said he, "I will be no farmer; I am foreman, and so I mean to keep, and be paid as we agreed." Finding he could do nothing with him, the farmer only begged one fortnight's respite, and called together all his friends, to ask their advice in the matter. They bethought themselves for a long time, and at last agreed that the shortest way was to kill this troublesome foreman. The next thing was to settle how it was to be done; and it was agreed that he should be ordered to carry into the yard some great mill-stones, and to put them on the edge of a well; that then he should be sent down to clean it out, and when he was at the bottom, the millstones should be pushed down upon his head. Everything went right, and when the foreman was safe in the well, the stones were rolled in. As they struck the bottom, the water splashed to the very top. Of course they thought his head must be crashed to pieces; but he only cried out, "Drive away the chickens from the well; they are pecking about in the sand above me, and throwing it into my eyes, so that I cannot see." When his job was done, up he sprung from the well, saying, "Look here! see what a fine neck-cloth I have!" as he pointed to one of the mill-stones, that had fallen over his head, and hung about his neck.

The farmer was again overcome with fear, and begged another fortnight to think of it. So his friends were called together again, and at last gave this advice; that the foreman should be sent and made to grind corn by night at the haunted mill, whence no man had ever yet come out in the morning alive. That very evening he was told to carry eight bushels of corn to the mill, and grind them in the night. Away he went to the loft, put two bushels in his right pocket, two in his left, and four in a long sack slung over his shoulders, and then set off to the mill. The miller told him he might grind there in the day-time, but not by night, for the mill was bewitched, and whoever went in at night had been found dead in the morning: "Never mind, miller, I shall come out safe," said he; "only make haste and get out of the way, and look out for me in the morning."

So he went into the mill and put the corn into the hopper, and about twelve o'clock sat himself down on the bench in the miller's room. After a little time the door all at once opened of itself, and in came a large table. On the table stood wine and meat, and many good things besides: all seemed placed there by themselves; at any rate there was no one to be seen. The chairs next moved themselves round it, but still neither guests nor servants came; till all at once he saw fingers handling the knives and forks and putting food on the plates, but still nothing else was to be seen. Now our friend felt somewhat hungry as he looked at the dishes, so he sat himself down at the table and ate whatever he liked best; and when he had had enough, and the plates were empty, on a sudden he heard something blow out the lights. When it was pitch dark he felt a tremendous blow upon his head; "If I get such another box on the ear," said he, "I shall just give it back again;" and this he really did, when the next blow came. Thus the game went on all night; and he never let fear get the better of him, but kept dealing his blows round, till at day-break all was still. "Well, miller," said he in the morning, "I have had some little slaps on the face, but I've given as good, I'll warrant you; and meantime I have eaten as much as I liked." The miller was glad to find the charm was broken, and would have given him a great deal of money; "I want no money, I have quite enough," said he, as he took the meal on his back, and went home to his master to claim his wages.

But the farmer was in a rage, knowing there was no help for him, and paced the room up and down till the drops of sweat ran down his forehead. Then he opened the window for a little fresh air, and before he was aware, his foreman gave him the first blow, and kicked him out of the window over the hills and far away, and next sent his wife after him; and there, for aught I know, they may be flying in the air still: but the young giant took up his iron walking-stick and walked off.

Perhaps this was the same giant that the Bold Little Tailor met, when he set out on his travels, as I will tell you next.

It was a fine summer morning when this little man bound his girdle round his body, and looked about his house to see if there was any thing good to take with him on his journey into the wide world. He could only find an old cheese; but that was better than nothing; so he took it up; and, as he was going out, the old hen met him at the door, and he packed her too into his wallet with the cheese. Then off he set, and when he had climbed a high hill, he found the giant sitting on the top. "Good day, comrade," said he; "there you sit at your ease, and look the wide world over: I have a mind to go and try my luck in that same world; what do you say to going with me?" Then the giant looked at him, and said, "You are

a poor trumpery little knave." "That may be," said the
tailor; "but we shall see who is the best man of the two."
The giant, finding the little man so bold, began to be a
little more respectful, and said they would soon try who
was master. So he took a large stone in his hand and
squeezed it till water dropped from it; "Do that," said
he, "if you have a mind to be thought a strong man." "Is
that all?" said the tailor; "I will soon do as much;" so he
put his hand in his wallet, pulled out the cheese (which
was quite new), and squeezed it till the whey ran out.
"What do you say now, Mr. Giant? my squeeze was a better one than yours." Then the giant, not seeing that it
was only a cheese, did not know what to say for himself,
though he could hardly believe his eyes; at last he took up a
stone, and threw it up so high that it went almost out of
sight; "Now then, little pygmy, do that if you can."
"Very good," said the other; "your throw was not a bad
one, but after all your stone fell to the ground; I will throw
something that shall not fall at all." "That you can't do,"
said the giant: but the tailor took his old hen out of the
wallet, and threw her up in the air, and she, pleased enough
to be set free, flew away out of sight. "Now, comrade,"
said he, "what do you say to that?" "I say you are a
clever hand," said the giant, "but we will now try how you
can work."

Then he led him into the wood, where a fine oak tree
lay felled. "Now let us drag it out of the wood together."
"Very well; do you take the thick end, and I will carry all
the top and branches, which are much the largest and
heaviest." So the giant took the trunk and laid it on his
shoulder; but the cunning little rogue, instead of carrying
anything, sat himself at his ease among the branches, and
let the giant carry stem, branches, and tailor into the bargain. All the way they went he made merry, and whistled

and sang his song as if carrying the tree were mere sport; while the giant after he had borne it a good way could carry it no longer, and said, "I must let it fall." Then the tailor sprung down and held the tree as if he were carrying it, saying, "What a shame that such a big lout as you cannot carry a tree like this!" Then on they went together till they came to a tall cherry tree; and the giant took hold of the top stem and bent it down to pluck the ripest fruit, and when he had done, gave it over to his friend that he too might eat; but the little man was so weak that he could not hold the tree down, and up he went with it swinging in the air. "Halloo!" said the giant, "what now? can't you hold that twig?" "To be sure I could," said the other; "but don't you see there's a huntsman, who is going to shoot into the bush where we stood? so I took a jump over the tree to be out of his way; do you do the same." The giant tried to follow, but the tree was far too high to jump over, and he only stuck fast in the branches, for the tailor to laugh at him. "Well! you are a fine fellow after all," said the giant; "so come home and sleep with me and a friend of mine in the mountains to-night."

The tailor had no business upon his hands, so he did as he was bid, and the giant gave him a good supper, and a bed to sleep upon; but the tailor was too cunning to lie down upon it, and crept slily into a corner, and slept there soundly. When midnight came, the giant came softly in with his iron walking-stick, and gave such a stroke upon the bed where he thought his guest was lying, that he said to himself, "It's all up now with that grasshopper; I shall have no more of his tricks." In the morning the giants went off into the woods, and quite forgot him, till all on a sudden they met him trudging along, whistling a merry tune; and so frightened were they at the sight, that they both ran away as fast as they could.

Then on went the little tailor following his spuddy nose, till at last he reached the king's court, and began to brag very loud of his mighty deeds, saying he was come to serve the king. To try him, they told him that the two giants who lived in a part of the kingdom a long way off, were become the dread of the whole land; for they had begun to rob, plunder and ravage all about them, and that if he was so great a man as he said, he should have a hundred soldiers and should set out to fight these giants, and if he beat them he should have half the kingdom. "With all my heart!" said he; "but as for your hundred soldiers, I believe I shall do as well without them." However, they set off together till they came to a wood: "Wait here, my friends," said he to the soldiers, "I will soon give a good account of these giants:" and on he went casting his sharp little eye here, there, and everywhere around him. After a while he spied them both lying under a tree, and snoring away till the very boughs whistled with the breeze. "The game's won, for a penny," said the little man, as he filled his wallet with stones, and climbed the tree under which they lay.

As soon as he was safely up, he threw one stone after another at the nearest giant, till at last he woke up in a rage, and shook his companion, crying out, "What did you strike me for?" "Nonsense! you are dreaming," said the other, "I did not strike you." Then both lay down to sleep again, and the tailor threw stones at the second giant, till he sprung up and cried, "What are you about? you struck me." "I did not," said the other; and on they wrangled for a while, till as both were tired they made up the matter, and fell asleep again. But then the tailor began his game once more, and flung the largest stone he had in his wallet with all his force and hit the first giant on the nose. "That is too bad," cried he, as if he was mad, "I will not bear it." So he struck the other a mighty blow; he of course was not pleased at this, and gave him just such another box on the ear; and at last a bloody battle began; up flew the trees by the roots, the rocks and stones went bang at one another's heads, and in the end both lay dead upon the spot. "It is a good thing," said the tailor, "that they let my tree stand, or I must have made a fine jump." Then down he ran, and took his sword and gave each of them a very fine wound or two on the breast and set off to look for the soldiers. "There lie the giants," said he; "I have killed them, but it has been no small job, for they even tore trees up in their struggle." "Have you any wounds?" asked they. "That is a likely matter, truly," said he; "they have not touched a hair of my head." But the soldiers would not believe him till they rode into the wood and found the giants weltering in their blood, and the trees lying around torn up by the roots.

The king, after he had got rid of his enemies, was not much pleased at the thoughts of giving up half his kingdom to a tailor; so he said, "You have not yet done; in the palace court lies a bear with whom you must pass the night, and if when I rise in the morning I find you still living, you shall then have your reward." Now he thought he had got rid of him, for the bear had never yet let any one go away alive who had come within reach of his claws. "Very well," said the tailor, "I am willing."

So when evening came our little tailor was led out and shut up in the court with the bear, who rose at once to give him a friendly welcome with his paw. "Softly, softly, my friend," said he; "I know a way to please you;" then at his ease and as if he cared nothing about the matter, he pulled out of his pocket some fine walnuts, cracked them, and ate the kernels. When the bear saw this, he took a great fancy to having some nuts too; so the tailor felt in his pocket and gave him a handful, not of walnuts, but nice round pebbles. The bear snapt them up, but could not crack one of them, do what he would. "What a clumsy thick head thou art!" thought the beast to itself; "thou canst not crack a nut to-day." Then said he to the tailor, "Friend, **pray** crack me the nuts." "Why, what a lout you are," said the tailor, "to have such a jaw as that, and not to be able to crack a little nut! Well! engage to be friends with me and I'll help you." So he took the stones, and slily changed them for nuts, put them in his mouth, and crack! they went. "I must try for myself, however," said the bear; "now I see how you do it, I am sure I can do it myself." Then the tailor gave him the cobble stones again, and the bear lay down and worked away as hard as he could, and bit and bit with all his force till he broke all his teeth, and lay down quite tired.

But the tailor began to think this would not last long, and that the bear might find him out and break the bargain; so he pulled a fiddle out from under his coat and played him a tune. As soon as the bear heard it, he could not help jumping up and beginning to dance; and when he had jigged away for a while, the thing pleased him so much that he said, "Hark ye, friend! is the fiddle hard to play upon?" "No! not at all!" said the other; "look ye, I lay my left hand here, and then I take the bow with my right hand thus, and scrape it over the strings there, and away it goes merrily, hop, sa, sa! fal, lal, la!" "Will you teach me to fiddle," said the bear, "so that I may have music whenever I want to dance?" "With all my heart; but let me look at your claws, they are so very long that I must first clip your nails a little bit." Then the bear lifted up his paws one after another, and the tailor screwed them down tight, and said, "Now wait till I come with my scissors." So he left the bear to growl as loud as he liked, and laid himself down on a heap of straw in the corner and slept soundly.   In the morning when the king came, he found the tailor sitting merrily eating his breakfast, and could no longer help keeping his word; and thus the little man became a great one.

The guard of the gate asked what trade he followed.

THE GIANT WITH THE THREE
GOLDEN HAIRS

Page 153

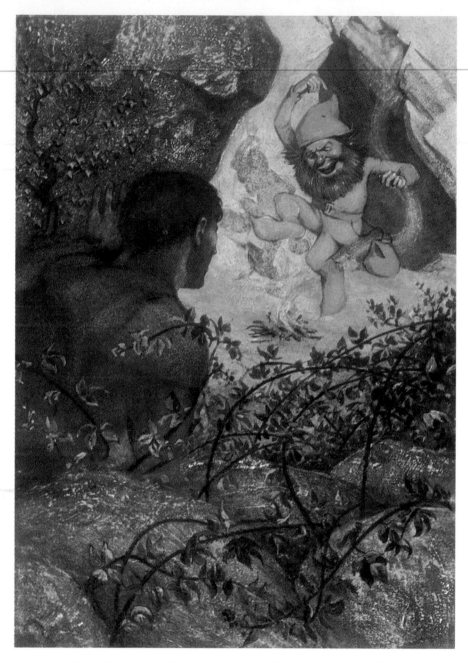

Round about the fire danced a funny little man upon one leg.

RUMPEL-STILTS-KIN

Page 167

The Crows and the Soldier

A WORTHY soldier had saved a good deal of money out of his pay; for he worked hard, and did not spend all he earned in eating and drinking, as many others do. Now he had two comrades who were great rogues, and wanted to rob him of his money, but behaved outwardly towards him in a friendly way. "Comrade," said they to him one day, "why should we stay here shut up in this town like prisoners, when you at any rate have earned enough to live upon for the rest of your days in peace and plenty at home by your own fireside?" They talked so often to him in this manner, that he at last said he would go and try his luck with them; but they all the time thought of nothing but how they should manage to steal his money from him.

When they had gone a little way, the two rogues said, "We must go by the right-hand road, for that will take us quickest into another country where we shall be safe." Now they knew all the while that what they were saying was untrue; and as soon as the soldier said, "No, that will take us straight back into the town we came from; we must keep on the left hand;" they picked a quarrel with him, and said, "What do you give yourself airs for? you know nothing about it;" and then they fell upon him and knocked him down, and beat him over the head till he was blind. Then they took all the money out of his pockets and dragged him to a gallows-tree that stood hard by, bound him fast down at the foot of it, and went back into the town with the money; but the poor blind man did not know where he was; and he felt all around him, and finding that he was bound to a large beam of wood, thought it was a cross, and said, "After all, they have done kindly in leaving me under a cross; now Heaven will guard me;" so he raised himself up and began to pray.

When night came on, he heard something fluttering over his head. It turned out to be three crows, who flew round and round, and at last perched upon the tree. By and by they began to talk together, and he heard one of them say, "Sister, what is the best news with you to-day?" "Oh, if men knew what we know!" said the other; "the princess is ill, and the king has vowed to marry her to any one who will cure her; but this none can do, for she will not be well until yonder flower is burnt to ashes and swallowed by her." "Oh, indeed," said the other crow, "if men did but know what we know! to-night will fall from heaven a dew of such healing power, that even the blind man who washes his eyes with it will see again;" and the third spoke, and said, "Oh, if men knew what we know! the flower is wanted but for one, the dew is wanted but for few; but there is a great dearth of water in the town; all the wells are dried up; and no one knows that they must take away the large square stone out of the market-place, and dig underneath it, and that then the finest water will spring up.

When the three crows had done talking, he heard them fluttering round again, and at last away they flew. Greatly wondering at what he had heard, and overjoyed at the thoughts of getting his sight, he tried with all his strength to break loose from his bonds; at last he found himself free, and plucked some of the grass that grew beneath him and washed his eyes with the dew that had fallen upon it. At once his eyesight came to him again, and he saw by the light of the moon and the stars that he was beneath the gallows-tree, and not the cross, as he had thought. Then he gathered together in a bottle as much of the dew as he could to take away with him, and looked around till he saw the flower that grew close by; and when he had burned it he gathered up the ashes, and set out on his way towards the king's court.

When he reached the palace, he told the king he was come to cure the princess; and when she had taken of the ashes and been made well, he claimed her for his wife, as the reward that was to be given; but the king looking upon him and seeing that his clothes were so shabby, would not keep his word, and thought to get rid of him by saying, "Whoever wants to have the princess for his wife, must find enough water for the use of the town, where there is this summer a great dearth." Then the soldier went out and told the people to take up the square stone in the market-place and dig for water underneath; and when they had done so there came up a fine spring, that gave enough water for the whole town. So the king could no longer get off giving him his daughter, and they were married and lived happily together.

Some time after, as he was walking one day through a field, he met his two wicked comrades who had treated him so basely. Though they did not know him, he knew them at once, and went up to them and said, "Look upon me, I am your old comrade whom you beat and robbed and left blind; Heaven has defeated your wicked wishes, and turned all the mischief which you brought upon me into good luck." When they heard this they fell at his feet and begged for pardon, and he had a kind and good heart, so he forgave them, and took them to his palace and gave them food and clothes. And he told them all that had happened to him, and how he had reached these honours.

After they had heard the whole story they said to themselves, "Why should not we go and sit some night under the gallows? we may hear something that will bring us good luck too."

Next night they stole away; and, when they had sat under the tree a little while, they heard a fluttering noise over their heads; and the three crows came and perched upon it. "Sisters," said one of them, "some one must have overheard us, for all the world is talking of the wonderful things that have happened: the princess is well; the flower has been plucked and burnt; a blind man's sight has been given him again, and they have dug a fresh well that gives water to the whole town: let us look about, perhaps we may find some one near; if we do he shall rue the day." Then they began to flutter about, and soon found out the two men below, and flew at them in a rage, beating and pecking them in the face with their wings and beaks till they were quite blind, and lay nearly dead upon the ground under the gallows. The next day passed over and they did not return to the palace; and their old comrade began to wonder where they had been, and went out the following morning in search of them, and at last found them where they lay, dreadfully repaid for all their folly and baseness.

Pee-Wit

A POOR countryman whose name was Pee-wit lived with his wife in a very quiet way in the parish where he was born. One day, as he was ploughing with his two oxen in the field, he heard all on a sudden some one calling out his name. Turning round, he saw nothing but a bird that kept crying Pee-wit! Pee-wit! Now this poor bird is called a Pee-wit, and like the cuckoo always keeps crying out its own name. But the countryman thought it was mocking him, so he took up a huge stone and threw at it; the bird flew off safe and sound, but the stone fell upon the head of one of the oxen, and killed him on the spot. "What is to be done with the odd one?" thought Pee-wit to himself as he looked at the ox that was left; so without more ado he killed him too, skinned them both, and set out for the neighbouring town, to sell the hides to the tanner for as much as he could get. He soon found out where the tanner lived, and knocked at the door. Before, however, the door was opened, he saw through the window that the mistress of the house was hiding in an old chest a friend of hers, whom she seemed to wish no one should see. By and by the door was opened, "What do you want?" said the woman. Then he told her that he wanted to sell his hides; and it came out that the tanner was not at home, and that no one there ever made bargains but himself. The countryman said he would sell cheap, and did not mind giving his hides for the old chest in the corner; meaning

219

the one he had seen the good woman's friend get into. Of course the wife would not agree to this; and they went on talking the matter over so long, that at last in came the tanner and asked what it was all about. Pee-wit told him the whole story, and asked him whether he would give the old chest for the hides. "To be sure I will," said he; and scolded his wife for saying nay to such a bargain, which she ought to have been glad to make if the countryman was willing. Then up he took the chest on his shoulders, and all the good woman could say mattered nothing; away it went into the countryman's cart, and off he drove. But when they had gone some way, the young man within began to make himself heard, and to beg and pray to be let out. Pee-wit, however, was not to be bought over; till at last after a long parley a thousand dollars were bid and taken; the money was paid, and at that price the poor fellow was set free, and went about his business.

Then Pee-wit went home very happy, and built a new house and seemed so rich that his neighbours wondered, and said, "Pee-wit must have been where the golden snow falls." So they took him before the next justice of the peace, to give an account of himself, and show that he came honestly by his wealth; and then he told them that he had sold his hides for one thousand dollars. When they heard it they all killed their oxen and would sell the hides to the same tanner; but the justice said, "My maid shall have the first chance;" so off she went, and when she came to the tanner, he laughed at them all, and said he had given their neighbour nothing but an old chest.

At this they were all very angry, and laid their heads together to work him some mischief, which they thought they could do while he was digging in his garden. All this, however, came to the ears of the countryman, who was plagued with a sad scold for his wife; and he thought to himself, "If any one is to come into trouble, I don't see why it should not be my wife, rather than me;" so he said to her that he wished she would humour him in a whim he had taken into his head, and would put on his clothes, and dig the garden in his stead. The wife did what was asked, and next morning began digging; but soon came some of the neighbours, and, thinking it was Pee-wit, threw a stone at her, (harder perhaps than they meant,) and killed her at once. Poor Pee-wit was rather sorry at this, but still thought that he had had a lucky escape for himself, and that perhaps he might after all turn the death of his wife to some account: so he dressed her in her own clothes, put a basket with fine fruit (which was now scarce, it being winter) into her hand, and set her by the road side on a broad bench.

After a while came by a fine coach with six horses, servants, and outriders, and within sat a noble lord who lived not far off. When his lordship saw the beautiful fruit, he sent one of the servants to the woman to ask what was the price of her goods. The man went and asked "What is the price of this fruit?" No answer. He asked again. No answer: and when this had happened three times, he became angry; and, thinking she was asleep, gave her a blow, and down she fell backwards into the pond that was behind the seat. Then up ran Pee-wit, and cried and sorrowed because they had drowned his poor wife, and threatened to have the lord and his servants tried for what they had done. His lordship begged him to be easy, and offered to give him the coach and horses, servants and all; so the countryman after a long time let himself be appeased a little, took what they gave, got into the coach and set off towards his own home again.

As he came near, the neighbours wondered much at the beautiful coach and horses, and still more when they stopped, and Pee-wit got out at his own door. Then he told them the whole story, which only vexed them still more; so they took him and fastened him up in a tub and were going to throw him into the lake that was hard by. Whilst they were rolling the tub on before them towards the water, they passed by an alehouse and stopped to re-fresh themselves a little before they put an end to Pee-wit; meantime they tied the tub to a tree and there left it while they were enjoying themselves within doors.

Pee-wit no sooner found himself alone than he began to turn over in his mind how he could get free. He listened, and soon heard Ba, ba! from a flock of sheep and lambs that were coming by.   Then he lifted up his voice, and shouted out, "I will not be burgomaster, I say; I will not be made burgomaster."   The shepherd hearing this went up, and said, "What is all this noise about?" "Oh!" said Pee-wit, "my neighbours will make me burgomaster against my will; and when I told them I would not agree, they put me into the cask and are going to throw me into the lake."   "I should like very well to be burgomaster if I were you," said the shepherd.   "Open the cask then," said the other, "and let me out, and get in yourself, and they will make you burgomaster instead of me."   No sooner said than done, the shepherd was in, Pee-wit was out; and as there was nobody to take care of the shepherd's flock, he drove it off merrily towards his own house.

When the neighbours came out of the alehouse, they rolled the cask on, and the shepherd began to cry out, "I *will* be burgomaster now; I *will* be burgomaster now."   "I dare say you will, but you shall take a swim first," said a neighbour, as he gave the cask the last push over into the lake.   This done, away they went home merrily, leaving the shepherd to get out as well as he could.

But as they came in at one side of the village, who

should they meet coming in the other way but Pee-wit driving a fine flock of sheep and lambs before him. "How came you here?" cried all with one voice. "Oh! the lake is enchanted," said he; "when you threw me in, I sank deep and deep into the water, till at last I came to the bottom; there I knocked out the bottom of the cask and found myself in a beautiful meadow with fine flocks grazing upon it, so I chose a few for myself, and here I am." "Cannot we have some too?" said they. "Why not? there are hundreds and thousands left; you have nothing to do but jump in and fetch them out."

So all agreed they would dive for sheep; the justice first, then the clerk, then the constables, and then the rest of the parish, one after the other. When they came to the side of the lake, the blue sky was covered with little white clouds like flocks of sheep, and all were reflected in the clear water: so they called out, "There they are, there they are already;" and fearing lest the justice should get everything, they jumped in all at once; and Pee-wit jogged home, and made himself happy with what he had got, leaving them to find their flocks by themselves as well as they could.

Hans and His Wife Grettel

I. Showing who Grettel was.

THERE was once a little maid named Grettel: she wore shoes with red heels, and when she went abroad she turned out her toes, and was very merry, and thought to herself, "What a pretty girl I am!" And when she came home, to put herself in good spirits, she would tipple down a drop or two of wine; and as wine gives a relish for eating, she would take a taste of everything when she was cooking, saying, "A cook ought to know whether a thing tastes well." It happened one day that her master said, "Grettel, this evening I have a friend coming to sup with me; get two fine fowls ready." "Very well, sir," said Grettel. Then she killed the fowls, plucked, and trussed them, put them on the spit, and when evening came put them to the fire to roast. The fowls turned round and round, and soon began to look nice and brown, but the guest did not come. Then Grettel cried out, "Master, if the guest does not come I must take up the fowls, but it will be a shame and a pity if they are not eaten while they are hot and good." "Well," said her master, "I'll run and tell him to come." As soon as he had turned his back, Grettel stopped the spit, and laid it with the fowls upon it on one side, and thought to herself, "Standing by the fire makes one very tired and thirsty; who knows how long they will be? meanwhile I will just step into the cellar and take a drop." So off she ran, put down her pitcher, and said, "Your health, Grettel," and took a good draught. "This wine is a good friend," said she to herself, "it breaks one's heart to leave it." Then up she trotted, put the fowls down to the fire, spread some butter over them, and turned the spit merrily round again.

The fowls soon smelt so good, that she thought to herself, "They are very good, but they may want something still; I had better taste them and see." So she licked her fingers, and said, "Oh! how good! what a shame and a pity that they are not eaten!" Away she ran to the window to see if her master and his friend were coming; but nobody was in sight: so she turned to the fowls again, and thought it would be better for her to eat a wing than that it should be burnt. So she cut one wing off, and ate it, and it tasted very well; and as the other was quite done enough, she thought it had better be cut off too, or else her master would see one was wanting. When the two wings were gone, she went again to look out for her master, but could not see him. "Ah!" thought she to herself, "who knows whether they will come at all? very likely they have turned into some tavern: Oh Grettel! Grettel! make yourself happy, take another draught, and eat the rest of the fowl; it looks so oddly as it is; when you have eaten all, you will be easy: why should such good things be wasted?" So she ran once more to the cellar, took another drink, and ate up the rest of the fowl with the greatest glee.

Still her master did not come, and she cast a lingering eye upon the other fowl, and said, "Where the other went, this had better go too; they belong to each other; they who have a right to one must have a right to the other; but if I were to take another draught first, it would not hurt me." So she tippled down another drop of wine, and sent the second fowl to look after the first. While she was making an end of this famous meal, her master came home and called out, "Now quick, Grettel, my friend is just at hand!" "Yes, master, I will dish up this minute," said she. In the meantime he looked to see if the cloth was laid, and took up the carving-knife to sharpen it. Whilst this was going on, the guest came and knocked softly and gently at the house door; then Grettel ran to see who was there, and when she saw him she put her finger upon her lips, and said, "Hush! hush! run away as fast as you can, for if my master catches you, it will be worse for you; he owes you a grudge, and asked you to supper only that he might cut off your ears; only listen how he is sharpening his knife." The guest listened, and when he heard the knife, he made as much haste as he could down the steps and ran off. Grettel was not idle in the meantime, but ran screaming, "Master! master! what a fine guest you have asked to supper!" "Why, Grettel, what's the matter?" "Oh!" said she, "he has taken both the fowls that I was going to bring up, and has run away with them." "That is a rascally trick to play," said the master, sorry to lose the fine chickens; "at least he might have left me one, that I might have had something to eat; call out to him to stay." But the guest would not hear; so he ran after him with his knife in his hand, crying out, "Only one, only one, I want only one;" meaning that the guest should leave him one of the fowls, and not take both: but he thought that his host meant nothing less than that he would cut off at least one of his ears; so he ran away to save them both, as if he had hot coals under his feet.

II.   HANS IN LOVE.

Hans's mother says to him, "Whither so fast?" "To see Grettel," says Hans. "Behave well." "Very well:

Good-bye, mother!" Hans comes to Grettel; "Good day, Grettel!" "Good day, Hans! do you bring me anything good?" "Nothing at all: have you anything for me?" Grettel gives Hans a needle. Hans says, "Good-bye, Grettel!" "Good-bye, Hans!" Hans takes the needle, sticks it in a truss of hay, and takes both off home. "Good evening, mother!" "Good evening, Hans! where have you been?" "To see Grettel." "What did you take her?" "Nothing at all." "What did she give you?" "She gave me a needle." "Where is it, Hans?" "Stuck in the truss." "How silly you are! you should have stuck it in your sleeve." "Let me alone! I'll do better next time."

"Where now, Hans?" "To see Grettel, mother." "Behave yourself well." "Very well: Good-bye, mother!" Hans comes to Grettel; "Good day, Grettel!" "Good day, Hans! what have you brought me?" "Nothing at all: have you anything for me?" Grettel gives Hans a knife. "Good-bye, Grettel!" "Good-bye, Hans!" Hans takes the knife, sticks it in his sleeve, and goes home. "Good evening, mother!" "Good evening, Hans! where have you been?" "To see Grettel." "What did you carry her?" "Nothing at all." "What has she given you?" "A knife." "Where is the knife, Hans?" "Stuck in my sleeve, mother." "You silly goose! you should have put it in your pocket." "Let me alone! I'll do better next time."

"Where now, Hans?" "To see Grettel." "Behave yourself well." "Very well: Good-bye, mother!" Hans comes to Grettel; "Good day, Grettel!" "Good day, Hans! have you anything good?" "No: have you anything for me?" Grettel gives Hans a kid. "Good-bye, Grettel!" "Good-bye, Hans!" Hans takes the kid, ties it up with a cord, stuffs it into his pocket, and chokes it to death. "Good evening, mother!" "Good evening, Hans! where have you been?" "To see Grettel, mother!" "What

did you take her?" "Nothing at all." "What did she
give you?" "She gave me a kid." "Where is the kid,
Hans?" "Safe in my pocket." "You silly goose! you
should have led it with a string." "Never mind, mother,
I'll do better next time."

"Where now, Hans?" "To Grettel's, mother." "Behave well." "Quite well, mother; Good-bye!" Hans
comes to Grettel; "Good day, Grettel!" "Good day,
Hans! what have you brought me?" "Nothing at all:
have you anything for me?" Grettel gives Hans a piece
of bacon; Hans ties the bacon to a string and drags it behind him; the dog comes after and eats it all up as he walks
home. "Good evening, mother!" "Good evening, Hans!
where have you been?" "To Grettel's." "What did you
take her?" "Nothing at all." "What did she give you?"
"A piece of bacon." "Where is the bacon, Hans?" "Tied
to the string, and dragged home, but somehow or other
all gone." "What a silly trick, Hans! you should have
brought it on your head." "Never mind, mother, I'll do
better another time."

"Where now, Hans?" "Going to Grettel." "Take
care of yourself." "Very well, mother: Good-bye." Hans
comes to Grettel; "Good day, Grettel!" "Good day,
Hans! what have you brought me?" "Nothing: have you
anything for me?" Grettel gives Hans a calf. Hans
sets it upon his head, and it kicks him in the face. "Good
evening, mother!" "Good evening, Hans! where have
you been?" "To see Grettel." "What did you take her?"
"Nothing." "What did she give you?" "She gave me a
calf." "Where is the calf, Hans?" "I put it on my
head, and it scratched my face." "You silly goose! you
should have led it home and put it in the stall." "Very
well; I'll do better another time."

"Where now, Hans?" "To see Grettel." "Mind and

behave well." "Good-bye, mother!" Hans comes to Grettel; "Good day, Grettel!" "Good day, Hans! what have you brought?" "Nothing at all: have you anything for me?" "I'll go home with you." Hans ties a string round her neck, leads her along, and ties her up in the stall. "Good evening, mother!" "Good evening, Hans! where have you been?" "At Grettel's." "What has she given you?" "She has come herself." "Where have you put her?" "Fast in the stall with plenty of hay." "How silly you are! you should have taken good care of her, and brought her home." Then Hans went back to the stall; but Grettel was in a great rage, and had got loose and run away: yet, after all, she was Hans' bride.

III. Hans Married.

Hans and Grettel lived in the village together, but Grettel did as she pleased, and was so lazy that she never would work; and when her husband gave her any yarn to spin she did it in a slovenly way; and when it was spun she did not wind it on the reel, but left it to lie all tangled about. Hans sometimes scolded, but she was always beforehand with her tongue, and said, "Why how should I wind it when I have no reel? go into the wood and make one." "If that's all," said he, "I will go into the wood and cut reel-sticks." Then Grettel was frightened lest when he had cut the sticks he should make a reel, and thus she would be forced to wind the yarn and spin again. So she pondered a while, till at last a bright thought came into her head, and she ran slyly after her husband into the wood. As soon as he had got into a tree and began to bend down a bough to cut it, she crept into the bush below, where he could not see her, and sang—

> "Bend not the bough;
> He who bends it shall die!
> Reel not the reel;
> He who reels it shall die!"

Hans listened a while, laid down his axe, and thought to himself, "What can that be?" "What indeed can it be?" said he at last; "it is only a singing in your ears, Hans! pluck up your heart, man!" So he raised up his axe again, and took hold of the bough, but once more the voice sang—

> "Bend not the bough;
> He who bends it shall die!
> Reel not the reel;
> He who reels it shall die!"

Once more he stopped his hand; fear came over him, and he began pondering what it could mean. After a while, however, he plucked up his courage again, and took up his axe and began for the third time to cut the wood; again the third time began the song—

> "Bend not the bough;
> He who bends it shall die!
> Reel not the reel;
> He who reels it shall die!"

At this he could hold no longer, down he dropped from the tree and set off homewards as fast as he could. Away too ran Grettel by a shorter cut, so as to reach home first, and when he opened the door met him quite innocently, as if nothing had happened, and said, "Well! have you brought a good piece of wood for the reel?" "No," said he, "I see plainly that no luck comes of that reel;" and then he told her all that had happened, and left her for that time in peace.

But soon afterwards Hans began again to reproach her

with the untidiness of her house. "Wife," said he; "is it not a sin and a shame that the spun yarn should lie all about in that way?" "It may be so," said she; "but you know very well that we have no reel; if it must be done, lie down there and hold up your hands and legs, and so I'll make a reel of you, and wind off the yarn into skeins." "Very well," said Hans (who did not much like the job, but saw no help for it if his wife was to be set to work); so he did as she said, and when all was wound, "The yarn is all in skeins," said he; "now take care and get up early and heat the water and boil it well, so that it may be ready for sale." Grettel disliked this part of the work very much, but said to him, "Very well, I'll be sure to do it very early to-morrow morning." But all the time she was thinking to herself what plan she should take for getting off such work for the future.

Betimes in the morning she got up, made the fire and put on the boiler; but instead of the yarn she laid a large ball of tow in it and let it boil. Then she went up to her husband, who was still in bed, and said to him, "I must go out, pray look meantime to the yarn in the boiler over the fire; but do it soon and take good care, for if the cock crows and you are not looking to it, they say it will turn to tow." Hans soon after got up that he might run no risk, and went (but not perhaps as quickly as he might have done) into the kitchen, and when he lifted up the boiler lid and looked in, to his great terror nothing was there but a ball of tow. Then off he slunk as dumb as a mouse, for he thought to himself that he was to blame for his laziness; and left Grettel to get on with her yarn and her spinning as fast as she pleased and no faster.

One day, however, he said to her, "Wife, I must go a little way this morning; do you go into the field and cut the corn." "Yes, to be sure, dear Hans!" said she; so when he was gone she cooked herself a fine mess and took it with her into the field.   When she came into the field, she sat down for a while and said to herself, "What shall I do? shall I sleep first or eat first?   Heigho! I'll first eat a bit."   Then she ate her dinner heartily, and when she had had enough she said again to herself, "What shall I do? shall I reap first or sleep first?   Heigho! I'll first sleep a bit."   So she laid herself down among the corn and went fast asleep.   By and by Hans came home, but no Grettel was to be seen, and he said to himself, "What a clever wife I have! she works so hard that she does not even come home to her dinner!"   Evening came and still she did not come; then Hans set off to see how much of the corn was reaped, but there it all stood untouched, and Grettel lay fast asleep in the middle.   So he ran home and got a string of little bells and tied them quietly round her waist, and went back and set himself down on his stool and locked the house door.

At last Grettel woke when it was quite dark, and as she rose up the bells jingled around her every step she took. At this she was greatly frightened, and puzzled to tell whether she was really Grettel or not.   "Is it I, or is it not?" said she as she stood doubting what she ought to think.   At last, after she had pondered a while, she thought to herself, "I will go home and ask if it is I or not; Hans will know."   So she ran to the house door, and when she found it locked she knocked at the window and cried out, "Hans! is Grettel within?"   "She is where she ought to be, to be sure," said Hans; "O dear then!" said she frightened, "this is not I."   Then away she went and knocked at the neighbours' doors; but when they heard her bells rattling no one would let her in, and so at last off she ran back to the field again.

Cherry, or the Frog-Bride

THERE was once a king who had three sons. Not far from his kingdom lived an old woman who had an only daughter called Cherry. The king sent his sons out to see the world, that they might learn the ways of foreign lands, and get wisdom and skill in ruling the kingdom that they were one day to have for their own. But the old woman lived at peace at home with her daughter, who was called Cherry, because she liked cherries better than any other kind of food, and would eat scarcely anything else. Now her poor old mother had no garden and no money to buy cherries every day for her daughter; and at last there was no other plan left but to go to a neighbouring nunnery-garden and beg the finest she could get of the nuns; for she dared not let her daughter go out by herself, as she was very pretty, and she feared some mischance might befall her. Cherry's taste was, however, very well known; and as it happened that the abbess was as fond of cherries as she was, it was soon found out where all the best fruit went; and the holy mother was not a little angry at missing some of her stock and finding whither it had gone.

The princes while wandering on came one day to the town where Cherry and her mother lived; and as they passed along the street saw the fair maiden standing at the window, combing her long and beautiful locks of hair.

235

Then each of the three fell deeply in love with her, and began to say how much he longed to have her for his wife! Scarcely had the wish been spoken, when all drew their swords, and a dreadful battle began; the fight lasted long, and their rage grew hotter and hotter, when at last the abbess hearing the uproar came to the gate. Finding that her neighbour was the cause, her old spite against her broke forth at once, and in her rage she wished Cherry turned into an ugly frog, and sitting in the water under the bridge at the world's end. No sooner said than done; and poor Cherry became a frog, and vanished out of their sight. The princes had now nothing to fight for; so sheathing their swords again, they shook hands as brothers, and went on towards their father's home.

The old king meanwhile found that he grew weak and ill fitted for the business of reigning: so he thought of giving up his kingdom; but to whom should it be? This was a point that his fatherly heart could not settle; for he loved all his sons alike. "My dear children," said he, "I grow old and weak, and should like to give up my kingdom; but I cannot make up my mind which of you to choose for my heir, for I love you all three; and besides, I should wish to give my people the cleverest and best of you for their king. However, I will give you three trials, and the one who wins the prize shall have the kingdom. The first is to seek me out one hundred ells of cloth, so fine that I can draw it through my golden ring." The sons said they would do their best, and set out on the search.

The two eldest brothers took with them many followers, and coaches and horses of all sorts, to bring home all the beautiful cloths which they should find; but the youngest went alone by himself. They soon came to where the roads branched off into several ways; two ran through smiling meadows, with smooth paths and shady groves,

but the third looked dreary and dirty, and went over barren wastes.   The two eldest chose the pleasant ways; and
the youngest took his leave and whistled along over the
dreary road.   Whenever fine linen was to be seen, the two
elder brothers bought it, and bought so much that their
coaches and horses bent under their burthen.   The youngest, on the other hand, journeyed on many a weary day,
and found not a place where he could buy even one piece
of cloth that was at all fine and good.   His heart sank
beneath him, and every mile he grew more and more heavy
and sorrowful.   At last he came to a bridge over a stream,
and there he sat himself down to rest and sigh over his
bad luck, when an ugly-looking frog popped its head out
of the water, and asked, with a voice that had not at all a
harsh sound to his ears, what was the matter.   The prince
said in a pet, "Silly frog! thou canst not help me."   "Who
told you so?" said the frog; "tell me what ails you."   After
a while the prince opened the whole story, and told why his
father had sent him out.   "I will help you," said the frog;
so it jumped back into the stream and soon came back
dragging a small piece of linen not bigger than one's hand,
and by no means the cleanest in the world in its look.
However, there it was, and the prince was told to take it
away with him.   He had no great liking for such a dirty
rag; but still there was something in the frog's speech that
pleased him much, and he thought to himself, "It can do
no harm, it is better than nothing;" so he picked it up, put
it in his pocket, and thanked the frog, who dived down
again, panting and quite tired, as it seemed, with its
work.   The further he went the heavier he found to his
great joy the pocket grow, and so he turned himself homewards, trusting greatly in his good luck.

He reached home nearly about the same time that his
brothers came up, with their horses and coaches all heavily

laden.   Then the old king was very glad to see his children again, and pulled the ring off his finger to try who had done the best; but in all the stock which the two eldest had brought there was not one piece a tenth part of which would go through the ring.   At this they were greatly abashed; for they had made a laugh of their brother, who came home, as they thought, empty-handed.   But how great was their anger, when they saw him pull from his pocket a piece that for softness, beauty, and whiteness, was a thousand times better than anything that was ever before seen!   It was so fine that it passed with ease through the ring; indeed, two such pieces would readily have gone in together.   The father embraced the lucky youth, told his servants to throw the coarse linen into the sea, and said to his children, "Now you must set about the second task which I am to set you;—bring me home a little dog, so small that it will lie in a nut-shell."

His sons were not a little frightened at such a task; but they all longed for the crown, and made up their minds to go and try their hands, and so after a few days they set out once more on their travels.   At the cross-ways they parted as before, and the youngest chose his old dreary rugged road with all the bright hopes that his former good luck gave him.   Scarcely had he sat himself down again at the bridge foot, when his old friend the frog jumped out, set itself beside him, and as before opened its big wide mouth, and croaked out, "What is the matter?"   The prince had this time no doubt of the frog's power, and therefore told what he wanted.   "It shall be done for you," said the frog; and springing into the stream it soon brought up a hazel-nut, laid it at his feet, and told him to take it home to his father, and crack it gently, and then see what would happen.   The prince went his way very well pleased, and the frog, tired with its task, jumped back into the water.

His brothers had reached home first, and brought with them a great many very pretty little dogs.   The old king, willing to help them all he could, sent for a large walnut-shell and tried it with every one of the little dogs; but one stuck fast with the hind-foot out, and another with the head, and a third with the forefoot, and a fourth with its tail,—in short, some one way and some another; but none were at all likely to sit easily in this new kind of kennel. When all had been tried, the youngest made his father a dutiful bow, and gave him the hazel-nut, begging him to crack it very carefully; the moment this was done out ran a beautiful little white dog upon the king's hand, wagged its tail, fondled his new master, and soon turned about and barked at the other little beasts in the most graceful manner, to the delight of the whole court.   The joy of every one was great; the old king again embraced his lucky son, told his people to drown all the other dogs in the sea, and said to his children, "Dear sons! your weightiest tasks are now over; listen to my last wish; whoever brings home the fairest lady shall be at once the heir to my crown."

The prize was so tempting and the chance so fair for all, that none made any doubts about setting to work, each in his own way, to try and be the winner.   The youngest was not in such good spirits as he was the last time; he thought to himself, "The old frog has been able to do a great deal for me; but all its power must be nothing to me now, for where should it find me a fair maiden, still less a fairer maiden than was ever seen at my father's court? The swamps where it lives have no living things in them, but toads, snakes, and such vermin."   Meantime he went on, and sighed as he sat down again with a heavy heart by the bridge.   "Ah frog!" said he, "this time thou canst do me no good." "Never mind," croaked the frog; "only tell me what is the matter now." Then the prince told his old friend what trouble had now come upon him. "Go thy ways home," said the frog; "the fair maiden will follow hard after; but take care and do not laugh at whatever may happen!" This said, it sprang as before into the water and was soon out of sight. The prince still sighed on, for he trusted very little this time to the frog's word; but he had not set many steps towards home before he heard a noise behind him, and looking round saw six large water rats dragging along a large pumpkin like a coach, full trot. On the box sat an old fat toad as coachman, and behind stood two little frogs as footmen, and two fine mice with stately whiskers ran before as outriders; within sat his old friend the frog, rather misshapen and unseemly to be sure, but still with somewhat of a graceful air as it bowed to him in passing. Much too deeply wrapt in thought as to his chance of finding the fair lady whom he was seeking, to take any heed of the strange scene before him, the prince scarcely looked at it, and had still less mind to laugh. The coach passed on a little way, and soon turned a corner that hid it from his sight; but how astonished was he, on turning the corner himself, to find a handsome coach and six black horses standing there, with a coachman in gay livery, and within, the most beautiful lady he had ever seen, whom he soon knew to be the fair Cherry, for whom his heart had so long ago panted! As he came up, the servants opened the coach door, and he was allowed to seat himself by the beautiful lady.

They soon came to his father's city, where his brothers also came, with trains of fair ladies; but as soon as Cherry was seen, all the court gave her with one voice the crown of beauty. The delighted father embraced his son, and named him the heir to his crown, and ordered all the other ladies to be thrown like the little dogs into the sea and drowned. Then the prince married Cherry, and lived long and happily with her, and indeed lives with her still—if he be not dead.

Mother Holle

A WIDOW had two daughters; one of them was very
pretty and thrifty, but the other was ugly and idle.
Odd as you may think it, she loved the ugly and idle
one much the best, and the other was made to do all the
work, and was in short quite the drudge of the whole house.
Every day she had to sit on a bench by a well on the side of
the high-road before the house, and spin so much that
her fingers were quite sore, and at length the blood would
come. Now it happened that once when her fingers had
bled and the spindle was all bloody, she dipt it into the
well, and meant to wash it, but unluckily it fell from her
hand and dropt in. Then she ran crying to her mother,
and told her what had happened; but she scolded her
sharply, and said, "If you have been so silly as to let the
spindle fall in, you must get it out again as well as you
can." So the poor little girl went back to the well, and
knew not how to begin, but in her sorrow threw herself
into the water, and sank down to the bottom senseless. In
a short time she seemed to awake as from a trance, and
came to herself again; and when she opened her eyes and
looked around, she saw she was in a beautiful meadow,
where the sun shone brightly, the birds sang sweetly on
the boughs, and thousands of flowers sprang beneath her
feet.

Then she rose up, and walked along this delightful
meadow, and came to a pretty cottage by the side of a

wood; and when she went in she saw an oven full of new bread baking, and the bread said, "Pull me out! pull me out! or I shall be burnt, for I am quite done enough."   So she stepped up quickly and took it all out.   Then she went on further, and came to a tree that was full of fine rosy-cheeked apples, and it said to her, "Shake me! shake me! we are all quite ripe!"   So she shook the tree, and the apples fell down like a shower, until there were no more upon the tree.   Then she went on again, and at length came to a small cottage where an old woman was sitting at the door: the little girl would have run away, but the old woman called out after her, "Don't be frightened, my dear child! stay with me, I should like to have you for my little maid, and if you do all the work in the house neatly you shall fare well; but take care to make my bed nicely, and shake it every morning out at the door, so that the feathers may fly, for then the good people below say it snows.—I am Mother Holle."

As the old woman spoke so kindly to her, the girl was willing to do as she said; so she went into her employ, and took care to do everything to please her, and always shook the bed well, so that she led a very quiet life with her, and every day had good meat both boiled and roast to eat for her dinner.

But when she had been some time with the old lady, she became sorrowful, and although she was much better off here than at home, still she had a longing towards it, and at length said to her mistress, "I used to grieve at my troubles at home, but if they were all to come again, and I were sure of faring ever so well here, I could not stay any longer."   "You are right," said her mistress; "you shall do as you like; and as you have worked for me so faith-fully, I will myself show you the way back again."   Then she took her by the hand and led her behind her cottage,

and opened a door, and as the girl stood underneath there
fell a heavy shower of gold, so that she held out her apron
and caught a great deal of it. And the fairy put a shining
golden dress over her, and said, "All this you shall have
because you have behaved so well;" and she gave her back
the spindle too which had fallen into the well, and led her
out by another door. When it shut behind her, she found
herself not far from her mother's house; and as she went
into the court-yard the cock sat upon the well-head and
clapt his wings and cried out,

"Cock a-doodle-doo!
Our golden lady's come home again."

Then she went into the house, and as she was so rich she
was welcomed home. When her mother heard how she
got these riches, she wanted to have the same luck for her
ugly and idle daughter, so she too was told to sit by the
well and spin. That her spindle might be bloody, she
pricked her fingers with it, and when that would not do she
thrust her hand into a thorn-bush. Then she threw
it into the well and sprang in herself after it. Like
her sister, she came to a beautiful meadow, and followed
the same path. When she came to the oven in the cottage,
the bread called out as before, "Take me out! take me out!
or I shall burn, I am quite done enough." But the lazy
girl said, "A pretty story, indeed! just as if I should dirty
myself for you!" and went on her way. She soon came to
the apple-tree that cried, "Shake me! shake me! for my apples are quite ripe!" but she answered, "I will take care
how I do that, for one of you might fall upon my head;" so
she went on. At length she came to Mother Holle's house,
and readily agreed to be her maid. The first day she behaved herself very well, and did what her mistress told her;

for she thought of the gold she would give her; but the second day she began to be lazy, and the third still more so, for she would not get up in the morning early enough, and when she did she made the bed very badly, and did not shake it so that the feathers would fly out. Mother Holle was soon tired of her, and turned her off; but the lazy girl was quite pleased at that, and thought to herself, "Now the golden rain will come." Then the fairy took her to the same door; but when she stood under it, instead of gold a great kettle full of dirty pitch came showering upon her. "That is your wages," said Mother Holle as she shut the door upon her. So she went home quite black with the pitch, and as she came near her mother's house the cock sat upon the well, and clapt his wings, and cried out—

"Cock a-doodle-doo!
Our dirty slut's come home again!"

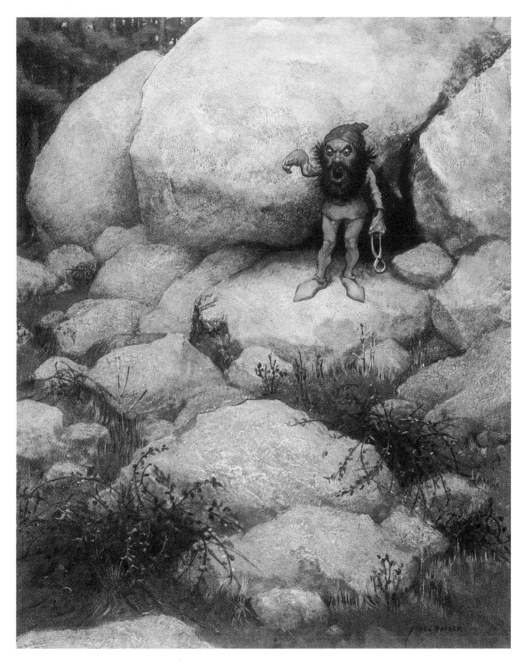

As he looked around, there stood above him
on one of the rocks a little dwarf.

THE WATER OF LIFE

Page 247

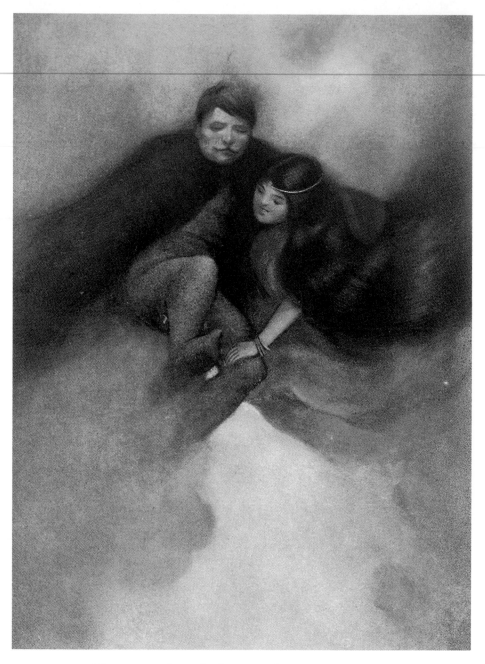

The moment he wished to be on the granite mountain,
they were both there.

THE SALAD

Page 277

The Water of Life

LONG before you and I were born there reigned, in a country a great way off, a king who had three sons. This king once fell very ill, so ill that nobody thought he could live. His sons were very much grieved at their father's sickness; and as they walked weeping in the garden of the palace, an old man met them and asked what they ailed. They told him their father was so ill that they were afraid nothing could save him. "I know what would," said the old man; "it is the Water of Life. If he could have a draught of it he would be well again, but it is very hard to get." Then the eldest son said, "I will soon find it," and went to the sick king, and begged that he might go in search of the Water of Life, as it was the only thing that could save him. "No," said the king; "I had rather die than place you in such great danger as you must meet with in your journey." But he begged so hard that the king let him go; and the prince thought to himself, "If I bring my father this water I shall be his dearest son, and he will make me heir to his kingdom."

Then he set out, and when he had gone on his way some time he came to a deep valley overhung with rocks and woods; and as he looked around there stood above him on one of the rocks a little dwarf, who called out to him and said, "Prince, whither hastest thou so fast?" "What is that to you, little ugly one?" said the prince sneeringly, and rode on his way. But the little dwarf fell into a great

247

rage at his behaviour, and laid a spell of ill luck upon him, so that, as he rode on, the mountain pass seemed to become narrower and narrower, and at last the way was so straitened that he could not go a step forward, and when he thought to have turned his horse round and gone back the way he came, the passage he found had closed behind also, and shut him quite up; he next tried to get off his horse and make his way on foot, but this he was unable to do, and so there he was forced to abide spell-bound.

Meantime the king his father was lingering on in daily hope of his return, till at last the second son said, "Father, I will go in search of this Water;" for he thought to himself, "My brother is surely dead, and the kingdom will fall to me if I have good luck in my journey." The king was at first very unwilling to let him go, but at last yielded to his wish. So he set out and followed the same road which his brother had taken, and met the same dwarf, who stopped him at the same spot, and said as before, "Prince, whither hastest thou so fast?" Mind your own affairs, busybody!" answered the prince scornfully, and rode off. But the dwarf put the same enchantment upon him, and when he came like the other to the narrow pass in the mountains he could neither move forward nor backward. Thus it is with proud silly people, who think themselves too wise to take advice.

When the second prince had thus staid away a long while, the youngest said he would go and search for the Water of Life, and trusted he should soon be able to make his father well again. The dwarf met him too at the same spot, and said, "Prince, whither hastest thou so fast?" and the prince said, "I go in search of the Water of Life, because my father is ill and like to die:—can you help me?" "Do you know where it is to be found?" asked the dwarf. "No," said the prince. "Then as you have spoken to me kindly and sought for advice, I will tell you how and where to go. The Water you seek springs from a well in an enchanted castle, and that you may be able to go in safety I will give you an iron wand and two little loaves of bread; strike the iron door of the castle three times with the wand, and it will open: two hungry lions will be lying down inside gaping for their prey; but if you throw them the bread they will let you pass; then hasten on to the well and take some of the Water of Life before the clock strikes twelve, for if you tarry longer the door will shut upon you for ever."

Then the prince thanked the dwarf for his friendly aid, and took the wand and the bread and went travelling on and on over sea and land, till he came to his journey's end, and found everything to be as the dwarf had told him. The door flew open at the third stroke of the wand, and when the lions were quieted he went on through the castle, and came at length to a beautiful hall; around it he saw several knights sitting in a trance; then he pulled off their rings and put them on his own fingers. In another room he saw on a table a sword and a loaf of bread, which he also took. Further on he came to a room where a beautiful young lady sat upon a couch, who welcomed him joyfully, and said, if he would set her free from the spell that bound her, the kingdom should be his if he would come back in a year and marry her; then she told him that the well that held the Water of Life was in the palace gardens, and bade him make haste and draw what he wanted before the clock struck twelve. Then he went on, and as he walked through beautiful gardens he came to a delightful shady spot in which stood a couch; and he thought to himself, as he felt tired, that he would rest himself for a while and gaze on the lovely scenes around him. So he laid himself down, and sleep fell upon him unawares and he did not wake up

till the clock was striking a quarter to twelve; then he
sprang from the couch dreadfully frightened, ran to the
well, filled a cup that was standing by him full of Water,
and hastened to get away in time.   Just as he was going
out of the iron door it struck twelve, and the door fell so
quickly upon him that it tore away a piece of his heel.

When he found himself safe he was overjoyed to think
that he had got the Water of Life; and as he was going on
his way homewards, he passed by the little dwarf, who
when he saw the sword and the loaf said, "You have made
a noble prize; with the sword you can at a blow slay whole
armies, and the bread will never fail."   Then the prince
thought to himself, "I cannot go home to my father without my brothers;" so he said, "Dear dwarf, cannot you tell
me where my two brothers are, who set out in search of the
Water of Life before me and never came back?"   "I have
shut them up by a charm between two mountains," said the
dwarf, "because they were proud and ill behaved, and
scorned to ask advice."   The prince begged so hard for his
brothers that the dwarf at last set them free, though unwillingly, saying, "Beware of them, for they have bad
hearts."   Their brother, however, was greatly rejoiced to
see them, and told them all that had happened to him, how
he had found the Water of Life, and had taken a cup full
of it, and how he had set a beautiful princess free from a
spell that bound her; and how she had engaged to wait a
whole year, and then to marry him and give him the kingdom.   Then they all three rode on together, and on their
way home came to a country that was laid waste by war
and a dreadful famine, so that it was feared all must die
for want.   But the prince gave the king of the land the
bread, and all his kingdom ate of it.   And he slew the
enemy's army with the wonderful sword, and left the kingdom in peace and plenty.   In the same manner he be-

friended two other countries that they passed through on their way.

When they came to the sea, they got into a ship, and during their voyage the two eldest said to themselves, "Our brother has got the Water which we could not find, therefore our father will forsake us, and give him the kingdom which is our right;" so they were full of envy and revenge, and agreed together how they could ruin him. They waited till he was fast asleep, and then poured the Water of Life out of the cup and took it for themselves, giving him bitter sea-water instead. And when they came to their journey's end, the youngest son brought his cup to the sick king, that he might drink and be healed. Scarcely, however, had he tasted the bitter sea-water when he became worse even than he was before, and then both the elder sons came in and blamed the youngest for what he had done, and said that he wanted to poison their father, but that they had found the Water of Life and had brought it with them. He no sooner began to drink of what they brought him, than he felt his sickness leave him, and was as strong and well as in his young days; then they went to their brother and laughed at him, and said, "Well, brother, you found the Water of Life, did you? you have had the trouble and we shall have the reward; pray, with all your cleverness why did not you manage to keep your eyes open? Next year one of us will take away your beautiful princess, if you do not take care; you had better say nothing about this to our father, for he does not believe a word you say, and if you tell tales, you shall lose your life into the bargain, but be quiet and we will let you off."

The old king was still very angry with his youngest son, and thought that he really meant to have taken away his life; so he called his court together and asked what should be done, and it was settled that he should be put to death. The prince knew nothing of what was going on, till one day when the king's chief huntsman went a-hunting with him, and they were alone in the wood together, the huntsman looked so sorrowful that the prince said, "My friend, what is the matter with you?" "I cannot and dare not tell you," said he. But the prince begged hard and said, "Only say what it is, and do not think I shall be angry, for I will forgive you." "Alas!" said the huntsman, "the king has ordered me to shoot you." The prince started at this, and said, "Let me live, and I will change dresses with you; you shall take my royal coat to show to my father, and do you give me your shabby one." "With all my heart," said the huntsman; "I am sure I shall be glad to save you, for I could not have shot you." Then he took the prince's coat, and gave him the shabby one, and went away through the wood.

Some time after, three grand embassies came to the old king's court, with rich gifts of gold and precious stones for his youngest son, which were sent from the three kings to whom he had lent his sword and loaf of bread, to rid them of their enemy, and feed their people. This touched the old king's heart, and he thought his son might still be guiltless, and said to his court, "Oh! that my son were still alive! how it grieves me that I had him killed!" "He still lives," said the huntsman; "and I rejoice that I had pity on him, and saved him, for when the time came, I could not shoot him, but let him go in peace and brought home his royal coat." At this the king was overwhelmed with joy, and made it known throughout all his kingdom, that if his son would come back to his court, he would forgive him.

Meanwhile the princess was eagerly waiting the return of her deliverer, and had a road made leading up to her palace all of shining gold; and told her courtiers that whoever came on horseback and rode straight up to the gate upon it, was her true lover, and that they must let him in; but whoever rode on one side of it, they must be sure was not the right one, and must send him away at once.

The time soon came, when the eldest thought he would make haste to go to the princess, and say that he was the one who had set her free, and that he should have her for his wife, and the kingdom with her. As he came before the palace and saw the golden road, he stopt to look at it, and thought to himself, "It is a pity to ride upon this beautiful road;" so he turned aside and road on the right of it. But when he came to the gate, the guards said to him, he was not what he said he was, and must go about his business. The second prince set out soon afterwards on the same errand; and when he came to the golden road, and his horse had set one foot upon it, he stopt to look at it, and thought it very beautiful, and said to himself, "What a pity it is that anything should tread here!" then he too turned aside and rode on the left of it. But when he came to the gate the guards said he was not the true prince, and that he too must go away.

Now when the full year was come, the third brother left the wood, where he had lain for fear of his father's anger, and set out in search of his betrothed bride. So he journeyed on, thinking of her all the way, and rode so quickly that he did not even see the golden road, but went with his horse straight over it; and as he came to the gate, it flew open, and the princess welcomed him with joy, and said he was her deliverer and should now be her husband and lord of the kingdom, and the marriage was soon kept with great feasting. When it was over, the princess told him she had heard of his father having forgiven him, and of his wish to have him home again: so he went to visit him, and told him everything, how his brothers had cheated and robbed him, and yet that he had borne all these wrongs for the love of his father. Then the old king was very angry, and wanted to punish his wicked sons; but they made their escape, and got into a ship and sailed away over the wide sea, and were never heard of any more.

Peter the Goatherd

IN the wilds of the Hartz Forest there is a high mountain, where the fairies and goblins dance by night, and
where they say the great Emperor Frederic Barbarossa
still holds his court among the caverns.   Now and then
he shows himself and punishes those whom he dislikes, or
gives some rich gift to the lucky wight whom he takes it
into his head to befriend.   He sits on a throne of marble
with his red beard sweeping on the ground, and once or
twice in a long course of years rouses himself for a while
from the trance in which he is buried, but soon falls again
into his former forgetfulness.   Strange chances have befallen many who have strayed within the range of his
court—you shall hear one of them.

A great many years ago there lived in the village at
the foot of the mountain, one Peter, a goatherd.   Every
morning he drove his flock to feed upon the green spots
that are here and there found on the mountain's side, and
in the evening he sometimes thought it too far to drive his
charge home, so he used in such cases to shut it up in a
spot amongst the woods, where an old ruined wall was
left standing, high enough to form a fold, in which he
could count his goats and rest in peace for the night.   One
evening he found that the prettiest goat of his flock had
vanished soon after they were driven into this fold, but
was there again in the morning.   Again and again he
watched, and the same strange thing happened.   He

thought he would look still more narrowly, and soon found a cleft in the old wall, through which it seemed that his favourite made her way. Peter followed, scrambling as well as he could down the side of the rock, and wondered not a little, on overtaking his goat, to find it employing itself very much at its ease in a cavern, eating corn, which kept dropping from some place above. He went into the cavern and looked about him to see where all this corn, that rattled about his ears like a hail-storm, could come from: but all was dark, and he could find no clue to this strange business. At last, as he stood listening, he thought he heard the neighing and stamping of horses. He listened again; it was plainly so; and after a while he was sure that horses were feeding above him, and that the corn fell from their mangers. What could these horses be, which were thus kept in a mountain where none but the goat's foot ever trod? Peter pondered a while; but his wonder only grew greater and greater, when on a sudden a little page came forth and beckoned him to follow; he did so, and came at last to a court-yard surrounded by an old wall. The spot seemed the bosom of the valley; above rose on every hand high masses of rock; wide branching trees threw their arms overhead, so that nothing but a glimmering twilight made its way through; and here, on the cool smooth shaven turf, were twelve old knights, who looked very grave and sober, but were amusing themselves with a game of nine-pins.

Not a word fell from their lips; but they ordered Peter by dumb signs to busy himself in setting up the pins, as they knocked them down. At first his knees trembled, as he dared to snatch a stolen sidelong glance at the long beards and old-fashioned dresses of the worthy knights. Little by little, however, he grew bolder; and at last he plucked up his heart so far as to take his turn in the

draught at the can, which stood beside him and sent up
the smell of the richest old wine. This gave him new
strength for his work; and as often as he flagged at all,
he turned to the same kind friend for help in his need.

Sleep at last overpowered him; and when he awoke
he found himself stretched out upon the old spot where
he had folded his flock. The same green turf was spread
beneath, and the same tottering walls surrounded him:
he rubbed his eyes, but neither dog nor goat was to be
seen, and when he had looked about him again the grass
seemed to be longer under his feet, and trees hung over
his head which he had either never seen before or had forgotten. Shaking his head, and hardly knowing whether
he were in his right mind, he wound his way among the
mountain steeps, through paths where his flocks were wont
to wander; but still not a goat was to be seen. Below
him in the plain lay the village where his home was, and
at length he took the downward path, and set out with
a heavy heart in search of his flock. The people who met
him as he drew near to the village were all unknown to
him; they were not even drest as his neighbours were, and
they seemed as if they hardly spoke the same tongue; and
when he eagerly asked after his goats, they only stared
at him and stroked their chins. At last he did the same
too, and what was his wonder to find that his beard was
grown at least a foot long! The world, thought he now
to himself, is turned over, or at any rate bewitched; and
yet he knew the mountain (as he turned round to gaze
upon its woody heights); and he knew the houses and
cottages also, with their little gardens, all of which were
in the same places as he had always known them; he
heard some children, too, call the village by its old name,
as a traveller that passed by was asking his way.

Again he shook his head and went straight through the

village to his own cottage. Alas! it looked sadly out of repair; and in the court-yard lay an unknown child, in a ragged dress, by the side of a rough, toothless dog, whom he thought he ought to know, but who snarled and barked in his face when he called him to him. He went in at an opening in the wall where a door had once stood, but found all so dreary and empty that he staggered out again like a drunken man, and called his wife and children loudly by their names; but no one heard, at least no one answered him.

A crowd of women and children soon flocked around the long gray-bearded man, and all broke upon him at once with the questions, "Who are you?" "Whom do you want?" It seemed to him so odd to ask other people at his own door after his wife and children, that in order to get rid of the crowd he named the first man that came into his head—"Hans, the blacksmith!" said he. Most held their tongues and stared, but at last an old woman said, "He went these seven years ago to a place that you will not reach to-day." "Frank the tailor, then!" "Heaven rest his soul!" said an old beldame upon crutches; "he has laid these ten years in a house that he'll never leave."

Peter looked at the old woman, and shuddered as he saw her to be one of his old friends, only with a strangely altered face. All wish to ask further questions was gone; but at last a young woman made her way through the gaping throng with a baby in her arms, and a little girl about three years old clinging to her other hand; all three looked the very image of his wife. "What is thy name?" asked he wildly. "Mary." "And your father's?" "Heaven bless him! Peter! It is now twenty years since we sought him day and night on the mountain; his flock came back, but he never was heard of any more. I was then seven years old." The goatherd could hold no longer. "I am Peter," cried he; "I am Peter, and no other;" as he took the child from his daughter's arms and kissed it. All stood gaping, and not knowing what to say or think, till at length one voice was heard, "Why, it is Peter!" and then several others cried, "Yes, it is, it is Peter! Welcome neighbour. welcome home, after twenty long years!"

The Four Clever Brothers

DEAR children," said a poor man to his four sons, "I have nothing to give you; you must go out into the world, and try your luck. Begin by learning some trade, and see how you can get on." So the four brothers took their walking-sticks in their hands, and their little bundles on their shoulders, and, after bidding their father good-bye, went all out at the gate together. When they had got on some way they came to four cross-ways, each leading to a different country. Then the eldest said, "Here we must part; but this day four years we will come back to this spot; and in the meantime each must try what he can do for himself." So each brother went his way; and as the oldest was hastening on, a man met him, and asked him where he was going and what he wanted. "I am going to try my luck in the world, and should like to begin by learning some trade," answered he. "Then," said the man, "go with me, and I will teach you how to become the cunningest thief that ever was." "No," said the other, "that is not an honest calling, and what can one look to earn by it in the end but the gallows?" "Oh!" said the man, "you need not fear the gallows; for I will only teach you to steal what will be fair game; I meddle with nothing but what no one else can get or care anything about, and where no one can find you out." So the young man agreed to follow his trade, and he soon showed himself so clever that nothing could escape him that he had once set his mind upon.

The second brother also met a man, who, when he found out what he was setting out upon, asked him what trade he meant to learn. "I do not know yet," said he. "Then come with me, and be a star-gazer. It is a noble trade, for nothing can be hidden from you when you understand the stars." The plan pleased him much, and he soon became such a skilful star-gazer, that when he had served out his time, and wanted to leave his master, he gave him a glass, and said, "With this you can see all that is passing in the sky and on earth, and nothing can be hidden from you."

The third brother met a huntsman, who took him with him, and taught him so well all that belonged to hunting, that he became very clever in that trade; and when he left his master he gave him a bow, and said, "Whatever you shoot at with this bow you will be sure to hit."

The youngest brother likewise met a man who asked him what he wished to do. "Would not you like," said he, "to be a tailor?" "Oh no!" said the young man; "sitting cross-legged from morning to night, working backwards and forwards with a needle and a goose, will never suit me." "Oh!" answered the man, "that is not my sort of tailoring; come with me, and you will learn quite another kind of trade from that." Not knowing what better to do, he came into the plan, and learnt the trade from the beginning; and when he left his master, he gave him a needle, and said, "You can sew anything with this, be it as soft as an egg, or as hard as steel, and the joint will be so fine that no seam will be seen."

After the space of four years, at the time agreed upon, the four brothers met at the four cross-roads, and having welcomed each other, set off towards their father's home, where they told him all that had happened to them, and how each had learned some trade. Then one day, as they were sitting before the house under a very high tree, the father said, "I should like to try what each of you can do in his trade." So he looked up, and said to the second son, "At the top of this tree there is a chaffinch's nest; tell me how many eggs there are in it." The star-gazer took his glass, looked up, and said, "Five." "Now," said the father to the eldest son, "take away the eggs without the bird that is sitting upon them and hatching them, knowing anything of what you are doing." So the cunning thief climbed up the tree, and brought away to his father the five eggs from under the bird, who never saw or felt what he was doing, but kept sitting on at her ease. Then the father took the eggs, and put one on each corner of the table and the fifth in the middle, and said to the huntsman, "Cut all the eggs in two pieces at one shot." The huntsman took up his bow, and at one shot struck all the five eggs as his father wished. "Now comes your turn," said he to the young tailor; "sew the eggs and the young birds in them together again, so neatly that the shot shall have done them no harm." Then the tailor took his needle, and sewed the eggs as he was told; and when he had done, the thief was sent to take them back to the nest, and put them under the bird, without its knowing it. Then she went on sitting, and hatched them; and in a few days they crawled out, and had only a little red streak across their necks where the tailor had sewed them together.

"Well done, sons!" said the old man, "you have made good use of your time, and learnt something worth the knowing; but I am sure I do not know which ought to have the prize. Oh! that a time might soon come for you to turn your skill to some account!"

Not long after this there was a great bustle in the

country; for the king's daughter had been carried off by a mighty dragon, and the king mourned over his loss day and night, and made it known that whoever brought her back to him should have her for a wife. Then the four brothers said to each other, "Here is a chance for us; let us try what we can do." And they agreed to see whether they could not set the princess free. "I will soon find out where she is, however," said the star-gazer as he looked through his glass, and soon cried out, "I see her afar off, sitting upon a rock in the sea, and I can spy the dragon close by, guarding her." Then he went to the king, and asked for a ship for himself and his brothers, and went with them upon the sea till they came to the right place. There they found the princess sitting, as the star-gazer had said, on the rock, and the dragon was lying asleep with his head upon her lap. "I dare not shoot at him," said the huntsman, "for I should kill the beautiful young lady also." "Then I will try my skill," said the thief; and went and stole her away from under the dragon so quickly and gently that the beast did not know it, but went on snoring.

Then away they hastened with her full of joy in their boat towards the ship; but soon came the dragon roaring behind them through the air, for he awoke and missed the princess; but when he got over the boat, and wanted to pounce upon them and carry off the princess, the huntsman took up his bow and shot him straight at the heart, so that he fell down dead. They were still not safe; for he was such a great beast, that in his fall he overset the boat, and they had to swim in the open sea upon a few planks. So the tailor took his needle, and with a few large stitches put some of the planks together, and sat down upon them, and sailed about and gathered up all the pieces of the boat, and tacked them together so quickly that the boat was soon ready, and they then reached the ship and got home safe.

When they had brought home the princess to her father, there was great rejoicing; and he said to the four brothers, "One of you shall marry her, but you must settle amongst yourselves which it is to be." Then there arose a quarrel between them; and the star-gazer said, "If I had not found the princess out, all your skill would have been of no use; therefore she ought to be mine." "Your seeing her would have been of no use," said the thief, "if I had not taken her away from the dragon; therefore she ought to be mine." "No, she is mine," said the huntsman; "for if I had not killed the dragon, he would after all have torn you and the princess into pieces." "And if I had not sewed the boat together again," said the tailor, "you would all have been drowned; therefore she is mine." Then the king put in a word, and said, "Each of you is right; and as all cannot have the young lady, the best way is for neither of you to have her; and to make up for the loss, I will give each, as a reward for his skill, half a kingdom." So the brothers agreed that would be much better than quarrelling; and the king then gave each half a kingdom, as he had said; and they lived very happily the rest of their days, and took good care of their father.

The Elfin-Grove

I HOPE," said a woodman one day to his wife, "that the children will not run into that fir-grove by the side of the river; who they are that have come to live there I cannot tell, but I am sure it looks more dark and gloomy than ever, and some queer-looking beings are to be seen lurking about it every night, as I am told." The woodman could not say that they brought any ill luck as yet, whatever they were; for all the village had thriven more than ever since they came; the fields looked gayer and greener, and even the sky was a deeper blue. Not knowing what to say of them, the farmer very wisely let his new friends alone, and in truth troubled his head very little about them.

That very evening little Mary and her playfellow Martin were playing at hide and seek in the valley. "Where can he be hid?" said she; "he must have gone into the fir-grove," and down she ran to look. Just then she spied a little dog that jumped round her and wagged his tail, and led her on towards the wood. Then he ran into it, and she soon jumped up the bank to look after him, but was overjoyed to see, instead of a gloomy grove of firs, a delightful garden, where flowers and shrubs of every kind grew upon turf of the softest green; gay butterflies flew about her, the birds sang sweetly, and, what was strangest, the prettiest little children sported about on all sides, some twining the flowers, and others dancing

267

in rings upon the shady spots beneath the trees. In the midst, instead of the hovels of which Mary had heard, there was a palace that dazzled her eyes with its brightness. For a while she gazed on the fairy scene around her, till at last one of the little dancers ran up to her, and said, "And you are come at last to see us? we have often seen you play about, and wished to have you with us." Then she plucked some of the fruit that grew near; and Mary at the first taste forgot her home, and wished only to see and know more of her fairy friends.

Then they led her about with them and showed her all their sports. One while they danced by moonlight on the primrose banks; at another time they skipped from bough to bough among the trees that hung over the cooling streams; for they moved as lightly and easily through the air as on the ground: and Mary went with them everywhere, for they bore her in their arms wherever they wished to go. Sometimes they would throw seeds on the turf, and directly little trees sprang up; and then they would set their feet upon the branches, while the trees grew under them, till they danced upon the boughs in the air, wherever the breezes carried them; and again the trees would sink down into the earth and land them safely at their bidding. At other times they would go and visit the palace of their queen; and there the richest food was spread before them, and the softest music was heard; and there all around grew flowers which were always changing their hues, from scarlet to purple and yellow and emerald. Sometimes they went to look at the heaps of treasure which were piled up in the royal stores; for little dwarfs were always employed in searching the earth for gold. Small as this fairyland looked from without, it seemed within to have no end; a mist hung around it to shield it from the eyes of men; and some of the little elves sat perched upon the outermost trees, to keep watch lest the step of man should break in and spoil the charm.

"And who are you?" said Mary one day. "We are what are called elves in your world," said one whose name was Gossamer, and who had become her dearest friend: "we are told you talk a great deal about us; some of our tribes like to work you mischief, but we who live here seek only to be happy: we meddle little with mankind; but when we do come among them, it is to do them good." "And where is your queen?" said little Mary. "Hush! hush! you cannot see or know her: you must leave us before she comes back, which will be now very soon, for mortal step cannot come where she is. But you will know that she is here when you see the meadows gayer, the rivers more sparkling, and the sun brighter."

Soon afterwards Gossamer told Mary the time was come to bid her farewell, and gave her a ring in token of their friendship, and led her to the edge of the grove. "Think of me," said she; "but beware how you tell what you have seen, or try to visit any of us again, for if you do, we shall quit this grove and come back no more." Turning back, Mary saw nothing but the gloomy fir-grove she had known before. "How frightened my father and mother will be!" thought she as she looked at the sun, which had risen some time. "They will wonder where I have been all night, and yet I must not tell them what I have seen." She hastened homewards, wondering however, as she went, to see that the leaves, which were yesterday so fresh and green, were now falling dry and yellow around her. The cottage too seemed changed, and, when she went in, there sat her father looking some years older than when she saw him last; and her mother, whom she hardly knew, was by his side. Close by was a young man; "Father," said Mary, "who is this?" "Who are you that

call me father?" said he; "are you—no you cannot be—
our long-lost Mary?" But they soon saw that it was their
Mary; and the young man, who was her old friend and
playfellow Martin, said, "No wonder you had forgotten
me in seven years; do not you remember how we parted
seven years ago while playing in the field? We thought
you were quite lost; but we are glad to see that some one
has taken care of you and brought you home at last."
Mary said nothing, for she could not tell all; but she
wondered at the strange tale, and felt gloomy at the change
from fairyland to her father's cottage.

Little by little she came to herself, thought of her
story as a mere dream, and soon became Martin's bride.
Everything seemed to thrive around them; and Mary
called her first little girl Elfie, in memory of her friends.
The little thing was loved by every one. It was pretty
and very good-tempered; Mary thought that it was very
like a little elf; and all, without knowing why, called it
the fairy child.

One day, while Mary was dressing her little Elfie, she
found a piece of gold hanging round her neck by a silken
thread, and knew it to be of the same sort as she had seen
in the hands of the fairy dwarfs. Elfie seemed sorry at
its being seen, and said that she had found it in the garden.
But Mary watched her, and soon found that she went every
afternoon to sit by herself in a shady place behind the
house: so one day she hid herself to see what the child did
there; and to her great wonder Gossamer was sitting by
her side. "Dear Elfie," she was saying, "your mother
and I used to sit thus when she was young and lived among
us. Oh! if you could but come and do so too! but since
our queen came to us it cannot be; yet I will come and
see you and talk to you, whilst you are a child; when you
grow up we must part for ever." Then she plucked one

of the roses that grew around them and breathed gently upon it, and said, "Take this for my sake. It will keep its freshness a whole year."

Then Mary loved her little Elfie more than ever; and when she found that she spent some hours of almost every day with the elf, she used to hide herself and watch them without being seen, till one day when Gossamer was bearing her little friend through the air from tree to tree, her mother was so frightened lest her child should fall that she could not help screaming out, and Gossamer set her gently on the ground and seemed angry, and flew away. But still she used sometimes to come and play with her little friend, and would soon have done so perhaps the same as before, had not Mary one day told her husband the whole story, for she could not bear to hear him always wondering and laughing at their little child's odd ways, and saying he was sure there was something in the fir-grove that brought them no good. So to show him that all she said was true, she took him to see Elfie and the fairy; but no sooner did Gossamer know that he was there, (which she did in an instant), than she changed herself into a raven and flew off into the fir-grove.

Mary burst into tears, and so did Elfie, for she knew she should see her dear friend no more: but Martin was restless and bent upon following up his search after the fairies; so when night came he stole away towards the grove. When he came to it nothing was to be seen but the gloomy firs and the old hovels; and the thunder rolled, and the wind groaned and whistled through the trees. It seemed that all about him was angry so he turned homewards frightened at what he had done.

In the morning all the neighbours flocked around, asking one another what the noise and bustle of the last night could mean; and when they looked about them, their trees looked blighted, and the meadows parched, the streams were dried up, and everything seemed troubled and sorrowful; but they all thought that somehow or other the fir-grove had not near so forbidding a look as it used to have. Strange stories were told, how one had heard flutterings in the air, another had seen the fir-grove as it were alive with little beings that flew away from it. Each neighbour told his tale, and all wondered what could have happened; but Mary and her husband knew what was the matter, and bewailed their folly; for they foresaw that their kind neighbours, to whom they owed all their luck, were gone for ever. Among the bystanders none told a wilder story than the old ferryman who plied across the river at the foot of the grove; he told how at midnight his boat was carried away, and how hundreds of little beings seemed to load it with treasures; how a strange piece of gold was left for him in the boat, as his fare; how the air seemed full of fairy forms, fluttering around; and how at last a great train passed over that seemed to be guarding their leader to the meadows on the other side; and how he heard soft music floating around as they flew; and how sweet voices sang as they hovered over his head,

> Fairy Queen!
> Fairy Queen!
> Mortal steps are on the green;
> Come away!
> Haste away!
>
> Fairies, guard your Queen!
> Hither, hither, fairy Queen!
> Lest thy silvery wing be seen;
> O'er the sky
> Fly, fly, fly!
> Fairies, guard your lady Queen!
> O'er the sky
> Fly, fly, fly!
> Fairies, guard your Queen!

Fairy Queen!
Fairy Queen!
Thou hast pass'd the treach'rous scene;
Now we may
Down and play
O'er the daisied green.
Lightly, lightly, fairy Queen!
Trip it gently o'er the green:
Fairies gay,
Trip away
Round about your lady Queen!
Fairies gay,
Trip away
Round about your Queen!

Poor Elfie mourned their loss the most, and would spend whole hours in looking upon the rose that her play-fellow had given her, and singing over it the pretty airs she had taught her; till at length when the year's charm had passed away and it began to fade, she planted the stalk in her garden, and there it grew and grew till she could sit under the shade of it and think of her friend Gossamer.

The Salad

AS a merry young huntsman was once going briskly along through a wood, there came up a little old woman, and said to him, "Good day, good day; you seem merry enough, but I am hungry and thirsty; do pray give me something to eat." The huntsman took pity on her, and put his hand in his pocket and gave her what he had. Then he wanted to go his way; but she took hold of him, and said, "Listen, my friend, to what I am going to tell you; I will reward you for your kindness; go your way, and after a little time you will come to a tree where you will see nine birds sitting on a cloak. Shoot into the midst of them, and one will fall down dead: the cloak will fall too; take it, it is a wishing-cloak, and when you wear it you will find yourself at any place where you may wish to be. Cut open the dead bird, take out its heart and keep it, and you will find a piece of gold under your pillow every morning when you rise. It is the bird's heart that will bring you this good luck."

The huntsman thanked her, and thought to himself, "If all this does happen, it will be a fine thing for me." When he had gone a hundred steps or so, he heard a screaming and chirping in the branches over him, and looked up and saw a flock of birds pulling a cloak with their bills and feet; screaming, fighting, and tugging at each other as if each wished to have it himself. "Well," said the huntsman, "this is wonderful; this happens just as the old woman said;" then he shot into the midst of them so that their feathers flew all about. Off went the flock chattering away; but one fell down dead, and the cloak with it. Then the huntsman did as the old woman told him, cut open the bird, took out the heart, and carried the cloak home with him.

The next morning when he awoke he lifted up his pillow, and there lay the piece of gold glittering underneath; the same happened next day, and indeed every day when he arose. He heaped up a great deal of gold, and at last thought to himself, "Of what use is this gold to me whilst I am at home? I will go out into the world and look about me."

Then he took leave of his friends, and hung his bag and bow about his neck, and went his way. It so happened that his road one day led through a thick wood, at the end of which was a large castle in a green meadow, and at one of the windows stood an old woman with a very beautiful young lady by her side looking about them. Now the old woman was a fairy, and said to the young lady, "There is a young man coming out of the wood who carries a wonderful prize; we must get it away from him, my dear child, for it is more fit for us than for him. He has a bird's heart that brings a piece of gold under his pillow every morning." Meantime the huntsman came nearer and looked at the lady, and said to himself, "I have been travelling so long that I should like to go into this castle and rest myself, for I have money enough to pay for anything I want;" but the real reason was, that he wanted to see more of the beautiful lady. Then he went into the house, and was welcomed kindly; and it was not long before he was so much in love that he thought of nothing else but looking at the lady's eyes, and doing everything that she wished. Then the old woman said, "Now is the time for getting the bird's heart." So the lady stole it away, and he never found any more gold under his pillow, for it lay now under the young lady's, and the old woman took it away every morning; but he was so much in love that he never missed his prize.

"Well," said the old fairy, "we have got the bird's heart, but not the wishing-cloak yet, and that we must also get." "Let us leave him that," said the young lady; "he has already lost his wealth." Then the fairy was very angry, and said, "Such a cloak is a very rare and wonderful thing, and I must and will have it." So she did as the old woman told her, and set herself at the window, and looked about the country and seemed very sorrowful; then the huntsman said, "What makes you so sad?" "Alas! dear sir," said she, "yonder lies the granite rock where all the costly diamonds grow, and I want so much to go there, that whenever I think of it I cannot help being sorrowful, for who can reach it? only the birds and the flies—man cannot." "If that's all your grief," said the huntsman, "I'll take you there with all my heart;" so he drew her under his cloak, and the moment he wished to be on the granite mountain they were both there. The diamonds glittered so on all sides that they were delighted with the sight and picked up the finest. But the old fairy made a deep sleep come upon him, and he said to the young lady, "Let us sit down and rest ourselves a little, I am so tired that I cannot stand any longer." So they sat down, and he laid his head in her lap and fell asleep; and whilst he was sleeping on she took the cloak from his shoulders, hung it on her own, picked up the diamonds, and wished herself home again.

When he awoke and found that his lady had tricked him, and left him alone on the wild rock, he said, "Alas! what roguery there is in the world!" and there he sat in great grief and fear, not knowing what to do. Now this rock belonged to fierce giants who lived upon it; and as he saw three of them striding about, he thought to himself, "I can only save myself by feigning to be asleep;" so he laid himself down as if he were in a sound sleep. When the giants came up to him, the first pushed him with his foot, and said, "What worm is this that lies here curled up?" "Tread upon him and kill him," said the second. "It's not worth the trouble," said the third; "let him live, he'll go climbing higher up the mountain, and some cloud will come rolling and carry him away." And they passed on. But the huntsman had heard all they said; and as soon as they were gone, he climbed to the top of the mountain, and when he had sat there a short time a cloud came rolling around him, and caught him in a whirlwind and bore him along for some time, till it settled in a garden, and he fell quite gently to the ground amongst the greens and cabbages.

Then he looked around him, and said, "I wish I had something to eat, if not I shall be worse off than before; for here I see neither apples nor pears, nor any kind of fruits, nothing but vegetables." At last he thought to himself, "I can eat salad, it will refresh and strengthen me." So he picked out a fine head and ate of it; but scarcely had he swallowed two bites when he felt himself quite changed, and saw with horror that he was turned into an ass. However, he still felt very hungry, and the salad tasted very nice; so he ate on till he came to another kind of salad, and scarcely had he tasted it when he felt another change come over him, and soon saw that he was lucky enough to have found his old shape again.

Then he laid himself down and slept off a little of his weariness; and when he awoke the next morning he broke off a head both of the good and the bad salad, and thought to himself, "This will help me to my fortune again, and enable me to pay off some folks for their treachery." So he went away to try and find the castle of his old friends; and after wandering about a few days he luckily found it. Then he stained his face all over brown, so that even his mother would not have known him, and went into the castle and asked for a lodging; "I am so tired," said he, "that I can go no further." "Countryman," said the fairy, "who are you? and what is your business?" "I am," said he, "a messenger sent by the king to find the finest salad that grows under the sun. I have been lucky enough to find it, and have brought it with me; but the heat of the sun scorches so that it begins to wither, and I don't know that I can carry it further."

When the fairy and the young lady heard of this beautiful salad, they longed to taste it, and said, "Dear countryman, let us just taste it." "To be sure," answered he; "I have two heads of it with me, and will give you one;" so he opened his bag and gave them the bad. Then the fairy herself took it into the kitchen to be dressed; and when it was ready she could not wait till it was carried up, but took a few leaves immediately and put them in her mouth, and scarcely were they swallowed when she lost her own form and ran braying down into the court in the form of an ass. Now the servant-maid came into the kitchen, and seeing the salad ready was going to carry it up; but in the way she too felt a wish to taste it as the old woman had done, and ate some leaves; so she also was turned into an ass and ran after the other, letting the dish with the salad fall on the ground. The messenger sat all this time with the beautiful young lady, and as nobody came with the salad and she longed to taste it, she said, "I don't know where the salad can be." Then he thought something must have happened, and said, "I will go into the kitchen and see." And as he went he saw two asses in the court running about, and the salad lying on the ground. "All right!" said he; "those two have had their share." Then he took up the rest of the leaves, laid them on the dish and brought them to the young lady, saying, "I bring you the dish myself that you may not wait any longer." So she ate of it, and like the others ran off into the court, braying away.

Then the huntsman washed his face and went into the court that they might know him. "Now you shall be paid for your roguery," said he; and tied them all three to a rope and took them along with him till he came to a mill and knocked at the window. "What's the matter?" said the miller. "I have three tiresome beasts here," said the other; "if you will take them, give them food and room, and treat them as I tell you, I will pay you whatever you ask." "With all my heart," said the miller; "but how shall I treat them?" Then the huntsman said, "Give the old one stripes three times a day and hay once; give the next (who was the servant-maid) stripes once a day and hay three times; and give the youngest (who was the beautiful lady) hay three times a day and no stripes:" for he could not find it in his heart to have her beaten. After this he went back to the castle, where he found everything he wanted.

Some days after the miller came to him, and told him that the old ass was dead; "the other two," said he, "are alive and eat, but are so sorrowful that they cannot last long." Then the huntsman pitied them, and told the miller to drive them back to him, and when they came, he gave them some of the good salad to eat. And the beautiful young lady fell upon her knees before him, and said, "Oh dearest huntsman! forgive me all the ill I have done you; my mother forced me to it, it was against my will, for I always loved you very much. Your wishing-cloak hangs up in the closet, and as for the bird's heart, I will give it you too." But he said, "Keep it, it will be just the same thing, for I mean to make you my wife." So they were married, and lived together very happily till they died.

The Nose

DID you ever hear the story of the three poor soldiers, who, after having fought hard in the wars, set out on their road home begging their way as they went?

They had journeyed on a long way, sick at heart with their bad luck at thus being turned loose on the world in their old days, when one evening they reached a deep gloomy wood through which they must pass; night came fast upon them, and they found that they must, however unwillingly, sleep in the wood; so to make all as safe as they could, it was agreed that two should lie down and sleep, while a third sat up and watched lest wild beasts should break in and tear them to pieces; when he was tired he was to wake one of the others and sleep in his turn, and so on with the third, so as to share the work fairly among them.

The two who were to rest first soon lay down and fell fast asleep, and the other made himself a good fire under the trees and sat down by the side to keep watch. He had not sat long before all on a sudden up came a little man in a red jacket. "Who's there?" said he. "A friend," said the soldier. "What sort of a friend?" "An old broken soldier," said the other, "with his two comrades who have nothing left to live on; come, sit down and warm yourself." "Well, my worthy fellow," said the little man, "I will do what I can for you; take this and show it to your comrades in the morning." So he took out an old cloak and gave it to the soldier, telling him that whenever he put it over his shoulders anything that he wished for would be fulfilled; then the little man made him a bow and walked away.

The second soldier's turn to watch soon came, and the first laid himself down to sleep; but the second man had not sat by himself long before up came the little man in the red jacket again. The soldier treated him in a friendly way as his comrade had done, and the little man gave him a purse, which he told him was always full of gold, let him draw as much as he would.

Then the third soldier's turn to watch came, and he also had the little man for his guest, who gave him a wonderful horn that drew crowds around it whenever it was played; and made every one forget his business to come and dance to its beautiful music.

In the morning each told his story and showed his treasure; and as they all liked each other very much and were old friends, they agreed to travel together to see the world, and for a while only to make use of the wonderful purse. And thus they spent their time very joyously, till at last they began to be tired of this roving life, and thought they should like to have a home of their own. So the first soldier put his old cloak on, and wished for a fine castle. In a moment it stood before their eyes; fine gardens and green lawns spread round it, and flocks of sheep and goats and herds of oxen were grazing about, and out of the gate came a fine coach with three dapple gray horses to meet them and bring them home.

All this was very well for a time; but it would not do to stay at home always, so they got together all their rich clothes and horses and servants, and ordered their coach with three horses, and set out on a journey to see a neighbouring king. Now this king had an only daughter, and as he took the three soldiers for kings' sons, he gave them a kind welcome. One day, as the second soldier was walking with the princess, she saw him with the wonderful purse in his hand; and having asked him what it was, he was foolish enough to tell her—though indeed it did not much signify, for she was a witch and knew all the wonderful things that the three soldiers brought. Now this princess was very cunning and artful; so she set to work and made a purse so like the soldier's that no one would know one from the other, and then asked him to come and see her, and made him drink some wine that she had got ready for him, till he fell fast asleep. Then she felt in his pocket, and took away the wonderful purse and left the one she had made in its place.

The next morning the soldiers set out home, and soon after they reached their castle, happening to want some money, they went to their purse for it, and found something indeed in it, but to their great sorrow when they had emptied it, none came in the place of what they took. Then the cheat was soon found out; for the second soldier knew where he had been, and how he had told the story to the princess, and he guessed that she had betrayed him, "Alas!" cried he, "poor wretches that we are, what shall we do?" "Oh!" said the first soldier, "let no gray hairs grow for this mishap; I will soon get the purse back." So he threw his cloak across his shoulders and wished himself in the princess's chamber. There he found her sitting alone, telling her gold that fell around her in a shower from the purse. But the soldier stood looking at her too long, for the moment she saw him she started up and cried out with all her force, "Thieves! Thieves!" so that the whole court came running in and tried to seize him. The poor soldier now began to be dreadfully frightened in his turn, and thought it was high time to make the best of his

way off; so without thinking of the ready way of travelling
that his cloak gave him, he ran to the window, opened it,
and jumped out; and unluckily in his haste his cloak
caught and was left hanging, to the great joy of the princess, who knew its worth.

The poor soldier made the best of his way home to his
comrades, on foot and in a very downcast mood; but
the third soldier told him to keep up his heart, and took
his horn and blew a merry tune. At the first blast a
countless troop of foot and horse came rushing to their
aid, and they set out to make war against their enemy.
Then the king's palace was besieged, and he was told that
he must give up the purse and cloak, or that not one
stone should be left upon another. And the king went
into his daughter's chamber and talked with her; but she
said, "Let me try first if I cannot beat them some other
way." So she thought of a cunning scheme to overreach
them, and dressed herself out as a poor girl with a basket
on her arm; and set out by night with her maid, and went
into the enemy's camp as if she wanted to sell trinkets.

In the morning she began to ramble about, singing
ballads so beautifully, that all the tents were left empty,
and the soldiers ran round in crowds and thought of nothing but hearing her sing. Amongst the rest came the
soldier to whom the horn belonged, and as soon as she
saw him she winked to her maid, who slipped slily through
the crowd and went into his tent where it hung, and stole
it away. This done, they both got safely back to the palace; the besieging army went away, the three wonderful
gifts were all left in the hands of the princess, and the
three soldiers were as penniless and forlorn as when the
little man with the red jacket found them in the wood.

Poor fellows! they began to think what was now to
be done. "Comrades," at last said the second soldier, who

had had the purse, "we had better part, we cannot live together, let each seek his bread as well as he can." So he turned to the right, and the other two to the left; for they said they would rather travel together. Then on he strayed till he came to a wood; (now this was the same wood where they had met with so much good luck before;) and he walked on a long time till evening began to fall, when he sat down tired beneath a tree, and soon fell asleep.

Morning dawned, and he was greatly delighted, at opening his eyes, to see that the tree was laden with the most beautiful apples. He was hungry enough, so he soon plucked and ate first one, then a second, then a third apple. A strange feeling came over his nose: when he put the apple to his mouth something was in the way; he felt it; it was his nose, that grew and grew till it hung down to his breast. It did not stop there, still it grew and grew; "Heavens!" thought he, "when will it have done growing?" And well might he ask, for by this time it reached the ground as he sat on the grass, and thus it kept creeping on till he could not bear its weight, or raise himself up; and it seemed as if it would never end, for already it stretched its enormous length all through the wood.

Meantime his comrades were journeying on, till on a sudden one of them stumbled against something. "What can that be?" said the other. They looked, and could think of nothing that it was like but a nose. "We will follow it and find its owner, however," said they; so they traced it up till at last they found their poor comrade lying stretched along under the apple tree. What was to be done? They tried to carry him, but in vain. They caught an ass that was passing by, and raised him upon its back; but it was soon tired of carrying such a load. So they sat down in despair, when up came the little man in the red jacket. "Why, how now, friend?" said he, laughing; "well, I must find a cure for you, I see." So he told them to gather a pear from a tree that grew close by, and the nose would come right again. No time was lost, and the nose was soon brought to its proper size, to the poor soldier's joy.

"I will do something more for you yet," said the little man; "take some of those pears and apples with you; whoever eats one of the apples will have his nose grow like yours just now; but if you give him a pear, all will come right again. Go to the princess and get her to eat some of your apples; her nose will grow twenty times as long as yours did; then look sharp, and you will get what you want of her."

Then they thanked their old friend very heartily for all his kindness, and it was agreed that the poor soldier who had already tried the power of the apple should undertake the task. So he dressed himself up as a gardener's boy, and went to the king's palace, and said he had apples to sell, such as were never seen there before. Every one that saw them was delighted and wanted to taste, but he said they were only for the princess; and she soon sent her maid to buy his stock. They were so ripe and rosy that she soon began eating, and had already eaten three when she too began to wonder what ailed her nose, for it grew and grew, down to the ground, out at the window, and over the garden, nobody knows where.

Then the king made known to all his kingdom, that whoever would heal her of this dreadful disease should be richly rewarded. Many tried, but the princess got no relief. And now the old soldier dressed himself up very sprucely as a doctor, who said he could cure her; so he chopped up some of the apple, and to punish her a little more gave her a dose, saying he would call to-morrow and see her again. The morrow came, and of course, instead of being better, the nose had been growing fast all night, and the poor princess was in a dreadful fright. So the doctor chopped up a very little of the pear and gave her, and said he was sure that would do good, and he would call again the next day. Next day came, and the nose was to be sure a little smaller, but yet it was bigger than it was when the doctor first began to meddle with it.

Then he thought to himself, "I must frighten this cunning princess a little more before I shall get what I want of her;" so he gave her another dose of the apple, and said he would call on the morrow. The morrow came, and the nose was ten times as bad as before. "My good lady," said the doctor; "something works against my medicine, and is too strong for it; but I know by the force of my art what it is; you have stolen goods about you, I am sure, and if you do not give them back, I can do nothing for you." But the princess denied very stoutly that she had anything of the kind. "Very well," said the doctor, "you may do as you please, but I am sure I am right, and you will die if you do not own it." Then he went to the king, and told him how the matter stood. "Daughter," said he, "send back the cloak, the ring, and the horn, that you stole from the right owners."

Then she ordered her maid to fetch all three, and gave them to the doctor, and begged him to give them back to the soldiers; and the moment he had them safe he gave her a whole pear to eat, and the nose came right. And as for the doctor, he put on the cloak, wished the king and all his court a good day, and was soon with his two brothers, who lived from that time happily at home in their palace, except when they took airings in their coach with the three dapple gray horses.

The Five Servants

SOME time ago there reigned in a country many thousands of miles off, an old queen who was very spiteful and delighted in nothing so much as mischief. She had one daughter, who was thought to be the most beautiful princess in the world; but her mother only made use of her as a trap for the unwary; and whenever any suitor who had heard of her beauty came to seek her in marriage, the only answer the old lady gave to each was, that he must undertake some very hard task and forfeit his life if he failed. Many, led by the report of the princess's charms, undertook these tasks, but failed in doing what the queen set them to do. No mercy was ever shown them; but the word was given at once, and off their heads were cut.

Now it happened that a prince who lived in a country far off, heard of the great beauty of this young lady, and said to his father, "Dear father, let me go and try my luck." "No," said the king; "if you go you will surely lose your life." The prince, however, had set his heart so much upon the scheme, that when he found his father was against it he fell very ill, and took to his bed for seven years, and no art could cure him, or recover his lost spirits: so when his father saw that if he went on thus he would die, he said to him with a heart full of grief, "If it must be so, go and try your luck." At this he rose from his bed, recovered his health and spirits, and went forward on his way light of heart and full of joy.

Then on he journeyed over hill and dale, through fair

weather and foul, till one day, as he was riding through a
wood, he thought he saw afar off some large animal upon
the ground, and as he drew near he found that it was a
man lying along upon the grass under the trees; but he
looked more like a mountain than a man, he was so fat
and jolly.   When this big fellow saw the traveller, he
arose, and said, "If you want any one to wait upon you,
you will do well to take me into your service."   "What
should I do with such a fat fellow as you?" said the prince.
"It would be nothing to you if I were three thousand times
as fat," said the man, "so that I do but behave myself
well."   "That's true," answered the prince; "so come
with me, I can put you to some use or another I dare say."
Then the fat man rose up and followed the prince, and
by and by they saw another man lying on the ground with
his ear close to the turf.   The prince said, "What are
you doing there?"   "I am listening," answered the man.
"To what?"   "To all that is going on in the world, for I
can hear everything, I can even hear the grass grow."
"Tell me," said the prince, "what you hear is going on at
the court of the old queen, who has the beautiful
daughter?"   "I hear," said the listener, "the noise of the
sword that is cutting off the head of one of her suitors."
"Well!" said the prince, "I see I shall be able to make
you of use—come along with me!"   They had not gone
far before they saw a pair of feet, and then part of the
legs of a man stretched out; but they were so long that
they could not see the rest of the body, till they had passed
on a good deal further, and at last they came to the body,
and, after going on a while further, to the head; "Bless
me!" said the prince, "what a long rope you are!"   "Oh!"
answered the tall man, "this is nothing, when I choose to
stretch myself to my full length, I am three times as high
as any mountain you have seen on your travels, I warrant

you; I will willingly do what I can to serve you if you will let me." "Come along then," said the prince, "I can turn you to account in some way."

The prince and his train went on further into the wood, and next saw a man lying by the road side basking in the heat of the sun, yet shaking and shivering all over, so that not a limb lay still. "What makes you shiver," said the prince, "while the sun is shining so warm?" "Alas!" answered the man, "the warmer it is, the colder I am; the sun only seems to me like a sharp frost that thrills through all my bones; and on the other hand, when others are what you call cold I begin to be warm, so that I can neither bear the ice for its heat nor the fire for its cold." "You are a queer fellow," said the prince; "but if you have nothing else to do, come along with me." The next thing they saw was a man standing, stretching his neck and looking around him from hill to hill. "What are you looking for so eagerly?" said the prince. "I have such sharp eyes," said the man, "that I can see over woods and fields and hills and dales;—in short, all over the world." "Well," said the prince, "come with me if you will, for I want one more to make up my train."

Then they all journeyed on, and met with no one else till they came to the city where the beautiful princess lived. The prince went straight to the old queen, and said, "Here I am, ready to do any task you set me, if you will give me your daughter as a reward when I have done." "I will set you three tasks," said the queen; "and if you get through all, you shall be the husband of my daughter. First, you must bring me a ring which I dropped in the red sea." The prince went home to his friends and said, "The first task is not an easy one; it is to fetch a ring out of the red sea, so lay your heads together and say what is to be done." Then the sharp-sighted one said, "I will see where it lies," and looked down into the sea, and cried out, "There it lies upon a rock at the bottom." "I would fetch it out," said the tall man, "if I could but see it." "Well!" cried out the fat one, "I will help you to do that," and laid himself down and held his mouth to the water, and drank up the waves till the bottom of the sea was as dry as a meadow. Then the tall man stooped a little and pulled out the ring with his hand, and the prince took it to the old queen, who looked at it, and wondering said, "It is indeed the right ring; you have gone through this task well: but now comes the second; look yonder at the meadow before my palace; see! there are a hundred fat oxen feeding there; you must eat them all up before noon: and underneath in my cellar there are a hundred casks of wine, which you must drink all up." "May I not invite some guests to share the feast with me?" said the prince. "Why, yes!" said the old woman with a spiteful laugh; "you may ask one of your friends to breakfast with you, but no more."

Then the prince went home and said to the fat man, "You must be my guest to-day, and for once you shall eat your fill." So the fat man set to work and ate the hundred oxen without leaving a bit, and asked if that was to be all he should have for his breakfast? and he drank the wine out of the casks without leaving a drop, licking even his fingers when he had done. When the meal was ended, the prince went to the old woman and told her the second task was done. "Your work is not all over, however," muttered the old hag to herself; "I will catch you yet, you shall not keep your head upon your shoulders if I can help it." "This evening," said she, "I will bring my daughter into your house and leave her with you; you shall sit together there, but take care that you do not fall asleep; for I shall come when the clock strikes

twelve, and if she is not then with you, you are undone."
"O!" thought the prince, "it is an easy task to keep such a
watch as that; I will take care to keep my eyes open."
So he called his servants and told them all that the old
woman had said. "Who knows though," said he, "but
there may be some trick at the bottom of this? it is as
well to be upon our guard and keep watch that the young
lady does not get away." When it was night the old
woman brought her daughter to the prince's house; then
the tall man twisted himself round about it, the listener put
his ear to the ground, the fat man placed himself before
the door so that no living soul could enter, and the sharp-
eyed one looked out afar and watched. Within sat the
princess without saying a word, but the moon shone bright
through the window upon her face, and the prince gazed
upon her wonderful beauty. And while he looked upon
her with a heart full of joy and love, his eyelids did not
droop; but at eleven o'clock the old woman cast a charm
over them so that they all fell asleep, and the princess vanished in a moment.

And thus they slept till a quarter to twelve, when the
charm had no longer any power over them, and they all
awoke. "Alas! alas! woe is me," cried the prince; "now
I am lost for ever." And his faithful servants began to
weep over their unhappy lot; but the listener said, "Be
still and I will listen;" so he listened a while, and cried
out, "I hear her bewailing her fate;" and the sharp-sighted
man looked, and said, "I see her sitting on a rock three
hundred miles hence; now help us, my tall friend; if you
stand up, you will reach her in two steps." "Very well,"
answered the tall man; and in an instant, before one could
turn one's head round, he was at the foot of the enchanted rock. Then the tall man took the young lady in
his arms and carried her back to the prince a moment

before it struck twelve; and they all sat down again and made merry. And when the clock struck twelve the old queen came sneaking by with a spiteful look, as if she was going to say "Now he is mine;" nor could she think otherwise, for she knew that her daughter was but the moment before on the rock three hundred miles off; but when she came and saw her daughter in the prince's room, she started, and said, "There is somebody here who can do more than I can." However, she now saw that she could no longer avoid giving the prince her daughter for a wife, but said to her in a whisper, "It is a shame that you should be won by servants, and not have a husband of your own choice."

Now the young lady was of a very proud haughty temper, and her anger was raised to such a pitch, that the next morning she ordered three hundred loads of wood to be brought and piled up; and told the prince it was true he had by the help of his servants done the three tasks, but that before she would marry him some one must sit upon that pile of wood when it was set on fire and bear the heat. She thought to herself that though his servants had done everything else for him, none of them would go so far as to burn themselves for him, and that then she should put his love to the test by seeing whether he would sit upon it himself. But she was mistaken; for when the servants heard this, they said, "We have all done something but the frosty man; now his turn is come;" and they took him and put him on the wood and set it on fire. Then the fire rose and burnt for three long days, till all the wood was gone; and when it was out, the frosty man stood in the midst of the ashes trembling like an aspen-leaf, and said, "I never shivered so much in my life; if it had lasted much longer, I should have lost the use of my limbs."

When the princess had no longer any plea for delay, she saw that she was bound to marry the prince; but when they were going to church, the old woman said, "I will never consent;" and sent secret orders out to her horseman to kill and slay all before them and bring back her daughter before she could be married. However, the listener had pricked up his ears and heard all that the old woman said, and told it to the prince. So they made haste and got to the church first, and were married; and then the five servants took their leave and went away saying, "We will go and try our luck in the world on our own account."

The prince set out with his wife, and at the end of the first day's journey came to a village, where a swineherd was feeding his swine; and as they came near he said to his wife, "Do you know who I am? I am not a prince, but a poor swineherd; he whom you see yonder with the swine is my father, and our business will be to help him to tend them." Then he went into the swineherd's hut with her, and ordered her royal clothes to be taken away in the night; so that when she awoke in the morning, she had nothing to put on, till the woman who lived there made a great favour of giving her an old gown and a pair of worsted stockings. "If it were not for your husband's sake," said she, "I would not have given you anything." Then the poor princess gave herself up for lost, and believed that her husband must indeed be a swineherd; but she thought she would make the best of it, and began to help him to feed them, and said, "It is a just reward for my pride." When this had lasted eight days she could bear it no longer, for her feet were all over wounds, and as she sat down and wept by the way-side, some people came up to her and pitied her, and asked if she knew what her husband really was. "Yes," said she; "a swineherd; he is just gone out to market with some of his stock." But they said, "Come along and we

will take you to him;" and they took her over the hill to
the palace of the prince's father; and when they came into
the hall, there stood her husband so richly drest in his royal
clothes that she did not know him till he fell upon her neck
and kissed her, and said, "I have borne much for your
sake, and you too have also borne a great deal for me."
Then the guests were sent for, and the marriage feast was
given, and all made merry and danced and sang, and the
best wish that I can wish is, that you and I had been
there too.

Cat-Skin

THERE was once a king, whose queen had hair of the purest gold, and was so beautiful that her match was not to be met with on the whole face of the earth. But this beautiful queen fell ill, and when she felt that her end drew near, she called the king to her and said, "Vow to me that you will never marry again, unless you meet with a wife who is as beautiful as I am, and who has golden hair like mine." Then when the king in his grief had vowed all she asked, she shut her eyes and died. But the king was not to be comforted, and for a long time never thought of taking another wife. At last, however, his counsellors said, "This will not do; the king must marry again, that we may have a queen." So messengers were sent far and wide, to seek for a bride who was as beautiful as the late queen. But there was no princess in the world so beautiful; and if there had been, still there was not one to be found who had such golden hair. So the messengers came home and had done all their work for nothing.

Now the king had a daughter who was just as beautiful as her mother, and had the same golden hair. And when she had grown up, the king looked at her and saw that she was just like his late queen: then he said to his courtiers, "May I not marry my daughter? she is the very image of my dead wife: unless I have her, I shall not find any bride upon the whole earth, and you say there must be a queen." When the courtiers heard this, they were shocked, and said, "Heaven forbid that a father should marry his daughter! out of so great a sin no good can come." And his daughter was also shocked, but hoped the king would soon give up such thoughts: so she said to him, "Before I marry any one I must have three dresses; one must be of gold like the sun, another must be of shining silver like the moon, and a third must be dazzling as the stars: besides this, I want a mantle of a thousand different kinds of fur put together, to which every beast in the kingdom must give a part of his skin." And thus she thought he would think of the matter no more. But the king made the most skilful workmen in his kingdom weave the three dresses, one as golden as the sun, another as silvery as the moon, and a third shining like the stars; and his hunters were told to hunt out all the beasts in his kingdom and take the finest fur out of their skins: and so a mantle of a thousand furs was made.

When all was ready, the king sent them to her; but she got up in the night when all were asleep, and took three of her trinkets, a golden ring, a golden necklace, and a golden brooch; and packed the three dresses of the sun, moon, and stars, up in a nut-shell, and wrapped herself up in the mantle of all sorts of fur, and besmeared her face and hands with soot. Then she threw herself upon heaven for help in her need, and went away and journeyed on the whole night, till at last she came to a large wood. As she was very tired, she sat herself down in the hollow of a tree and soon fell asleep: and there she slept on till it was mid-day: and it happened, that as the king to whom the wood belonged was hunting in it, his dogs came to the tree, and began to snuff about and run round and round, and then to bark. "Look sharp," said the king to the huntsmen, "and see what sort of game lies there." And the huntsmen went up to the tree, and when they came back again said, "In the hollow tree there lies a most wonderful beast, such as we never saw before; its skin seems of a thousand kinds of fur, but there it lies fast asleep. "See," said the king, "if you can catch it alive, and we will take it with us." So the huntsmen took it up, and the maiden awoke and was greatly frightened, and said, "I am a poor child that has neither father nor mother left; have pity on me and take me with you." Then they said, "Yes, Miss Cat-skin, you will do for the kitchen; you can sweep up the ashes and do things of that sort." So they put her in the coach and took her home to the king's palace. Then they showed her a little corner under the staircase where no light of day ever peeped in, and said, "Cat-skin, you may lie and sleep there." And she was sent into the kitchen, and made to fetch wood and water, to blow the fire, pluck the poultry, pick the herbs, sift the ashes, and do all the dirty work.

Thus Cat-skin lived for a long time very sorrowfully. "Ah! pretty princess!" thought she, "what will now become of thee!" But it happened one day that a feast was to be held in the king's castle; so she said to the cook, "May I go up a little while and see what is going on? I will take care and stand behind the door." And the cook said, "Yes, you may go, but be back again in half an hour's time to rake out the ashes." Then she took her little lamp, and went into her cabin, and took off the fur skin, and washed the soot from off her face and hands, so that her beauty shone forth like the sun from behind the clouds. She next opened her nutshell, and brought out of it the dress that shone like the sun, and so went to the feast. Every one made way for her, for nobody knew her, and they thought she could be no less than a king's daughter. But the king came up to her and held out his hand and danced with her, and he thought in his heart, "I never saw any one half so beautiful."

When the dance was at an end, she curtsied; and when the king looked round for her, she was gone, no one knew whither. The guards who stood at the castle gate were called in; but they had seen no one. The truth was, that she had run into her little cabin, pulled off her dress, blacked her face and hands, put on the fur-skin cloak, and was Cat-skin again. When she went into the kitchen to her work, and began to rake the ashes, the cook said, "Let that alone till the morning, and heat the king's soup; I should like to run up now and give a peep; but take care you don't let a hair fall into it, or you will run a chance of never eating again."

As soon as the cook went away, Cat-skin heated the king's soup and toasted up a slice of bread as nicely as ever she could; and when it was ready, she went and looked in the cabin for her little golden ring, and put it into the dish in which the soup was. When the dance was over, the king ordered his soup to be brought in, and it pleased him so well, that he thought he had never tasted any so good before. At the bottom he saw a gold ring lying, and as he could not make out how it had got there, he ordered the cook to be sent for. The cook was frightened when she heard the order, and said to Cat-skin, "You must have let a hair fall into the soup; if it be so, you will have a good beating." Then she went before the king, and he asked her who had cooked the soup. "I did," answered she. But the king said, "That is not true; it was better done than you could do it." Then she answered, "To tell the truth, I did not cook it, but Cat-skin did." "Then let Cat-skin come up," said the king: and when she came, he said to her, "Who are you?" "I am a poor child," said she, "who has lost both father and mother." "How came you in my palace?" asked he. "I am good for nothing," said she, "but to be scullion girl, and to have boots and shoes thrown at my head." "But how did you get the ring that was in the soup?" asked the king. But she would not own that she knew anything about the ring; so the king sent her away again about her business.

After a time there was another feast, and Cat-skin asked the cook to let her go up and see it as before. "Yes," said she, "but come back again in half an hour, and cook the king the soup that he likes so much." Then she ran to her little cabin, washed herself quickly, and took the dress out which was silvery as the moon, and put it on; and when she went in looking like a king's daughter, the king went up to her and rejoiced at seeing her again, and when the dance began, he danced with her. After the dance was at an end, she managed to slip out so slily that the king did not see where she was gone; but she sprang into her little cabin and made herself into Cat-skin again, and went into the kitchen to cook the soup. Whilst the cook was above, she got the golden necklace, and dropped it into the soup; then it was brought to the king, who ate it, and it pleased him as well as before; so he sent for the cook, who was again forced to tell him that Cat-skin had cooked it. Cat-skin was brought again before the king; but she still told him that she was only fit to have the boots and shoes thrown at her head.

But when the king had ordered a feast to be got ready for the third time, it happened just the same as before. "You must be a witch, Cat-skin," said the cook; "for you always put something into the soup, so that it pleases the king better than mine." However, she let her go up as before. Then she put on the dress which sparkled like the stars, and went into the ballroom in it; and the king danced with her again, and thought she had never looked so beautiful as she did then: so whilst he was dancing with her, he put a gold ring on her finger without her seeing it, and ordered that the dance should be kept up a long time. When it was at an end, he would have held her fast by the hand; but she slipt away and sprang so quickly through the crowd that he lost sight of her; and she ran as fast as she could into her little cabin under the stairs. But this time she kept away too long, and staid beyond the half-hour; so she had not time to take off her fine dress, but threw her fur mantle over it, and in her haste did not soot herself all over, but left one finger white.

Then she ran into the kitchen, and cooked the king's soup; and as soon as the cook was gone, she put the golden brooch into the dish. When the king got to the bottom, he ordered Cat-skin to be called once more, and soon saw the white finger and the ring that he had put on it whilst they were dancing: so he seized her hand, and kept fast hold of it, and when she wanted to loose herself and spring away, the fur cloak fell off a little on one side, and the starry dress sparkled underneath it. Then he got hold of the fur and tore it off, and her golden hair and beautiful form were seen, and she could no longer hide herself: so she washed the soot and ashes from off her face, and showed herself to be the most beautiful princess upon the face of the earth. But the king said, "You are my beloved bride, and we will never more be parted from each other." And the wedding feast was held, and a merry day it was.

The Robber-Bridegroom

THERE was once a miller who had a pretty daughter; and when she was grown up, he thought to himself, "If a seemly man should come to ask her for his wife, I will give her to him that she may be taken care of." Now it so happened that one did come, who seemed to be very rich, and behaved very well; and as the miller saw no reason to find fault with him, he said he should have his daughter. Yet the maiden did not love him quite so well as a bride ought to love her bridegroom, but, on the other hand, soon began to feel a kind of inward shuddering whenever she saw or thought of him.

One day he said to her, "Why do you not come and see my home, since you are to be my bride?" "I do not know where your house is," said the girl. "'Tis out there," said her bridegroom, "yonder in the dark green wood." Then she began to try and avoid going, and said, "But I cannot find the way thither." "Well, but you must come and see me next Sunday," said the bridegroom; "I have asked some guests to meet you, and that you may find your way through the wood, I will strew ashes for you along the path."

When Sunday came and the maiden was to go out, she felt very much troubled, and took care to put on two pockets, and filled them with peas and beans. She soon came to the wood, and found her path strewed with ashes; so she followed the track, and at every step threw a pea on the right and a bean on the left side of the road; and thus she journeyed on the whole day till she came to a house which stood in the middle of the dark wood. She saw no one within, and all was quite still, till on a sudden she heard a voice cry,

"Turn again, bonny bride!
Turn again home!
Haste from the robber's den,
Haste away home!"

She looked around, and saw a little bird sitting in a cage that hung over the door; and he flapped his wings, and again she heard him cry,

"Turn again, bonny bride!
Turn again home!
Haste from the robber's den,
Haste away home!"

However, the bride went in, and roamed along from one room to another, and so over all the house; but it was quite empty, and not a soul could she see. At last she came to a room where a very very old woman was sitting. "Pray, can you tell me, my good woman," said she, "if my bridegroom lives here?" "Ah! my dear child!" said the old woman, "you are come to fall into the trap laid for you: your wedding can only be with Death, for the robber will surely take away your life; if I do not save you, you are lost!" So she hid the bride behind a large cask, and then said to her, "Do not stir or move yourself at all, lest some harm should befall you; and when the robbers are asleep we will run off; I have long wished to get away."

She had hardly done this when the robbers came in, and brought another young maiden with them that had been ensnared like the bride. Then they began to feast and drink, and were deaf to her shrieks and groans: and they gave her some wine to drink, three glasses, one of white, one of red, and one of yellow; upon which she fainted and fell down dead. Now the bride began to grow very uneasy behind the cask, and thought that she too must die in her turn. Then the one that was to be her bridegroom saw that there was a gold ring on the little finger of the maiden they had murdered; and as he tried to snatch it off, it flew up in the air and fell down again behind the cask just in the bride's lap. So he took a light and searched about all round the room for it, but could not find anything; and another of the robbers said, "Have you looked behind the large cask yet?" "Pshaw!" said the old woman, "Come, sit still and eat your supper now, and leave the ring alone till to-morrow; it won't run away, I'll warrant."

So the robbers gave up the search, and went on with their eating and drinking; but the old woman dropped a sleeping-draught into their wine, and they laid themselves down and slept, and snored roundly. And when the bride heard this, she stepped out from behind the cask; and as she was forced to walk over the sleepers, who were lying about on the floor, she trembled lest she should awaken some of them. But heaven aided her, so that she soon got through her danger; and the old woman went upstairs with her, and they both ran away from this murderous den. The ashes that had been strewed were now all blown away, but the peas and beans had taken root and were springing up, and showed her the way by the light of the moon. So they walked the whole night, and in the morning reached the mill; when the bride told her father all that had happened to her.

As soon as the day arrived when the wedding was to take place, the bridegroom came; and the miller gave orders that all his friends and relations should be asked to the feast. And as they were all sitting at table, one of them proposed that each of the guests should tell some tale. Then the bridegroom said to the bride, when it came to her turn, "Well, my dear, do you know nothing? come, tell us some story." "Yes," answered she, "I can tell you a dream that I dreamt. I once thought I was going through a wood, and went on and on till I came to a house where there was not a soul to be seen, but a bird in a cage, that cried out twice,

> "Turn again, bonny bride!
>   Turn again home!
> Haste from the robber's den,
>   Haste away home!"

—I only dreamt that, my love. Then I went through all the rooms, which were quite empty, until I came to a room where there sat a very old woman; and I said to her, 'Does my bridegroom live here?' but she answered, 'Ah! my dear child! you have fallen into a murderer's snare; your bridegroom will surely kill you'—I only dreamt that, my love. But she hid me behind a large cask; and hardly had she done this, when the robbers came in, dragging a young woman along with them; then they gave her three kinds of wine to drink, white, red, and yellow, till she fell dead upon the ground—I only dreamt that, my love. After they had done this, one of the robbers saw that there was a gold ring on her little finger, and snatched at it; but it flew up to the ceiling, and then fell behind the great cask just where I was, and into my lap; and here is the ring!" At these words she brought out the ring and showed it to the guests.

When the robber saw all this, and heard what she said,

he grew as pale as ashes with fright, and wanted to run off; but the guests held him fast and gave him up to justice, so that he and all his gang met with the due reward of their wickedness.

The Three Sluggards

THE king of a country a long way off had three sons. He liked one as well as another, and did not know which to leave his kingdom to after his death: so when he was dying he called them all to him, and said, "Dear children, the laziest sluggard of the three shall be king after me." "Then," said the eldest, "the kingdom is mine; for I am so lazy that when I lie down to sleep, if anything were to fall into my eyes so that I could not shut them, I should still go on sleeping." The second said, "Father, the kingdom belongs to me; for I am so lazy that when I sit by the fire to warm myself, I would sooner have my toes burnt than take the trouble to draw my legs back." The third said, "Father, the kingdom is mine; for I am so lazy that if I were going to be hanged, with the rope round my neck, and somebody were to put a sharp knife into my hands to cut it, I had rather be hanged than raise my hand to do it." When the father heard this, he said, "You shall be the king; for you are the fittest man."

The Seven Ravens

THERE was once a man who had seven sons, and last of all one daughter. Although the little girl was very pretty, she was so weak and small that they thought she could not live; but they said she should at once be christened.

So the father sent one of his sons in haste to the spring to get some water, but the other six ran with him. Each wanted to be first at drawing the water, and so they were in such a hurry that all let their pitchers fall into the well, and they stood very foolishly looking at one another, and did not know what to do, for none dared go home. In the meantime the father was uneasy, and could not tell what made the young men stay so long. "Surely," said he, "the whole seven must have forgotten themselves over some game of play;" and when he had waited still longer and they yet did not come, he flew into a rage and wished them all turned into ravens. Scarcely had he spoken these words when he heard a croaking over his head, and looked up and saw seven ravens as black as coals flying round and round. Sorry as he was to see his wish so fulfilled, he did not know how what was done could be undone, and comforted himself as well as he could for the loss of his seven sons with his dear little daughter, who soon became stronger and every day more beautiful.

For a long time she did not know that she had ever had any brothers; for her father and mother took care not to speak of them before her: but one day by chance she heard the people about her speak of them. "Yes," said they, "she is beautiful indeed, but still 'tis a pity that her brothers should have been lost for her sake." Then she was much grieved, and went to her father and mother, and asked if she had any brothers, and what had become of them. So they dared not longer hide the truth from her, but said it was the will of heaven, and that her birth was only the innocent cause of it; but the little girl mourned sadly about it every day, and thought herself bound to do all she could to bring her brothers back; and she had neither rest nor ease, till at length one day she stole away, and set out into the wide world to find her brothers, wherever they might be, and free them, whatever it might cost her.

She took nothing with her but a little ring which her father and mother had given her, a loaf of bread in case she should be hungry, a little pitcher of water in case she should be thirsty, and a little stool to rest upon when she should be weary. Thus she went on and on, and journeyed till she came to the world's end: then she came to the sun, but the sun looked much too hot and fiery; so she ran away quickly to the moon, but the moon was cold and chilly, and said, "I smell flesh and blood this way!" so she took herself away in a hurry and came to the stars, and the stars were friendly and kind to her, and each star sat upon his own little stool; but the morning-star rose up and gave her a little piece of wood, and said, "If you have not this little piece of wood, you cannot unlock the castle that stands on the glass-mountain, and there your brothers live." The little girl took the piece of wood, rolled it up in a little cloth, and went on again until she came to the glass-mountain, and found the door shut. Then she felt for the little piece of wood; but when she unwrapped the cloth it was not there, and she saw she had lost the gift of the good stars. What was to be done? she wanted to save her brothers, and had no key of the castle of the glass-mountain; so this faithful little sister took a knife out of her pocket and cut off her little finger, that was just the size of the piece of wood she had lost, and put it in the door and opened it.

As she went in, a little dwarf came up to her, and said, "What are you seeking for?" "I seek for my brothers, the seven ravens," answered she. Then the dwarf said, "My masters are not at home; but if you will wait till they come, pray step in." Now the little dwarf was getting their dinner ready, and he brought their food upon seven little plates, and their drink in seven little glasses, and set them upon the table, and out of each little plate their sister ate a small piece, and out of each little glass she drank a small drop; but she let the ring that she had brought with her fall into the last glass.

On a sudden she heard a fluttering and croaking in the air, and the dwarf said, "Here come my masters." When they came in, they wanted to eat and drink, and looked for their little plates and glasses. Then said one after the other, "Who has eaten from my little plate? and who has been drinking out of my little glass?

> "Caw! Caw! well I ween
> Mortal lips have this way been."

When the seventh came to the bottom of his glass, and found there the ring, he looked at it, and knew that it was his father's and mother's, and said, "Oh that our little sister would but come! then we should be free." When the little girl heard this (for she stood behind the door all the time and listened), she ran forward, and in an instant all the ravens took their right form again; and all hugged and kissed each other, and went merrily home.

Roland and May-Bird

THERE was once a poor man who went every day to cut wood in the forest. One day as he went along he heard a cry like a little child's; so he followed the sound till at last he looked up a high tree, and on one of the branches sat a very little girl. Its mother had fallen asleep, and a vulture had taken it out of her lap and flown away with it and left it on the tree. Then the wood-cutter climbed up, took the little child down, and said to himself, "I will take this poor child home and bring it up with my own son Roland." So he brought it to his cottage, and both grew up together; and he called the little girl May-bird, because he had found her on a tree in May; and May-bird and Roland were so very fond of each other that they were never happy but when they were together.

But the wood-cutter became very poor, and had nothing in the world he could call his own, and indeed he had scarcely bread enough for his wife and the two children to eat. At last the time came when even that was all gone, and he knew not where to seek for help in his need. Then at night, as he lay on his bed and turned himself here and there, restless and full of care, his wife said to him, "Husband, listen to me, and take the two children out early to-morrow morning; give each of them a piece of bread, and then lead them into the midst of the wood where it is thickest, make a fire for them, and go away and leave them alone to shift for themselves, for we can no longer keep them here." "No, wife," said the husband, "I cannot find it in my heart to leave the children to the wild beasts of the forest, who would soon tear them to pieces." "Well, if you will not do as I say," answered the wife, "we must all starve together:" and she let him have no peace until he came into her plan.

Meantime the poor children too were lying awake restless, and weak from hunger, so that they heard all that their mother said to her husband. "Now," thought May-bird to herself, "it is all up with us:" and she began to weep. But Roland crept to her bedside, and said, "Do not be afraid, May-bird, I will find out some help for us." Then he got up, put on his jacket, and opened the door and went out.

The moon shone bright upon the little court before the cottage, and the white pebbles glittered like daisies on the green meadows. So he stooped down, and put as many as he could into his pocket, and then went back to the house. "Now, May-bird," said he, "rest in peace;" and he went to bed and fell fast asleep.

Early in the morning, before the sun had risen, the woodman's wife came and woke them. "Get up, children," said she, "we are going into the wood; there is a piece of bread for each of you, but take care of it and keep some for the afternoon." May-bird took the bread and carried it in her apron, because Roland had his pocket full of stones, and they made their way into the wood.

After they had walked on for a time, Roland stood still and looked towards home, and after a while turned again, and so on several times. Then his father said, "Roland, why do you keep turning and lagging about so? move your legs on a little faster." "Ah! father," answered Roland, "I am stopping to look at my white cat that sits on the roof, and wants to say good-bye to me." "You little fool!" said his mother, "that is not your cat; 'tis the morning sun shining on the chimney top." Now Roland had not been looking at the cat, but had all the while been staying behind to drop from his pocket one white pebble after another along the road.

When they came into the midst of the wood, the woodman said, "Run about, children, and pick up some wood, and I will make a fire to keep us all warm." So they piled up a little heap of brush-wood, and set it a-fire; and as the flame burnt bright, the mother said, "Now set yourselves by the fire and go to sleep, while we go and cut wood in the forest; be sure you wait till we come again and fetch you." Roland and May-bird sat by the fire-side till the afternoon, and then each of them ate their piece of bread. They fancied the woodman was still in the wood, because they thought they heard the blows of his axe; but it was a bough which he had cunningly hung upon a tree, so that the wind blew it backwards and forwards, and it sounded like the axe as it hit the other boughs. Thus they waited till evening; but the woodman and his wife kept away, and no one came to fetch them.

When it was quite dark May-bird began to cry; but Roland said, "Wait awhile till the moon rises." And when the moon rose, he took her by the hand, and there lay the pebbles along the ground, glittering like new pieces of money, and marked the way out. Towards morning they came again to the woodman's house, and he was glad in his heart when he saw the children again; for he had grieved at leaving them alone. His wife also seemed to be glad; but in her heart she was angry at it.

Not long after there was again no bread in the house, and May-bird and Roland heard the wife say to her husband, "The children found their way back once, and I took it in good part; but there is only half a loaf of bread left

for them in the house; to-morrow you must take them
deeper into the wood, that they may not find their way out,
or we shall all be starved." It grieved the husband in his
heart to do as his wife wished, and he thought it would be
better to share their last morsel with the children; but as
he had done as she said once, he did not dare to say no.
When the children had heard all their plan, Roland got
up and wanted to pick up pebbles as before; but when he
came to the door he found his mother had locked it. Still
he comforted May-bird, and said, "Sleep in peace, dear
May-bird; God is very kind and will help us." Early in
the morning a piece of bread was given to each of them,
but still smaller than the one they had before. Upon the
road Roland crumbled his in his pocket, and often stood
still, and threw a crumb upon the ground. "Why do you
lag so behind, Roland?" said the woodman; "go your ways
on before." "I am looking at my little dove that is sitting
upon the roof and wants to say good-bye to me." "You
silly boy!" said the wife, "that is not your little dove, it is
the morning sun that shines on the chimney top." But
Roland went on crumbling his bread, and throwing it on
the ground. And thus they went on still further into the
wood, where they had never been before in all their life.
There they were again told to sit down by a large fire, and
sleep; and the woodman and his wife said they would come
in the evening and fetch them away. In the afternoon
Roland shared May-bird's bread, because he had strewed
all his upon the road; but the day passed away, and evening passed away too, and no one came to the poor children.
Still Roland comforted May-bird, and said, "Wait till the
moon rises; then I shall see the crumbs of bread which I
have strewed, and they will show us the way home."

The moon rose; but when Roland looked for the
crumbs, they were gone; for thousands of little birds in

the wood had found them and picked them up. Roland, however, set out to try and find his way home; but they soon lost themselves in the wilderness, and went on through the night and all the next day, till at last they lay down and fell asleep for weariness: and another day they went on as before, but still did not reach the end of the wood, and were as hungry as could be, for they had nothing to eat.

In the afternoon of the third day they came to a strange little hut, made of bread, with a roof of cake, and windows of sparkling sugar. "Now we will sit down and eat till we have had enough," said Roland; "I will eat off the roof for my share; do you eat the windows, May-bird, they will be nice and sweet for you." Whilst May-bird, however, was picking at the sugar, a sweet pretty voice called from within:

"Tip, tap! who goes there?"

But the children answered:

"The wind, the wind,
That blows through the air;"

and went on eating; and May-bird broke out a round pane of the window for herself, and Roland tore off a large piece of cake from the roof, when the door opened, and a little old fairy came gliding out. At this May-bird and Roland were so frightened, that they let fall what they had in their hands. But the old lady shook her head, and said, "Dear children, where have you been wandering about? come in with me; you shall have something good." So she took them both by the hand, and led them into her little hut, and brought out plenty to eat—milk and pancakes, with sugar, apples, and nuts; and then two beautiful little beds were got ready, and May-bird and Roland laid themselves down, and thought they were in heaven: but the fairy was a spiteful one, and had made her pretty sweetmeat house to entrap little children. Early in the morning, before they were awake, she went to their little beds, and when she saw the two sleeping and looking so sweetly, she had no pity on them, but was glad they were in her power. Then she took up Roland, and put him in a little coop by himself; and when he awoke, he found himself behind a grating, shut up as little chickens are: but she shook May-bird, and called out, "Get up, you lazy little thing, and fetch some water; and go into the kitchen and cook something good to eat: your brother is shut up yonder; I shall first fatten him, and when he is fat, I think I shall eat him."

When the fairy was gone, the little girl watched her time and got up and ran to Roland, and told him what she had heard, and said, "We must run away quickly, for the old woman is a bad fairy, and will kill us." But Roland said, "You must first steal away her fairy wand, that we may save ourselves, if she should follow." Then the little maiden ran back, and fetched the magic wand, and away they went together; so when the old fairy came back, she could see no one at home, and sprang in a great rage to the window, and looked out into the wide world (which she could do far and near), and a long way off she spied May-bird running away with her dear Roland; "You are already a great way off," said she; "but you will still fall into my hands." Then she put on her boots, which walked several miles at a step, and scarcely made two steps with them, before she overtook the children: but May-bird saw that the fairy was coming after them, and by the help of the wand turned her dear Roland into a lake, and herself into a swan which swam about in the middle of it. So the fairy set herself down on the shore, and took a great deal of trouble to decoy the swan, and threw crumbs of bread to it; but it would not come near her, and she was forced to go home in the evening, without taking her revenge. And May-bird changed herself and her dear Roland back into their own forms once more and they went journeying on the whole night until the dawn of day; and then the maiden turned herself into a beautiful rose, which grew in the midst of a quickset hedge, and Roland sat by the side and played upon his flute.

The fairy soon came striding along. "Good piper," said she, "may I pluck the beautiful rose for myself?" "Oh yes," answered he; "and I will play to you meantime." So when she had crept into the hedge in a great hurry to gather the flower (for she well knew what it was), he began to play upon his flute; and, whether she liked it or not, such was the wonderful power of the music that she was forced to dance a merry jig, on and on without any rest. And as he did not cease playing a moment, the thorns at length tore the clothes from off her body, and pricked her sorely, and there she stuck quite fast.

Then May-bird was free once more; but she was very tired, and Roland said, "Now I will hasten home for help, and by and by we will be married." And May-bird said, "I will stay here in the meantime and wait for you; and, that no one may know me, I will turn myself into a stone and lie in the corner of yonder field." Then Roland went away, and May-bird was to wait for him. But Roland met with another maiden, who pleased him so much that he stopped where she lived, and forgot his former friend; and when May-bird had staid in the field a long time, and found he did not come back, she became quite sorrowful, and turned herself into a little daisy, and thought to herself, "Some one will come and tread me under foot, and so my sorrows will end." But it so happened that as a shepherd was keeping watch in the field he found the flower, and thinking it very pretty, took it home, placed it in a box in his room, and said, "I have never found so pretty a flower before." From that time everything throve wonderfully at the shepherd's house: when he got up in the morning, all the household work was ready done; the room was swept and cleaned; the fire made, and the water fetched: and in the afternoon, when he came home, the table-cloth was laid and a good dinner ready set for him. He could not make out how all this happened; for he saw no one in his house; and although it pleased him well enough, he was at length troubled to think how it could be, and went to a cunning woman who lived hard by, and asked her what he should do. She said, "There must be witchcraft in it; look out to-morrow morning early, and see if anything stirs about in the room; if it does, throw a white cloth at once over it, and then the witchcraft will be stopped." The shepherd did as she said, and the next morning saw the box open and the daisy come out: then he sprang up quickly and threw a white cloth over it: in an instant the spell was broken, and May-bird stood before him; for it was she who had taken care of his house for him; and as she was so beautiful he asked her if she would marry him. She said "No," because she wished to be faithful to her dear Roland; but she agreed to stay and keep house for him.

Time passed on, and Roland was to be married to the maiden that he had found; and according to an old custom in that land, all the maidens were to come and sing songs in praise of the bride and bridegroom. But May-bird was so grieved when she heard that her dearest Roland had forgotten her, and was to be married to another, that her heart seemed as if it would burst within her, and she would not go for a long time.   At length she was forced to go with the rest; but she kept hiding herself behind the others until she was left the last.   Then she could not any longer help coming forward; and the moment she began to sing, Roland sprang up, and cried out, "That is the true bride; I will have no other but her"; for he knew her by the sound of her voice; and all that he had forgotten came back into his mind, and his heart was opened towards her. So faithful May-bird was married to her dear Roland, and there was an end of her sorrows; and from that time forward she lived happily till she died.

The Mouse, the Bird, and the Sausage

ONCE upon a time a mouse, a bird, and a sausage took it into their heads to keep house together: and to be sure they managed to live for a long time very comfortably and happily; and beside that added a great deal to their store, so as to become very rich. It was the bird's business to fly every day into the forest and bring wood; the mouse had to carry the water, to make the fire, and lay the cloth for dinner; but the sausage was cook to the household.

He who is too well off often begins to be lazy and to long for something fresh. Now it happened one day that our bird met with one of his friends, to whom he boasted greatly of his good plight. But the other bird laughed at him for a poor fool, who worked hard, whilst the two at home had an easy job of it: for when the mouse had made her fire and fetched the water, she went and laid down in her own little room till she was called to lay the cloth; and the sausage sat by the pot, and had nothing to do but to see that the food was well cooked; and when it was meal time, had only to butter, salt, and get it ready to eat, which it could do in a minute. The bird flew home, and having laid his burden on the ground, they all sat down to table, and after they had made their meal slept soundly until the next morning. Could any life be more glorious than this?

The next day the bird, who had been told what to do by his friend, would not go into the forest, saying, he had waited on them, and been made a fool of long enough; they should change about, and take their turns at the work.

327

Although the mouse and the sausage begged hard that things might go on as they were, the bird carried the day. So they cast lots, and the lot fell upon the sausage to fetch wood, while the mouse was to be cook, and the bird was to bring the water.

What happened by thus taking people from their proper work? The sausage set out towards the wood, the little bird made a fire, the mouse set on the pot, and only waited for the sausage to come home and bring wood for the next day. But the sausage kept away so long that they both thought something must have happened to him, and the bird flew out a little way to look out for him; but not far off he found a dog on the road, who said he had met with a poor little sausage, and taking him for fair prey, had laid hold of him and knocked him down. The bird made a charge against the dog of open robbery and murder; but words were of no use; for the dog said, he found the sausage out of its proper work, and under false colours; and so he was taken for a spy and lost his life. The little bird took up the wood very sorrowfully and went home and told what he had seen and heard. The mouse and he were very much grieved, but agreed to do their best and keep together.

The little bird undertook to spread the table, and the mouse got ready the dinner; but when she went to dish it up, she fell into the pot and was drowned. When the bird came into the kitchen and wanted the dinner to put upon the table, no cook was to be seen; so he threw the wood about here, there, and everywhere, and called and sought on all sides, but still could not find the cook. Meantime the fire fell upon the wood and set it on fire; the bird hastened away to get water, but his bucket fell into the well, and he after it; and so ends the story of this clever family.

The Juniper Tree

A LONG while ago, perhaps as much as two thousand years, there was a rich man who had a wife of whom he was very fond; but they had no children. Now in the garden before the house where they lived, there stood a juniper tree; and one winter's day as the lady was standing under the juniper tree, paring an apple, she cut her finger, and the drops of blood trickled down upon the snow. "Ah!" said she, sighing deeply and looking down upon the blood, "how happy should I be if I had a little child as white as snow and as red as blood!" And as she was saying this, she grew quite cheerful, and was sure her wish would be fulfilled. And after a little time the snow went away, and soon afterwards the fields began to look green. Next the spring came, and the meadows were dressed with flowers; the trees put forth their green leaves; the young branches shed their blossoms upon the ground; and the little birds sang through the groves. And then came summer, and the sweet-smelling flowers of the juniper tree began to unfold; and the lady's heart leaped within her, and she fell on her knees for joy. But when autumn drew near, the fruit was thick upon the trees. Then the lady plucked the red berries from the juniper tree, and looked sad and sorrowful; and she called her husband to her, and said, "If I die, bury me under the juniper tree." Not long after this a pretty little child was born; it was, as the lady wished, as red as blood, and as white as snow; and as soon as she had looked upon it, her joy overcame her, and she fainted away and died.

Then her husband buried her under the juniper tree, and wept and mourned over her; but after a little while he grew better, and at length dried up his tears, and married another wife.

Time passed on, and he had a daughter born; but the child of his first wife, that was as red as blood, and as white as snow, was a little boy. The mother loved her daughter very much, but hated the little boy, and bethought herself how she might get all her husband's money for her own child; so she used the poor fellow very harshly, and was always pushing him about from one corner of the house to another, and thumping him one while and pinching him another, so that he was for ever in fear of her, and when he came home from school, could never find a place in the house to play in.

Now it happened that once when the mother was going into her store-room, the little girl came up to her, and said, "Mother, may I have an apple?" "Yes, my dear," said she, and gave her a nice rosy apple out of the chest. Now you must know that this chest had a very thick heavy lid, with a great sharp iron lock upon it. "Mother," said the little girl, "pray give me one for my little brother too." Her mother did not much like this; however, she said, "Yes, my child; when he comes from school, he shall have one too." As she was speaking, she looked out of the window and saw the little boy coming; so she took the apple from her daughter, and threw it back into the chest and shut the lid, telling her that she should have it again when her brother came home. When the little boy came to the door, this wicked woman said to him with a kind voice, "Come in, my dear, and I will give you an apple." "How kind you are, mother!" said the little boy; "I should like to have an apple very much." "Well, come with me then," said she. So she took him into the store-room and lifted up the cover of the chest, and said, "There, take one out for yourself"; and then, as the little boy stooped down to reach one of the apples out of the chest, bang! she let the lid fall, so hard that his head fell off amongst the apples. When she found what she had done, she was very much frightened, and did not know how she should get the blame off her shoulders. However, she went into her bedroom, and took a white handkerchief out of a drawer, and then fitted the little boy's head upon his neck, and tied the handkerchief round it, so that no one could see what had happened, and seated him on a stool before the door with the apple in his hand.

Soon afterwards Margery came into the kitchen to her mother, who was standing by the fire, and stirring about some hot water in a pot. "Mother," said Margery, "my brother is sitting before the door with an apple in his hand; I asked him to give it me, but he did not say a word, and looked so pale that I was quite frightened." "Nonsense!" said her mother; "go back again, and if he won't answer you, give him a good box on the ear." Margery went back, and said, "Brother, give me that apple." But he answered not a word; so she gave him a box on the ear; and immediately his head fell off. At this, you may be sure she was sadly frightened, and ran screaming out to her mother, that she had knocked off her brother's head, and cried as if her heart would break. "O Margery!" said her mother, "what have you been doing? However, what is done cannot be undone; so we had better put him out of the way, and say nothing to any one about it."

When the father came home to dinner, he said, "Where is my little boy?" And his wife said nothing, but put a large dish of black soup upon the table; and Margery wept bitterly all the time, and could not hold up her head. And the father asked after his little boy again. "Oh!" said his wife, "I should think he is gone to his uncle's." "What business could he have to go away without bidding me good-bye?" said his father. "I know he wished very much to go," said the woman; "and begged me to let him stay there some time; he will be well taken care of there." "Ah!" said the father, "I don't like that; he ought not to have gone away without wishing me good-bye." And with that he began to eat; but he seemed still sorrowful about his son, and said, "Margery, what do you cry so for? your brother will come back again, I hope." But Margery by and by slipped out of the room and went to her drawers and took her best silk handkerchief out of them, and tying it round her little brother's bones, carried them out of the house weeping bitterly all the while, and laid them under the juniper tree; and as soon as she had done this, her heart felt lighter, and she left off crying. Then the juniper tree began to move itself backwards and forwards, and to stretch its branches out, one from another, and then bring them together again, just like a person clapping hands for joy; and after this, a kind of cloud came from the tree, and in the middle of the cloud was a burning fire, and out of the fire came a pretty bird, that flew away into the air, singing merrily. And as soon as the bird was gone, the handkerchief and the little boy were gone too, and the tree looked just as it had done before; but Margery felt quite happy and joyful within herself, just as if she had known that her brother had been alive again, and went into the house and ate her dinner.

But the bird flew away, and perched upon the roof of a goldsmith's house, and sang:

> "My mother slew her little son;
> My father thought me lost and gone:
> But pretty Margery pitied me,
> And laid me under the juniper tree;
> And now I rove so merrily,
> As over the hills and dales I fly:
> Oh, what a fine bird am I!"

The goldsmith was sitting in his shop finishing a gold chain; and when he heard the bird singing on the house-top, he started up so suddenly that one of his shoes slipped off; however, without stopping to put it on again, he ran out into the street with his apron on, holding his pincers in one hand, and the gold chain in the other. And when he saw the bird sitting on the roof with the sun shining on its bright feathers, he said, "How sweetly you sing, my pretty bird! pray sing that song again." "No," said the bird, "I can't sing twice for nothing; if you will give me that gold chain, I'll try what I can do." "There," said the goldsmith, "take the chain, only pray sing that song again." So the bird flew down, and taking the chain in its right claw, perched a little nearer to the goldsmith, and sang:

> "My mother slew her little son;
> My father thought me lost and gone:
> But pretty Margery pitied me,
> And laid me under the juniper tree;
> And now I rove so merrily,
> As over the hills and dales I fly:
> Oh, what a fine bird am I!"

After that the bird flew away to a shoemaker's, and sitting upon the roof of the house, sang the same song as it had done before.

When the shoemaker heard the song, he ran to the door without his coat, and looked up to the top of the house; but he was obliged to hold his hand before his eyes, because

the sun shone so brightly. "Bird," said he, "how sweetly
you sing!" Then he called into the house, "Wife! wife!
come out here, and see what a pretty bird is singing on the
top of our house!" And he called out his children and
workmen; and they all ran out and stood gazing at the
bird, with its beautiful red and green feathers, and the
bright golden ring about its neck, and eyes which glittered
like the stars. "O bird!" said the shoemaker, "pray sing
that song again." "No," said the bird, "I cannot sing
twice for nothing; you must give me something if I do."
"Wife," said the shoemaker, "run upstairs into the work-
shop, and bring me down the best pair of new red shoes
you can find." So his wife ran and fetched them. "Here,
my pretty bird," said the shoemaker, "take these shoes;
but pray sing that song again." The bird came down,
and taking the shoes in his left claw, flew up again to the
house-top, and sang:

> "My mother slew her little son;
> My father thought me lost and gone:
> But pretty Margery pitied me,
> And laid me under the juniper tree;
> And now I rove so merrily,
> As over the hills and dales I fly:
>   Oh, what a fine bird am I!"

And when he had done singing, he flew away, holding
the shoes in one claw and the chain in the other. And he
flew a long, long way off, till at last he came to a mill. The
mill was going clipper! clapper! clipper! clapper! and in
the mill were twenty millers, who were all hard at work
hewing a millstone; and the millers hewed, hick! hack! hick!
hack! and the mill went on, clipper! clapper! clipper! clapper!

So the bird perched upon a linden tree close by the mill,
and began its song:

"My mother slew her little son;
My father thought me lost and gone:"

here two of the millers left off their work and listened:

"But pretty Margery pitied me,
And laid me under the juniper tree;"

now all the millers but one looked up and left their work;

"And now I rove so merrily,
As over the hills and dales I fly:
Oh, what a fine bird am I!"

Just as the song was ended, the last miller heard it, and started up, and said, "O bird! how sweetly you sing! do let me hear the whole of that song; pray, sing it again!" "No," said the bird, "I cannot sing twice for nothing; give me that millstone, and I'll sing again." "Why," said the man, "the millstone does not belong to me; if it was all mine, you should have it and welcome." "Come," said the other millers, "if he will only sing that song again, he shall have the millstone." Then the bird came down from the tree: and the twenty millers fetched long poles and worked and worked, heave, ho! heave, ho! till at last they raised the millstone on its side; and then the bird put its head through the hole in the middle of it, and flew away to the linden tree, and sang the same song at it had done before.

And when he had done, he spread his wings, and, with the chain in one claw, and the shoes in the other, and the millstone about his neck, he flew away to his father's house.

Now it happened that his father and mother and Margery were sitting together at dinner. His father was saying, "How light and cheerful I am!" But his mother said, "Oh, I am so heavy and so sad, I feel just as if a great storm was coming on." And Margery said nothing, but sat and cried. Just then the bird came flying along, and perched upon the top of the house; "Bless me!" said the father, "how cheerful I am; I feel as if I was about to see an old friend again." "Alas!" said the mother, "I am so sad, and my teeth chatter so, and yet it seems as if my blood was all on fire in my veins!" and she tore open her gown to cool herself. And Margery sat by herself in a corner, with her plate on her lap before her, and wept so bitterly that she cried her plate quite full of tears.

And the bird flew to the top of the juniper tree and sang:

> "My mother slew her little son;—"

Then the mother held her ears with her hands, and shut her eyes close, that she might neither see nor hear; but there was a sound in her ears like a frightful storm, and her eyes burned and glared like lightning.

> "My father thought me lost and gone:—"

"O wife!" said the father, "what a beautiful bird that is, and how finely he sings; and his feathers glitter in the sun like so many spangles!"

> "But pretty Margery pitied me,
> And laid me under the juniper tree;—"

At this Margery lifted up her head and sobbed sadly, and her father said, "I must go out, and look at that bird a little nearer." "Oh! don't leave me alone," said his wife; "I feel just as if the house was burning." However, he would go out to look at the bird; and it went on singing:

"But now I rove so merrily,
  As over the hills and dales I fly:
Oh, what a fine bird am I!"

As soon as the bird had done singing, he let fall the gold chain upon his father's neck, and it fitted so nicely that he went back into the house and said, "Look here, what a beautiful chain the bird has given me; only see how grand it is!" But his wife was so frightened that she fell all along on the floor, so that her cap flew off, and she lay as if she were dead. And when the bird began singing again, Margery said, "I must go out and see whether the bird has not something to give me." And just as she was going out of the door, the bird let fall the red shoes before her; and when she had put on the shoes, she all at once became quite light and happy, and jumped into the house and said, "I was so heavy and sad when I went out, and now I'm so happy! see what fine shoes the bird has given me!" Then the mother said, "Well, if the world should fall to pieces, I must go out and try whether I shall not be better in the air." And as she was going out, the bird let fall the millstone upon her head and crushed her to pieces.

The father and Margery hearing the noise ran out, and saw nothing but smoke and fire and flame rising up from the place; and when this was passed and gone, there stood the little boy beside them; and he took his father and Margery by the hand, and they went into the house, and ate their dinner together very happily.

Rapunzel

THERE was once a man and a woman who wished very much to have a child. Near their cottage was a beautiful garden, which belonged to a Witch. One day the wife looked over the garden wall and saw a bed full of the finest lettuce, and she longed so to have some to eat, that she gave her husband no peace till he climbed over the wall and brought her some. She made a salad, and ate it with great enjoyment.

In a few days she began to long for more lettuce, and she again made her husband climb over the wall to fetch her some. He had no sooner seized a handful than he saw the Witch standing beside him.

"How dare you come into my garden?" she exclaimed fiercely. "You have stolen my lettuces, and now you must pay for them. Promise that, if you have a child, you will give it to me."

The husband, in great fear, gave his promise. Soon after a little daughter was born, and the Witch came and took her away. She named her Rapunzel, and put her in a high tower in the forest. This tower had no stairs, and no door, and only one small window. When the Witch visited Rapunzel, she stood beneath the window, and cried:

> "Rapunzel, let down your golden hair
> That I may climb it like a stair."

Rapunzel had the most beautiful long hair, and when she heard the voice of the Witch, she let it hang over the window-sill right down to the ground, to such a length that the Witch could draw herself up as if it had been a ladder.

When Rapunzel was grown into a beautiful maiden, it happened one day that the King's son was passing the tower and heard her singing. Her voice was so sweet that he longed to see her. The next day he came again to listen, and the next. Then he heard the Witch call to Rapunzel beneath the window, and saw her climb up by the maiden's long hair. The following night, when it was dark, he placed himself beneath the window, and said:

> "Rapunzel, let down your golden hair
> That I may climb it like a stair."

Immediately the hair fell down, and he quickly climbed up and entered the tower.

Rapunzel was dreadfully frightened when she saw the Prince, for she had never seen a man before; but she soon lost all fear. After a time he asked her if she would marry him, and she consented, for he was a tall and handsome Prince, and she thought, "He will love me better than the old Witch."

"I will bring you a strong silk cord," said the Prince, "and you shall weave a ladder by which you will be able to descend from the tower. Then I will carry you to my father's castle, and we will be married."

Now the Witch had watched very carefully over Rapunzel, and she soon found out about the Prince's visits. She was very angry, and seized poor Rapunzel's golden hair and cut it off. Then she dragged her to a lonely place in the depths of the forest, and left her there.

At sunset the Prince came to the tower, and cried:

> "Rapunzel, let down your golden hair
> And I will climb it like a stair."

The Witch let the hair down, and the Prince climbed up to the window. What was his horror to see, instead of Rapunzel, a hideous old Witch!

"Ah!" she cried, with a sneer, "you have come to carry off your bride! Rapunzel has gone away, and you will never see her again."

On hearing this, the Prince was so overcome with grief that he sprang out of the window and fell among the thorn-trees beneath. The thorns stuck into his eyes and blinded him, and he wandered away into the wood, lamenting and calling the name of his lost bride.

For a whole year he wandered so, till at last he came to the lonely place where the Witch had left Rapunzel. He heard her singing, and followed the sound until, on coming near, he was clasped in her arms. When she saw that he was blind she began to weep bitterly, and two of her tears fell on his eyes and healed them. Then they travelled back to his father's kingdom, and soon afterwards they were married, and lived in peace and happiness for the rest of their lives.